MURDER
AMONG THE
OWLS

Also by Bill Crider

MURDER
AMONG THE
OWLS

▼

BILL CRIDER

THOMAS DUNNE BOOKS
ST. MARTIN'S MINOTAUR
NEW YORK

This is a work of fiction. All of the characters, organizations, and events portrayed in this novel are either products of the author's imagination or are used fictitiously.

THOMAS DUNNE BOOKS.
An imprint of St. Martin's Press.

www.thomasdunnebooks.com
www.minotaurbooks.com

Library of Congress Cataloging-in-Publication Data

Crider, Bill, 1941–
    Murder among the OWLS : a Sheriff Dan Rhodes mystery / Bill Crider—
1st ed.
        p. cm.
    ISBN-13: 978-0-34809-0
    ISBN-10: 0-312-34809-6
    1. Rhodes, Dan (Fictitious character)—Fiction. 2. Sheriffs—Fiction. 3.
Texas—Fiction. I. Title.

PS3553.R497 M85 2007
813'.54—dc22
                                                              2006050613

First Edition: January 2007

10 9 8 7 6 5 4 3 2 1

To Mary Jane in the Hill Country
and
the Manvel, Texas, OWLS

MURDER AMONG THE OWLS

Chapter 1

▼

WHEN SHERIFF DAN RHODES OPENED THE SCREEN DOOR OF HIS back porch, the cat was there.

It was an inky black, and it stared up at Rhodes with greenish yellow eyes, like a fugitive from a Halloween cartoon. It was an ordinary cat, he supposed, the kind the local vet would label a DHC, for Domestic House Cat. After giving Rhodes the once-over, it walked past him into his kitchen, pausing just long enough to arch its back and rub against Rhodes's leg, leaving behind some black hairs on his khaki pants.

Rhodes sneezed and looked around at the cat as it sniffed around the kitchen. The cat ignored Rhodes.

Rhodes turned back and looked out into the yard at Speedo, the border collie who inhabited it. Speedo wagged his tail. He didn't seem to mind that he'd allowed a strange cat to walk right past him. Rhodes thought that if dogs could shrug and talk, Speedo would have shrugged and said, "Hey, don't blame me for letting him get by. Cats are sneaky!"

Rhodes closed the door and went into the kitchen, where the cat was sniffing around the legs of the table. It appeared to be perfectly at ease. Rhodes saw that it was wearing a collar, a red one, and that a silver aluminum tag was hanging from it. He was about to have a look at the tag when Yancey bounded into the room.

Yancey was a Pomeranian and spent most of his time in the house, where he did a lot of bounding. He looked to Rhodes like a giant, hyperactive dust bunny. With eyes and legs.

Yancey froze when he saw the cat. Rhodes began to count silently. He had never seen Yancey stand still for more than five seconds.

The cat either didn't notice Yancey or didn't care about him if it did. It walked around under the table and then strolled over to the refrigerator, where warm air was being forced out from beneath by the exhaust fan. The cat sniffed at the air.

Rhodes had reached the count of seven-Mississippi, a new record, before Yancey went ballistic. The little dog bounced up and down in place, yipping. When it came to bounding, bouncing, and yipping, Yancey was a champ.

The cat was unperturbed, and Rhodes wondered if it might be deaf. It walked away from the refrigerator and over to where Yancey's food bowl sat.

Yancey stopped yipping and gave Rhodes an aggrieved look. Rhodes didn't say anything. He was curious to see what would happen.

The cat didn't seem interested in Yancey's food, which was just as well. Rhodes remembered having heard somewhere that dog food wasn't good for cats.

Turning away from the food, the cat leveled its gaze on Yancey and walked over to investigate him. Rhodes wished he'd been counting, because Yancey was still silent and immobile. He seemed paralyzed with either fear or indecision.

The cat walked right up to him and sniffed his nose.

Yancey hopped backward down the hall and went into a paroxysm of yipping.

The cat followed along, taking its time. If it had had a white stripe down its back, Rhodes thought, it would have been a ringer for Pepe Le Pew.

Yancey stopped yipping long enough to give a low, halfhearted growl as the cat neared him. Rhodes had never heard Yancey growl before, and it was such an ineffective sound that Rhodes thought the cat might burst out laughing. Far from being intimidated, the cat reached out with one paw and gave Yancey a gentle swat on the nose.

The cat's claws were sheathed, but it didn't matter as far as the effect on Yancey went. The little dog's eyes bugged out, and he began trembling all over, now resembling a dust bunny with eyes, legs, and a vibrator inside.

The cat stood where it was, giving Yancey a cool stare, as if daring him to strike back. Yancey clearly had no intention of trying any such thing. He turned and fled from the hall, yipping all the way.

The cat watched until Yancey disappeared, then returned to its exploration of the kitchen, sniffing along the baseboards of the cabinets.

"What on earth is going on in here?" Ivy asked Rhodes as she came into the kitchen. She gave Rhodes an accusatory look. "Have you been mean to Yancey?"

"I'm completely innocent," Rhodes told her.

"That's what they all say when you arrest them. Didn't you tell me that?"

"I may have, but it's an exaggeration. Some of them don't say anything at all. Where did Yancey go?"

"He's hiding under the bed." Ivy looked around and saw the cat. "Who's that?"

"We haven't been introduced," Rhodes said.

"How did it get in here?"

"It came though the door."

Ivy put her hands on her hips. "You let a cat in the house?"

Ivy was shorter than Rhodes and didn't weigh nearly as much, but she could be imposing at times.

"It came in when I opened the door," he said. "It's all Speedo's fault. He's supposed to be the watchdog."

"They all say they're innocent, and they all blame it on somebody else. Isn't that what you told me?"

"I don't remember telling you that last part."

"Well, you did."

Rhodes wasn't convinced, but Ivy didn't seem to mind. She walked over to the stove, where the cat was pawing at a crumb that had somehow eluded the broom.

"Hey, cat," Ivy said.

The cat ignored her and continued to paw at the crumb. Rhodes grinned. He didn't know much about cats, but he knew they were good at ignoring people.

Ivy stood patiently until the cat knocked the crumb under the stove.

The cat tried to reach under the stove and retrieve its prey, but its paw wouldn't quite fit.

"That's the last you'll ever see of that crumb," Rhodes told the cat, which naturally ignored him.

But Ivy didn't. "Are you implying something about my house-cleaning techniques?"

"I'm completely innocent," Rhodes said, holding up both hands, palms out.

"Don't start that innocent business again. We both know better than that. What are we going to do about the cat?"

Before Rhodes could answer, the cat turned from the stove and started arching its back against the leg of Ivy's slacks. It purred so loudly that Rhodes could hear it from where he stood across the room.

"We'll call him Sam," Ivy said.

Rhodes sneezed.

"Bless you," Ivy said.

"I'm allergic to cats," Rhodes said.

Ivy shook her head. "That's not so. It's all psychological. You're not really allergic to anything."

Rhodes didn't think that was true, but he didn't argue. Instead he changed the subject, which he'd often found was the safest course of action.

"You can't just give the cat a name. You're not even sure it's a he."

"Sam, for Sam Spade," Ivy said. "It's a he, all right. Except that he's been fixed."

Rhodes figured she knew what she was talking about, but he had never liked the term *fixed,* since it implied that a healthy male animal could be improved by castration. He wondered why they hadn't called it being *broken* or *impaired.*

"He's not our cat," Rhodes said. "That's why we can't name him. He's wearing a collar."

Ivy bent down and picked up the cat. It continued to purr while she looked at the tag on the collar.

"There's no name and address on here," she said. "Just a number."

"The vet can find its owner from the number," Rhodes said. "I'll check it out."

"You won't have to do that. I happen to be familiar with this cat. That's how I know his name is Sam."

"You know who he belongs to?"

"Cats don't belong to anybody but themselves. But this one lives with Helen Harris."

Helen Harris lived a couple of blocks down the street. She was a former elementary-school teacher, about seventy, short and white-haired, and very active. Rhodes saw her out in her yard now and then, picking up small branches that had fallen from the pecan trees. Sometimes he saw her mowing the lawn. She always made him feel guilty because he hated mowing the lawn. But he had to do it. He figured that if a woman her age could mow, so could he.

Her husband, W. H. Harris, had been a teacher as well. He'd taught at Clearview High School until his retirement at age sixty-five, and he'd been Rhodes's algebra teacher, or as Harris had called it, "algebry." Rhodes hadn't learned much in the class, as Mr. Harris spent most of the time telling about how he'd lost two fingers of his left hand when working at the sawmill one summer when he was in college. Rhodes had often wondered if he'd have become a scientist or engineer instead of a sheriff if he'd learned more math. Probably not.

Mr. Harris had gotten a Realtor's license during the time he'd taught school, and he'd bought and sold a few properties after he retired. A few years later, he'd died, and Mrs. Harris had lived alone ever since.

"The funny thing is that Sam shouldn't be here," Ivy said.

Rhodes agreed.

"I don't mean it like that," Ivy said. "I mean that Helen never lets him out of the house. That's why he feels so much at home here. He's strictly an indoor cat."

"For an indoor cat, he seems to have had plenty of experience with dogs."

"He probably never saw one before. That's why he's not scared of Yancey."

Rhodes didn't think any cat, no matter how nervous, would have been scared of Yancey, who was most likely still cowering under the bed.

"I think you should go check on Helen," Ivy told Rhodes. "I can't think of any reason she'd let Sam out."

"You seem to know a lot about it."

"Helen's a member of the OWLS."

The Harrises had never had children, and they hadn't had many close friends that Rhodes knew about. Mrs. Harris had a brother in Montana, where he'd retired after making a lot of money as an attorney in Houston. He'd never visited her, and the two must not have been close. After her husband died, Mrs. Harris had joined several groups that had social activities because they gave her something to do, and they got her out of the house. OWLS was an acronym for Older Women's Literary Society. Ivy occasionally attended the meetings as Helen's guest because, as she said, it made her feel like a teenager to be surrounded by women who were all thirty or forty years older than she was. The women met in the library to talk about the books they were reading. Some of them brought homemade snacks to the meetings, such as chocolate chip cookies, pies, and cakes, though Ivy said she didn't eat them.

Rhodes would have gone for the snacks alone. And he would have eaten them. He probably wouldn't have read the books they discussed, however, as he preferred watching old movies, the kind that used to be shown on TV late at night and which now turned up on bargain-priced DVDs. He'd recently picked up a copy of *The Last Man on Earth* with Vincent Price from a bargain bin, but he hadn't had time to watch it. He wondered sometimes if he ever would.

"I'd go check on Helen myself," Ivy said, "but I don't want to be late to work."

Ivy worked at an insurance agency downtown, and no one had to punch a time clock. But Ivy liked to be punctual, as Rhodes well knew.

"What about . . . the cat?" he said.

Rhodes couldn't bring himself to say its name. Once you named a cat, it was your responsibility, and he didn't want to take any chances.

Ivy set the cat on the floor. "He'll be just fine. I'm sure he'll be right here when you get back."

That was what Rhodes was afraid of. "Maybe I should take him with me."

"That might not be a smart idea. What if he got away from you and got lost?"

That was a good possibility, so Rhodes tried another tack.

"If he stays here, he might terrorize Yancey."

"Not unless he can find him," Ivy said. "I wish you'd go. I'm worried about Helen. Sam wouldn't be out and about if everything was normal."

A note of concern was in her voice, and Rhodes thought that maybe she had a point.

"I'll go look in on her," he said. "Sam probably slipped out the door while she was sweeping the house or something like that."

"Maybe. If that's what happened, she'll be looking for him. You be sure to call me and let me know if everything's all right."

"I'll call," Rhodes said. "You don't have to worry. I'm sure Helen is just fine."

But he was wrong about that.

Chapter 2

▼

IT WAS A BEAUTIFUL SPRING DAY, A WEEK AFTER EASTER, WITH-
out a cloud to hide the pure blue of the sky, and Rhodes enjoyed
the walk down the block. So did Speedo, who'd gone along for the
fun of it. He ran into and out of every yard they passed, seemingly
excited by all the new and exotic smells.

He ran ahead of Rhodes and then ran back to meet him, as if
trying to hurry him along. But Rhodes wasn't going to be rushed.
The air was dry and cool, and he didn't often get a chance to go
for a leisurely walk. No one else was out and about, so he and
Speedo had the neighborhood of the silent houses to themselves.
Some of the houses were empty because the owners had gone to
work, and in some of them people were eating breakfast, watching
TV, maybe reading last evening's *Clearview Herald*.

Helen Harris's yard, when they reached it, was immaculate, not
a twig to be seen, not that Rhodes had expected anything else. It
had been mowed only a day or so earlier, and the edges of the

grass along the sidewalks were trimmed. In the flower beds, which were completely free of weeds, purple irises bloomed, along with white narcissuses and yellow jonquils. Or maybe it was the jonquils that were white and the narcissuses that were yellow. Rhodes was never sure about flowers.

The house itself was old, dating from the 1930s or earlier, white frame with freshly painted trim and a clean-swept concrete porch walled with brick.

Rhodes and Speedo went up on the porch. Speedo ran from one corner of the wall to the other, as if something might be hiding in plain sight, but there was nothing, not so much as a spider. The floor of the porch was as clean as the floor in most people's living rooms.

A black-painted iron doorknocker was nailed to the frame beside the screen. It was shaped like a boot. Rhodes lifted it and gave a couple of taps.

No answer came from inside the house, so Rhodes knocked again, making the taps a bit louder. Still no answer. Rhodes figured that Helen was in the kitchen, which would be at the back of the house. Maybe she was busy or couldn't hear well. He went down the steps and around to the backyard, which was enclosed with Hurricane fencing that was beginning to rust in a few places. Rhodes opened the gate and went through, followed by Speedo, who ran to the other end of the yard before charging back toward the gate, hoping that Rhodes would play with him.

Rhodes told Speedo to mind his manners and not to mess up Helen's backyard, which was just as neatly kept as the front. There were no flower beds, but gardenia bushes lined the fences. Rhodes knew about gardenias. In June the smell of the flowers on so many bushes would be almost overpoweringly sweet.

The back porch was screened in. Rhodes stood on top of the concrete steps and knocked on the frame of the screen door with one knuckle. The door bounced a little when he struck it, as if it were loose, maybe not latched. Rhodes waited for several seconds, but no one responded.

Looking through the screen, Rhodes saw a little porch. A covered litterbox sat near the inner door beside a well-ripped scratching post. The inner door, which led into the kitchen, was open, but no one was in sight.

Thinking of the way the door had bounced, Rhodes gave it a try. Sure enough, it wasn't latched. He opened it and looked at the hook and loop arrangement. Nothing wrong with it. Maybe Mrs. Harris wasn't afraid of burglars, not that a hook-latch would do any good at all if anyone wanted in.

Rhodes could remember a time when hardly anyone in Clearview locked the doors, but that was in the past. Now, most people did, especially people living alone.

"Mrs. Harris?" he said.

Speedo ran over to see if Rhodes might have been calling him. Seeing that wasn't the case, he sat at the foot of the steps and looked up at Rhodes, who called out Mrs. Harris's name again, louder.

No answer, and Rhodes looked down at Speedo.

"Behave yourself," he said.

Speedo wagged his tail, brushing it across the short-cropped grass, and Rhodes went on inside.

A white washer and dryer sat on the wooden floor of the back porch. The painted hardwood floor was so clean that it gleamed. Rhodes passed the washer and dryer and went through the open door into the kitchen.

It was like stepping back into an earlier time. The linoleum on the floor had been new about forty years earlier, but it was still shiny. Rhodes wondered if they still made Johnson's Glo-Coat.

The kitchen cabinets were original to the house, and there was no dishwasher. The stove was a white Chambers range. Rhodes's parents had owned one exactly like it. It had once been the top of the line, but now it was a collector's item.

A divided sink had been installed in the counter at one time, but it was by now forty years old or more, and a chip of enamel was missing on one edge. The Formica-covered countertops were clean but worn, lined with canisters, a chrome toaster, and a coffee percolator. An old wooden table stood on the faded linoleum at the opposite end of the room, near a door leading into a dining room. Near the table a bowl of cat food and a bowl of water sat on a rubber mat.

The only jarring note in the room was the body lying on the floor in front of the sink.

It looked as if there had been an accident.

Helen Harris lay motionless with an overturned stool beside her. She lay on one side, almost as if she were asleep, but Rhodes had seen enough dead bodies to be pretty sure that Mrs. Harris wouldn't ever be waking up. He didn't want to take any chances that he was wrong, however, so he walked over and knelt down to check for a pulse. There was none.

The stool was made of wood and had four legs, which would supposedly make it fairly stable. Apparently it hadn't been.

The cover of the light over the sink had been removed and was sitting on the counter, and a lightbulb with a dark spot on it lay beside it. Rhodes stood up and looked into the sink. A broken bulb lay in the bottom.

So Mrs. Harris had been standing on the stool, trying to replace the bulb. Something had happened to the stool, it had become overbalanced, and she had fallen. The new bulb had landed in the sink, and she had landed on the floor.

That wouldn't have been enough to kill her. Her head, covered with wispy white hair, was beside the stool, and a pair of glasses lay not far away. Rhodes supposed that she might have hit one of the rounded corners of the stool when she fell. He saw a couple of white hairs caught on the wood, but he didn't make any firm conclusions.

He felt a kind of sadness that was a little different from that which usually came over him at someone's death. Mrs. Harris had been a part of the community for far longer than Rhodes could remember. For longer than most people in town could remember. Rhodes hadn't known her well, but he had vivid memories of her husband's algebry classes.

After looking down at the body for a couple of seconds, Rhodes sighed and went to check the rest of the house to make sure that no one else was hiding there. First he checked the front door. It was locked.

The furnishings in all the rooms were as old as the house, except for the TV set, which might not have been much more than twenty years old. There was only one telephone, an old black handset with a rotary dial, sitting in a little niche in a hallway. Rhodes didn't think there were many of those left in use even in a small town like Clearview.

Every room was as clean as the kitchen. The hardwood floors were smooth and shiny, the throw rugs hardly seemed to have been stepped on, and there was no cat hair that Rhodes could see. He wondered if there was a single dust bunny to be found under any of the beds. Probably not.

In one of the bedrooms on a low bookshelf there were all sorts of interesting items: pieces of old glass and metal objects, including a few coins. One was a half-dollar. Rhodes hadn't seen one of those in years. Some things Rhodes couldn't identify. Most of them appeared to be not much more than junk: an old ice pick, what looked like a rust-covered hood ornament from the days before they'd been eliminated, even some rusty bottle caps. Junk or not, everything was clean and dusted.

The bed in Helen's room had already been made up, and her purse sat on the dresser. Rhodes would check it later, but it didn't appear to have been disturbed.

A tall jewelry box sat in front of the dresser mirror. Rhodes opened the little doors and saw necklaces draped over small hangers. He opened the drawers to see if any rings were inside. Several rings were there, and it didn't appear that any had been taken. Whatever had happened in the kitchen, robbery didn't seem to have entered into it.

After peeking into the rest of the rooms and finding no one, Rhodes went back to the kitchen. Nothing in the house had been disturbed. Everything pointed to an accidental death, but Rhodes somehow didn't believe that was the case. He suspected that Helen Harris had been murdered. There was no proof of that as yet, and in fact nothing in the deserted house suggested it, but Rhodes couldn't shake the feeling.

The setup was obvious enough. When Mrs. Harris had gone into the kitchen that morning, she'd discovered that the bulb over her sink was burned out and decided to change it. Then the accident had happened. It was even possible that events had gone exactly that way.

But a few things were wrong. For one, the back screen door hadn't been latched. Rhodes thought that a meticulously careful person like Helen Harris would latch the door, especially if the door leading from the screened porch into the kitchen was open and unlocked.

It wasn't the doors that bothered Rhodes the most, though. It was the cat. Ivy said that Mrs. Harris never let the cat leave the house, but it had left, and it had been outside long enough to wander a couple of blocks to Rhodes's house. Who had let it out? Rhodes was convinced that someone besides Helen Harris had been in the house, someone who had gone out the back door and then gone somewhere else.

Rhodes thought about going to the black telephone and making the necessary calls, but he didn't want to mess up any fingerprints that might be there. He wished he'd brought a cell phone with him, but he didn't like cell phones. He thought about the odds of someone other than Mrs. Harris having made any phone calls. He decided there was next to no chance that anyone had, so he went into the hall and called the jail, dialing awkwardly because he was out of practice.

Hack Jensen, the dispatcher, answered, and Rhodes told him to have Ruth Grady, one of the deputies, meet him at Helen Harris's house.

"What's the matter?" Hack said. "Something happen to Helen?"

"I'll tell you later," Rhodes said, and hung up the phone, knowing that he'd just ruined Hack's day. The dispatcher wanted to know everything as soon as it happened, so he could lord it over Lawton, the jailer.

Rhodes then called the ambulance and the justice of the peace. He called Ivy last.

"That's terrible," Ivy said when he'd told her about Mrs. Harris. "I can't imagine why a woman of her age would want to climb up on a stool. She's frail and not exactly steady."

"I'm not sure she climbed on anything."

"What do you mean?"

"I don't know exactly. A few things don't seem quite right to me. I need to find out more about Helen Harris."

"Are you suggesting that it wasn't an accident?"

"I don't mean to suggest anything."

There was a pause, then Ivy said, "It's Sam, isn't it."

Rhodes wished she hadn't used the cat's name, but he said, "Yes. Didn't you say she never let him outside?"

"That's right. Someone had to open the door, or he'd still be in the house. I know Helen wouldn't have let him leave, and certainly not before she tried to change a lightbulb. Someone who didn't know about Sam's habits must have done it. Or someone who knew and didn't notice Sam slipping past."

That was what Rhodes thought, too. He said, "I don't know a lot about cats, but if S—if the cat hadn't been outside before, why would it go out now?"

"Because it was scared? Or bothered by a stranger being in the house?"

It sounded right to Rhodes.

"How many women are in the OWLS?" he asked.

"About six regulars, but Helen was in several other groups. She joined some of them when her husband was still alive."

That would complicate things, Rhodes thought. The more acquaintances a person had, the more potential suspects in a murder case. If this was a murder case. And that didn't even begin to account for the possibility of a stranger who might have wandered by.

"Do you know anything about those other groups?" he said.

Ivy didn't, not really.

"One of them was a metal-detecting club," she said, and Rhodes thought about the things he'd seen on the shelves. "But I don't know who else was in it," Ivy continued. "I don't even know for sure if she was still a member, but she used to talk about it now and then. You'll have to ask some of the OWLS."

Rhodes told her that he would and asked if she had a membership list.

"No," Ivy said, "but you can bet that Helen did. She was very particular about things like that."

Rhodes said that he believed it. "Where would the list be?"

"Isn't there a little black desk in one of the spare bedrooms?"

Rhodes said that he'd seen it. There had been a desk calendar with daily Bible verses on it, but that was all. Helen kept the top of the desk as clean as everything else in the house.

"That's where the list would be," Ivy said. "In one of the drawers, probably."

Rhodes said he'd look there and hung up the phone. Maybe he was being overly suspicious. Maybe Mrs. Harris had simply had an accident and, being old and frail, had died as a result.

Rhodes sighed. It was easy enough to tell himself that, but he didn't believe it for a minute.

Chapter 3

▼

RHODES RETURNED TO THE BACKYARD, WHERE SPEEDO SAT WAITing. As soon as Speedo saw Rhodes, he charged to the other side of the yard, probably hoping that Rhodes would follow and play.

Rhodes did follow, but only to check the gate in the rusty fence. It was between two of the gardenia bushes, and it was closed. It opened to the white-graveled alley that led away behind houses in both directions. Whoever had been in the house, if anyone had been, could have gone just about anywhere without much danger of being seen, since most of the yards backing up to the alley had either high wooden fences or trees or both hiding it from sight of the houses.

If Rhodes was right about someone having left by the back door, it meant that whoever had let the cat escape had walked to the house, but probably not through the alley. Most people used the sidewalk. Maybe someone had been outside and seen whoever it was, so Rhodes would have to talk to everyone who was home along both sides of the street.

Speedo tried to nudge past Rhodes and see what was so interesting in the alley, but Rhodes didn't open the gate.

"Can't touch it," he told the dog. "There might be fingerprints."

Speedo sat back on his haunches and looked wise, as if he understood completely.

Rhodes wished that he understood things as well as Speedo seemed to. He was sure he didn't have any solid reasons for his suspicions, but they didn't go away. They just kept getting stronger.

Rhodes heard a car pull into the driveway. He told Speedo to behave himself and went to see who'd arrived.

It was Ruth Grady, who got out of the county car and asked what was going on.

"Mrs. Helen Harris is in the kitchen," Rhodes told her. "She's dead. It looks like an accident."

"You wouldn't have called me for an accident," Ruth said.

She was short and stout and one of the best deputies Rhodes had ever worked with. She'd gotten a law enforcement degree at a community college in south Texas before coming to work in Blacklin County, and Rhodes trusted her to work a crime scene without making any mistakes.

"It might be an accident," Rhodes said. "But it might not." He told her about the cat. "So we're not going to take any chances."

"This is your neighborhood, isn't it?" Ruth said.

"Yes, but we'd do the same anywhere."

"I know that. I was just commenting. Did you know the victim?"

"She might not be a victim. But I knew her. Not well. Ivy knew her better. Her husband taught me algebra when I was in high school."

"I was pretty good in algebra," Ruth said.

Rhodes didn't want to get into a discussion of his high school accomplishments, or lack thereof, especially one in which he'd come off badly, so he told Ruth what he wanted her to do as soon as the justice of the peace got through with his business.

"I'll be interviewing the people who live up and down the block," Rhodes said, "in case they've noticed anything unusual."

Ruth looked both ways along the street, then back at Rhodes.

"I don't see anybody."

"If anybody's home, they know we're here. Not too many county cars pull into driveways in this part of town."

"Except for yours."

"That's right, but nobody even notices mine anymore. There's never been one in this driveway, though."

Rhodes heard a siren in the distance. Speedo, in the backyard, heard it, too, and started howling in accompaniment.

"That'll really get people's attention," Rhodes told Ruth. "You go on in and look things over."

"You haven't already done that?"

"Yes, but I didn't touch a thing. Treat it like a crime scene. Get pictures of everything before they move the body."

The ambulance parked at the curb, and its siren wound down. Speedo's howling did, too.

"That dog you hear is Speedo," Rhodes told Ruth. "You might want to say 'hey' to him when you go in."

"I like Speedo," Ruth said.

"Everybody does. He won't bother you."

"I know. He likes me, too."

Rhodes grinned and went to talk to the EMTs while Ruth was looking things over. After a few more minutes the JP arrived, and Rhodes left them there to begin walking the block.

He went to three houses before he found anybody who knew anything. In the first house, no one was home. In the second, a man named Grover Middleton was plenty willing to talk, but not about anything related to Helen Harris. He mainly wanted to quiz Rhodes about the ambulance and the patrol car being at Mrs. Harris's house. After finding out that Middleton had nothing to contribute, Rhodes told him as little as possible and left.

In the third house, Francine Oates had a lot to say, as if the idea of her neighbor's death had made her nervous. Francine was about Helen's age, and the two had known each other for many years, ever since the Harrises had moved to Clearview. Like Mrs. Harris, Francine had taught elementary school.

Francine was a tough, wiry woman whose hair was dyed a reddish brown. She'd been married at one time. Rhodes didn't remember her husband, who had been dead for years. Francine seemed to have given up wearing her wedding band, or any other rings, for that matter.

"I always did worry about Helen," Francine said after Rhodes had explained the reason for his visit. "She was entirely too active if you ask me, even when we were teaching together, and especially now. Women our age shouldn't be out mowing the yard and pruning trees."

Rhodes said what Francine wanted to hear.

"You don't look as old as Helen."

Francine smiled, revealing a set of good teeth.

"That's because I take care of myself, not like Helen, out sweating in the yard. It's hardly ladylike, if you know what I mean."

Francine dated back to the time when the word *ladylike* had been acceptable. More than that, it had meant something good, at least to people like Francine. Ladies wore hats and gloves when they went to church, which they did twice on Sunday and often on Wednesday. They didn't smoke, swear, or sweat, and they always let men hold the door for them. On the other hand, she was currently dressed in a pair of new-looking blue jeans and a man's long-sleeved shirt, which didn't look ladylike to Rhodes, though he refrained from saying so.

"You mentioned that it was an accident," Francine said. "You're probably right. Helen wasn't always as careful as she should be. Always climbing around."

"Was she careful about other things?" Rhodes said. "Like locking her doors?"

Francine hesitated for a couple of seconds. "I guess she was. A lady has to be careful these days." Francine had small eyes set too close together, and Rhodes detected a hint of nervous anxiety in her tone. "If it was an accident, then why are you here? I didn't think the sheriff investigated accidents."

"We have to make sure," Rhodes said. "Sometimes things aren't the way they seem."

"I'm sure they are in this case. Helen was always careless."

"Did you happen to see a car parked at Mrs. Harris's house this morning?"

"No, but that doesn't mean anything. I've been busy and haven't been outside. Anybody could have parked there, and I wouldn't have known. Would you like some coffee?"

Rhodes didn't drink coffee, so he declined politely.

"I have some Dublin Dr Pepper if you'd like a soft drink."

Rhodes couldn't resist an offer like that. The bottling company in Dublin still made Dr Pepper with real sugar, and it tasted the way it had when Rhodes had been growing up.

"I ordered it off the Internet," Francine said. "I don't think Helen even had a computer."

Rhodes hadn't seen one, but there could have been a laptop in a drawer. Or it could have been taken from the house.

"Come on in the kitchen," Francine said. "We can talk there. I'd be glad to help if I can."

Rhodes followed her to the back of the house, which was as old as the Harris home but with more up-to-date furnishings. The kitchen had a dishwasher, and the floor was tiled.

"Have a seat," Francine said, and Rhodes sat in a captain's chair at the square wooden table while she got the Dr Pepper out of the refrigerator. It was in a can, but Rhodes didn't mind, not if it was a real Dublin Dr Pepper.

"Aren't you going to have one?" Rhodes said, after she'd wrapped the can in a napkin and set it in front of him.

"I drink one a day, in the afternoon. I have to watch my weight."

Rhodes again said the expected, and it was true enough that Francine looked thin and fit.

"You don't seem to have a weight problem."

"That's because I work at it." Francine got a glass from a cabinet and put it on a coaster beside the Dr Pepper can. "Go ahead and drink. I'll talk while you do."

Rhodes popped the can open and poured about half the Dr Pepper into the glass. He took a swallow and smiled. It was the Real Thing for sure.

Francine smiled and laced her fingers together. "Helen and I were in the OWLS together, you know."

Rhodes hadn't known that Francine was in the OWLS. And he hadn't looked for the membership list in the Harris house. He'd have to do that if Ruth Grady didn't come across it.

"We were two of the founding members," Francine went on, "and we try . . . *tried* to keep the group on track. Lately some of them have suggested outlandish books for discussion."

She paused, and Rhodes was about to ask what books she meant, but she went on without prodding.

"Helen and I prefer Texas writers. Like Vernell Lindsey."

Vernell was a local success story. She'd had several romance novels published and had even sponsored a writing workshop at the old college campus in Obert. The workshop hadn't turned out so well, and the college's old main building now housed a church. There had been a murder there only two weeks earlier, and Rhodes sometimes wondered if Obert was jinxed.

"But some of the ladies wanted to read racier books," Francine said. "Like something by Joe Lansdale. Have you ever heard of him?"

Rhodes said that he hadn't.

"His books are just *filthy*." Francine giggled and put her hand to her mouth. "But they're very funny." Her face assumed a pious blandness. "He does have serious themes, you know."

Rhodes said that he didn't know.

"They're about the real Texas, not like some things we've read," Francine said. "They're about murders and things. Do you think Helen was murdered?"

Rhodes, who wasn't sure that murders and things were the real Texas, said that he didn't know anything for sure.

"If she died under suspicious circumstances," Francine said, "I think you should talk to Alton Brant."

Rhodes knew the name. Brant was a veteran of the Korean War and the person the *Clearview Herald* always interviewed on patriotic holidays. He'd once been quite a good-looking man, and he still made a good appearance in a photo on the *Herald*'s front page, even though he'd gained weight and become a bit stooped.

"He and Helen have been courting, you know," Francine said.

Rhodes said that he hadn't known.

"Oh, my, yes. They've been going at it hot and heavy."

Rhodes didn't think *hot and heavy* was a ladylike expression, but he didn't mention that to Francine. He said, "Does Alton stop by Helen's house often?"

"Certainly. They're not being discreet about anything. He visits several times a week. I wouldn't be surprised if they, well, it wouldn't be nice to say."

Rhodes didn't want to get into that kind of speculation. He said, "Do you know if she had a will?"

Francine paused and looked away. "Yes, she did. I witnessed it, in fact."

Rhodes took another drink of the Dr Pepper. It hit the spot. He should order a case for himself, he thought. Maybe two cases. He'd ordered it before, and while it was expensive, it was well worth the money.

"I didn't think Helen had a lot of money," Francine said when he set the glass back on the coaster. "Or anything else. Of course, that was before."

"Before what?"

"Before the big gas boom."

Rhodes nodded. In the last couple of years, the price of natural gas had risen to highs that would have been unbelievable not so very long ago. There had always been gas under the ground in parts of Blacklin County, but it had been deep, so it hadn't been economically feasible to drill for it. Now it was, and quite a few landowners had become much better off as a result. Instead of griping about the lack of rain in the summer and the cold weather in the winter, they complained about their taxes. It was always something.

"So Mrs. Harris had a gas well?" Rhodes said.

"Not yet," Francine said. "But she owned a good bit of property in the south part of the county where there's a lot of drilling. Her husband bought it years ago just for speculation. He never realized a thing from it, but Helen would have. Or she *thought* she would. She told everybody all about it at an OWLS meeting. Some of the property had very good leases on it, and one of the big gas companies started drilling on the property only a few days ago. Helen just knew it was going to be a good well."

Rhodes didn't keep up with all the drilling activity, and Ivy hadn't been to an OWLS meeting in a while. So he hadn't known about Helen's good fortune. Which was now the good fortune of whoever might be her heir. That was something else Rhodes would have to consider if the death wasn't accidental.

"Maybe Alton Brant is in her will," Francine said, interrupting Rhodes's thoughts. "I didn't look at it, naturally. I just signed where she showed me. But maybe Alton killed her for the money. I wouldn't be surprised if that was it, not in the least."

Rhodes said he didn't think anyone had killed Mrs. Harris, that her death was probably just an accident.

"I don't doubt it. She was always too careless about climbing on things."

The thought of Mrs. Harris's heirs reminded Rhodes of something. "Wasn't she related to Leonard Thorpe? I seem to remember hearing that sometime or other, but I don't know how they're related."

"He's not a Harris," Francine said, as if she knew all about it. "He's a cousin, related to Helen on her mother's side."

She didn't seem to want to talk about Thorpe, which wasn't surprising. He lived in Clearview's only trailer park, out past the city limits on the west side of town. It wasn't called a trailer park, of course. It was the Tranquility Mobile Home Park. It usually lived up to its name, but not always. Some of the people who lived there were interesting characters, and Leonard was definitely part of that group, except that *interesting* wasn't precisely the right word. Rhodes had dealt with him more than once when he'd disturbed the public tranquillity.

"I think you need to investigate the alley-walker," Francine said.

"The alley-walker?"

"You know who I mean. I forget his name. He's always walking the alleys and snooping in the trash. He can be scary."

Billy Joe Byron, Rhodes thought, and he felt something that might have been his conscience give him a jab in the ribs. He'd had dealings with Billy Joe, too. He'd made a decision that he'd never regretted, though he'd never been certain that it had been the right one. The situation, when he thought about it, was uncomfortably similar to the one with Mrs. Harris, or it could be. Rhodes hoped it wasn't.

"The alley-walker might have done it," Francine said. "Or it could have been some tramp."

Rhodes hadn't heard that last word in years. He said, "Have you seen any tramps around lately?"

"I really don't recall. Do you really think some tramp might have killed Helen?"

"I don't think anybody killed her. I was just wondering who might have visited her this morning. If anybody did."

"I wish I could help, but I spend most of my time on the computer. I don't see much of what's going on outside."

Rhodes thought that might be a familiar story these days, even among people Mrs. Oates's age, though she seemed to know a lot about Alton Brant's visits.

"I'm writing a book," she said. "A romance novel. Vernell Lindsey is my inspiration. I think people need a little more romance in their lives, and I believe I can bring it to them with my book."

"I hope your book is a big success." Rhodes stood up and thanked her again for the Dr Pepper. "If you think of anything else, or if you remember seeing anybody, call the office."

"I'll be sure to do that. I just can't imagine that Helen is dead. She always seemed so alive."

"I used to see her mowing that lawn."

"Yes." Francine shook her head in disapproval. "She shouldn't have done that. Very unladylike."

Rhodes said he appreciated Francine's help and started to leave. But he turned back at the door to ask if Francine wanted a cat.

"You mean Helen's cat?"

"That's the one. Somebody will have to take care of it."

Francine looked away from Rhodes. She twitched slightly and rubbed her arms as if fleas were hopping around on her skin underneath the shirtsleeves.

"I don't like cats," she said. "Cats are sneaky and hateful. Just turn it over to your animal control officer."

Rhodes was sure that Speedo would have agreed with her characterization of cats.

"They're dirty, too," Francine continued, "and they have fleas. I've never understood how a woman with Helen's habits was able to have one in the house with her."

Rhodes started to say that the cat had lived inside and wasn't likely to have fleas, but he didn't think Francine would be convinced. He left to see if he could get any better information from someone else along the block.

He didn't.

Chapter 4

▼

BACK AT THE HARRIS HOUSE, RHODES FOUND THAT MRS. HARris's body had been removed. Because he wasn't sure about the circumstances of her death, he'd considered having it sent to the Southwest Forensics Laboratory for autopsy, but Dr. White had been doing autopsies for the county for years, and Rhodes figured he could handle this one, too. So far, nothing had proved too tricky for him.

Ruth Grady was still going through the house, and she had only one question for Rhodes. It was about the bookshelf Rhodes had noticed earlier.

"Do you think something's missing?" Ruth asked.

Rhodes didn't see how she could tell. On some shelves he could name, it would be easy to see if something had been moved because the lack of dust would reveal where it had been sitting. These shelves were spotless.

"Look." Ruth counted off the items on each shelf.

"Ten on all of them," Rhodes said when she finished. "Except the top one."

"That's right. You can tell by looking around the house that Mrs. Harris was a particular person. Very precise. So shouldn't there be ten things on every shelf?"

Rhodes didn't know. It seemed likely, but it wasn't a certainty.

"There's no empty space," he said.

"It wouldn't take much to nudge a couple of things around. Like these two." Ruth moved a rusty belt buckle and a corroded penny. "See?"

Rhodes nodded. "Why those two?"

"Look a little closer."

Rhodes got his reading glasses from his pocket. He hated using them, and he'd even thought about having Lasik surgery until someone told him that it wasn't always successful. He put the glasses on and looked at the shelf again. He had to bend down until his nose was almost touching the wood, but he finally saw a tiny scratch. He straightened and put the glasses back into his pocket.

"So?" he said.

"You don't think Mrs. Harris would stand for a scratch like that, do you? She'd have taken care of it as soon as she noticed it."

"*If* she noticed it," Rhodes said, but he knew that people like Mrs. Harris always noticed things like that, no matter how small, no matter how bad their eyesight.

"I think it's a fresh scratch," Ruth said. "I think something's missing, and I think whoever took it made that scratch."

It was pretty far-fetched, Rhodes thought, but no more than the assumptions he'd already made. He felt as if he was getting way ahead of himself. He'd have to sit down and think everything over.

Maybe there was nothing missing at all. Maybe Mrs. Harris had simply had an accident, after all.

"Why would anybody as clean as Mrs. Harris keep junk like this around in the first place?" Ruth asked.

Rhodes told her about the metal-detecting club. "I think these things were souvenirs from some of her treasure hunts."

"Well, I think one thing is missing, but I could be wrong."

It was one more item for Rhodes to add to his list of suspicions. He asked Ruth if she'd gone through Mrs. Harris's desk.

"Not yet."

"Let's have a look, then," Rhodes said, and they went into the room where the desk stood.

A piece of plate glass had been cut to cover the wooden top of the desk. The glass was spotless, of course, and so clean that it was hard to tell it was even there. Pictures were beneath it, and Rhodes recognized Mr. and Mrs. Harris in one of them. They had been young and on vacation somewhere. They stood in front of a mountainous backdrop that Rhodes didn't recognize.

He opened one of the two desk drawers. A manila folder lay inside, along with a couple of ballpoint pens. Black lettering on the outside of the folder told Rhodes that it held *Membership Lists*.

He opened the folder. Inside were several sheets of notebook paper, each one with a neatly printed heading, with block letters large enough for Rhodes to read without putting on his glasses. The one on top said *OWLS*. The one beneath it said *Rusty Nuggets*, which Rhodes assumed was the name of the metal-detecting club. The next said *Red Hats*. He didn't look at the others.

"Bring all of these with you when you're finished," Rhodes told

Ruth, putting the folder back into the drawer. "We need to make copies."

Ruth said she'd bring it, and Rhodes opened the other drawer, which held several more folders, all of them labeled in Helen Harris's careful printing. One held *Bills*. Another was for *Canceled Checks*. Rhodes flipped through the folders until he came to one labeled *Last Will and Testament*.

"We'll need a copy of this, too," Rhodes said, handing her the folder. "If it's a murder investigation, that is."

"It seems to be," Ruth said.

Rhodes returned the folders to their places. "We'll just go along pretending it is until we know better."

Before he could say more, he was interrupted by Speedo, who was barking in the backyard.

"He's hungry," Rhodes said. "I was going out to feed him this morning, but I never got around to it. Come to think of it, there's a cat at my house, and he might be hungry, too."

Ruth gave him a quizzical look. "A cat?"

Rhodes shook his head. "It's a long story. You finish up here and we'll talk about this back at the jail."

On his way out of the house, Rhodes stopped in the kitchen and picked up the bowl of dry cat food. Feeling guilty for taking anything at all from a crime scene before the investigation was complete, he called out to Ruth to let her know what he was doing.

"They never do things like that on *CSI*," she said.

Rhodes didn't answer. He went out into the backyard, where Speedo was barking at a squirrel in a pecan tree. Speedo lost interest in the squirrel as soon as he noticed Rhodes and ran over to him.

"You ready to eat?" Rhodes said.

Speedo wagged his tail and looked hopefully at the bowl of food Rhodes was holding.

"Not this stuff. Let's go home and get you something of your own."

On the walk back to the house, Speedo made his usual detours, but he didn't spend long on them. For his part, Rhodes couldn't enjoy the walk. The town was quiet and seemed peaceful enough, but Rhodes felt a hollow sadness inside because of Helen Harris's death. It seemed senseless to him, accident or not.

Looking at the houses he passed, he didn't think they seemed as peaceful as before. Any one of them might be holding secrets that no one outside ever imagined, and the secrets weren't always pleasant.

When they got to the backyard of his house, Rhodes left Speedo and went inside, but only after telling the dog that he'd be right back.

Speedo sat down in the shade of a pecan tree and thumped his tail on the grass, watching Rhodes until he was inside.

In the kitchen Rhodes looked around for Yancey, who should have come bouncing in to greet him. Yancey wasn't there, but the cat was. It wasn't going to bounce out and greet anybody. It lay under the table, stretched out to its full length and taking its ease as if it had lived in the house all its life. Yancey, Rhodes presumed, was still cowering under a bed somewhere.

Rhodes put the bowl of cat food he'd brought from Mrs. Harris's house down on the floor beside Yancey's water bowl. The cat (Rhodes still refused to use its name) heard the sound and got up slowly. Then it stretched, looked at Rhodes, stretched again, and walked over to the food. It sniffed it a couple of times and started to eat.

Rhodes sighed. He knew that he'd just made a big mistake. Feeding a cat was worse than naming it, much worse. Cats made themselves at home wherever the food was, and they didn't have a great deal of loyalty. Whoever fed them last was going to be blessed with their presence.

Rhodes sneezed, and the cat stopped eating to look up at him.

"It's not psychological," Rhodes said, "and don't try to tell me that it is."

The cat didn't try to tell him anything. It went right back to crunching the dry food between its teeth.

Rhodes got out the dog food and went into the backyard to feed Speedo, who was much more appreciative than the cat had appeared to be.

When Rhodes went back in the house, the cat was sprawled under the table again. Rhodes sneezed and put away the dog food. Then he sat down at the table. The cat wasn't disturbed. Rhodes thought about disturbing it, but he decided that wouldn't be a good idea. Instead he thought over everything he'd seen and heard that morning.

If Mrs. Harris's death was an accident, then someone would have to explain why the cat was in Rhodes's kitchen. Rhodes still didn't believe Mrs. Harris would have allowed it to go outside.

Rhodes, however, couldn't think of any reason why someone would have killed her. Maybe the will would give him a clue if Francine Oates's information about the gas wells was accurate. He had no reason to doubt that it was.

And it might be that something was missing from the bookshelf, as Ruth had pointed out, but Rhodes wasn't convinced of that. The scratch wasn't exactly powerful evidence, and there was no other indication that anybody had been in the house. Besides,

Rhodes couldn't imagine what might have been on the shelf to attract anyone's notice.

Another problem with the murder theory was that nobody Rhodes had talked to along the block had seen a car at the house, and nobody had seen anyone walking along the sidewalk or in the alley.

That didn't prove anything, either. People didn't keep a watch on the sparse traffic, and the alley was usually concealed by fences, trees, and bushes.

It would be best for all concerned if the autopsy proved that Mrs. Harris had simply had an unfortunate accident, but Rhodes couldn't rid himself of the nagging feeling that it hadn't been that way.

He heard a noise in the hallway and turned to see Yancey, who had established all kinds of records for keeping silent, peeking around the door facing. Rhodes started to tell Yancey not to worry about the cat, but before Rhodes could get the words out, the cat stretched, and Yancey was gone.

"You're a disruptive influence," Rhodes told the cat, which took no notice of him at all.

Rhodes smiled. You had to give the cat credit for impudence. Or something like that.

Rhodes stood up. He'd have to go back to the Harris house and pick up a couple of things.

Ruth was taking photographs in the kitchen. Rhodes let her know that he was taking the litterbox and the scratching post. She said that would be all right.

Back at home, Rhodes installed the box and post on his own little inside porch and pointed them out to the cat, who seemed bored with the whole thing.

"You just be sure you use the facilities I've provided instead of the floor or the furniture," Rhodes said.

The cat yawned widely.

Rhodes sometimes wondered about his ability to communicate with humans, though he thought he did all right with dogs. On the other hand, he was absolutely convinced that he had no ability at all to communicate with cats.

It was time he went to the jail to see what else was going on in the town, so he told the cat to leave Yancey alone, reminded him again about the litterbox, and went out to the county car. He had a feeling it was going to be a long day.

Chapter 5

▼

RHODES EXPECTED HACK TO START QUESTIONING HIM THE
minute he walked through the door, but the dispatcher surprised
him. He didn't say a word.

Neither did Lawton. Both men were looking at Hack's computer monitor and pretending that they didn't even know that
Rhodes had come into the room.

It was just a question of who would crack first, Rhodes thought
as he walked over to his desk. The two men were invariably curious about everything that happened in Clearview, and they usually
wanted Rhodes to divulge everything as soon as possible. On the
other hand, they preferred to keep Rhodes in the dark as long as
possible when they knew something he didn't. That much, at
least, was normal.

When Rhodes sat down, his chair squeaked, and Hack looked
up from the computer.

"I didn't think you'd be coming in today," he said. He ran a finger along one side of his thin mustache, which was mostly white with a little touch of brown. "It's getting on toward lunchtime."

It was only a little after ten thirty, but Rhodes didn't bother to point that out.

"Might be a little hard to get lunch, though," Hack continued.

"Depends on where you eat," Lawton said. "Might not be so hard if you went to the Dairy Queen. This is bean day, ain't it? Beans got a lot of fiber, they say."

"Fiber's good for you," Hack said. "Cleans out your system."

Rhodes didn't know where the discussion was headed, but that was often the case when Hack and Lawton got started. He knew they'd get to the point sooner or later. Most likely later, since they liked to draw things out as long as possible. It was their way of getting revenge on him for not always telling them all he knew.

"It's not bean day at the Dairy Queen," he said. "That's tomorrow."

"You still oughta go to the DQ if you want to eat anything about now," Hack said. "You might not be able to get served at McDonald's."

"That's right," Lawton said, "not unless Buddy's got things straightened out down there."

Hack glowered at Lawton, and Rhodes suppressed a smile. Lawton had spouted more information than Hack had planned, at least this early in the give-and-take.

"So there's a problem at McDonald's?" Rhodes said.

Lawton started to speak, but Hack gave him another glare. It was almost as if they were doing an Abbott and Costello routine, and they even resembled the comedians, a pair that Rhodes always liked to watch on cable, especially their movie that had them meeting Frankenstein's monster, Dracula, and the Wolf Man.

"Won't be a problem by now," Hack said. "Not if Buddy's on the job."

"Right," Lawton said. "It's probably all taken care of. Nothing to worry about."

Whenever one of them said that, Rhodes automatically began to worry.

"Tell me about it." His tone didn't give them any wiggle room, so Hack gave in.

"I got a call a little bit ago from the McDonald's. It was some customer in the drive-through line. He said they wouldn't serve him."

"Why not?" Rhodes said.

"Bad timin'," Lawton said. "He wanted a sausage biscuit, but—"

Hack swiveled his chair, the better to glower at Lawton, who gave him a hard stare right back. Hack, however, always won those contests. Lawton dropped his eyes after only a couple of seconds, and the dispatcher turned around to face Rhodes again.

"Like I was about to say before I got interrupted, this fella wanted a sausage biscuit. Just a plain one, no cheese, no egg, just sausage and a biscuit."

"Nothing wrong with that," Rhodes said, knowing that there had to be a catch. "Sounds like a reasonable request."

"Yeah, if had been made earlier, but it was after ten. They don't serve breakfast at McDonald's after ten. The fella complained, and they brought him what he said was an old leftover sausage biscuit with egg on it. They told him it was all they had left. That's when he called us."

"Why?" Rhodes said.

"'Cause he didn't get what he wanted," Lawton said, and before Hack could turn to him, he looked up at the ceiling and started to whistle a tune that Rhodes thought might be "Jesus Loves Me."

Hack waited for him to stop, which he did after four or five bars. Then Hack said, "The fella on the phone said that we were the law here and that it was up to us to protect him. 'Protect and serve,' that's what he said. You got a duty to 'protect and serve.'"

"What are we supposed to protect him from?" Rhodes asked. "The wrong breakfast?"

"That's what I asked him."

"Did he have an answer?"

"Sure he did. He said we had to protect him from idiotic business practices. He wanted a sausage biscuit, plain, with no egg, and they could damn well make him one."

"Did you tell him to take off the egg?"

"He didn't want to do that. Said it had already contaminated the sausages. Besides, the biscuit was cold. Said he wouldn't get out of the drive-through line until we came and made them obey the law."

"You told him that the law didn't have anything to do with sausage biscuits, I hope."

Hack nodded. "Sure did. Didn't make any difference, though. I could hear horns honking by that time, so I told him I'd send an officer. That's when I called Buddy."

Buddy had a strong puritanical streak, and Rhodes could just imagine what he told the caller when he arrived on the scene.

"Have you heard from Buddy?" Rhodes asked.

"Nope. Soon's I hung up on the first guy, the manager of McDonald's called. He wanted us to send somebody over there to arrest the fella who was blockin' his drive-through lane. I told him there was already an officer on the way. Kind of surprised him that we were so efficient, I think."

"I'll bet," Rhodes said. "See if you can get Buddy on the radio."

"Won't need to. I talked to him just before you came in. He's on his way here."

"Good," Rhodes said, and turned to his desk. He had to write a report on Mrs. Harris's death, and he was still learning to use the new computer the county commissioners had bought for him recently.

It was quiet for about ten seconds. Then Lawton said, "You don't have anything to tell us?"

Rhodes turned back around and gave him a puzzled look. "Tell you about what?"

"You know what," Hack said.

Rhodes could have toyed with them awhile longer, but instead he told them about the cat and about finding Mrs. Harris's body.

"That's too bad," Hack said. "Miz Harris was a fine woman. Not afraid of hard work."

"Some people wouldn't see it that way," Rhodes said, thinking of Francine Oates.

"They'd be wrong, then," Lawton said. "I like a woman who'll get out and do a little work. Shows you she's got character. How'd it happen?"

Rhodes told them that it appeared to have been an accident, but that he had his doubts.

"That's why you're the sheriff," Hack said. "You can see things the rest of us can't."

Rhodes was never quite sure if Hack was kidding when he said things like that.

"I'm not sure about it," Rhodes said. "Either of you need a cat?"

"I like cats, but I don't need another one," Lawton said. "I got two already."

"I'm allergic," Hack said.

"I've heard that's psychological," Rhodes said.

Hack shook his head. "Maybe it is, and maybe it ain't. All I know's that I sneeze when I'm around 'em, and at my age I don't like sneezin'."

Rhodes wasn't sure how old Hack was, except that he could have retired years ago if he'd wanted to. He didn't want to, however. He liked his job at the jail, and Rhodes suspected that he also enjoyed tormenting Rhodes and Lawton.

Before they could get any further into their discussion of cats and allergies, Buddy came in. Rhodes was glad to see that he didn't have a prisoner with him.

"How'd things shake out at the hamburger place?" Hack said. "Have to shoot anybody?"

Buddy grinned a thin grin. Everything about him was thin, including his hair. He had hardly any hips at all.

"I wanted to shoot that fella who called," he said, "but I didn't think I could get away with it."

"Self-defense," Lawton said. "Tell the judge he attacked you with a sausage biscuit."

"With egg on it," Hack added.

"I'm a peaceable man," Buddy said, in what Rhodes thought was a barely passable imitation of John Wayne. "So I just told him to drive on into the parking lot where we could talk. That got the lane unblocked."

"What'd you tell him?" Hack asked.

"I told him that there was no law that regulated when a business served breakfast and that there wasn't a thing I could do for him. I told him to act like a grown-up and go talk to the manager and get his money back if he didn't like what he'd been served." Buddy looked at Rhodes. "I told him that if he didn't like it, he could come down and talk to the sheriff."

"Great," Rhodes said. "I'm sure I can count on his vote in the next election."

"I don't think so. He told me that talking to you'd be a waste of time because you'd just back up your hirelings."

"He said *hirelings*?" Rhodes didn't think he'd ever heard the word used before.

"That's what he said. He was an educated kind of a guy. Probably teaches English at the community college."

"Those English teachers are sensitive," Lawton said.

"Anyway, he went in," Buddy said. "I think he was a little ashamed of himself by that time. I waited outside, and when he came back, I asked him if he'd got it all sorted out. He said he had. He was carrying a little sack."

"What'd he have in it?" Hack said.

"I didn't ask him."

"You mean we went through all of that, and you didn't even ask him what he bought?"

"I didn't think it was any of my business," Buddy said. "Should I do an incident report, Sheriff?"

"No crime, no report," Rhodes said. "You can get back on patrol."

As soon as Buddy was out the door, Hack said, "I can't believe he didn't even find out what that fella bought. After all that fuss, I'd kinda like to know."

"Not any of our business," Lawton said.

"It sure is our business. He called here, causin' a ruckus, and we got a right to know."

Rhodes knew they could carry on like that indefinitely. The law enforcement business in Blacklin County might not be quite like it was on a TV show like *Law & Order,* but it was never dull. Rhodes shut his ears to the office chatter and started to work on his own report, which was considerably more serious than the one Buddy had just made.

The trouble was that he didn't know what kind of report to write. He thought it might be best to wait until he heard from Dr. White.

While he was trying to make up his mind, Ruth Grady came in with the folders from Helen Harris's desk. Hack and Lawton started to quiz her about the crime scene as she was copying the documents, but she put a stop to their chatter when she opened the folder labeled *Last Will and Testament* and said, "That's interesting."

"What is?" Rhodes said.

Ruth held up the folder by the edge and let it flop open for Rhodes to see. It was empty.

Chapter 6

▼

"Maybe she didn't have a will," Ruth said. "She might have made the folder but never gotten around to writing a will. We could find out if she had a lawyer."

"You don't need a lawyer to make a will," Hack said. "You can just write one out longhand or get you a form from some computer software. That's what I did."

"Yeah," Lawton said, "but you don't have anything to leave anybody."

"That's all you know. I got a house and a savin's account at the First National Bank."

"Nobody to leave it to, though. Not chick nor child." Lawton rubbed his chin. "There's always Miz McGee, I guess. She's prob'ly just waitin' for you to pass so she can get her hands on that savin's account."

Miz McGee was the woman with whom Hack had been keeping company for a while, and there was no better way to rile him than to make a slighting reference to her.

Rhodes spoke up before things got out of hand. "Do you have a will, Lawton?"

Lawton turned the smooth, bland face that belied his age to look at Rhodes. "I sure do. I got a boy lives up in Dallas. He'll get all my worldly goods."

"Such as they are," Hack said.

"What about you, Ruth?" Rhodes said, before Lawton could reply.

"I have one. I didn't think I needed to at my age, but my parents told me I should have one, just in case."

"And I have one, too," Rhodes said. "That makes it unanimous. So you think a woman as particular as Helen Harris might not have had one?"

Nobody thought it was likely.

"There are a lot of reasons the will might not be in the folder, though," Ruth said. "She could have put it in a safe-deposit box or somewhere like that."

"I think she'd have kept a copy," Rhodes said, knowing Francine had witnessed a will.

"So you think somebody took the will?"

Rhodes said he didn't know what to think, and that was when Jennifer Loam walked in. She was a reporter for the *Clearview Herald* and, in fact, wrote most of the stories that appeared in the paper except for the ones on the sports page. She was young, blond, and determined. She was also an excellent writer, and Rhodes was a little surprised that she was still working for the *Herald*. He thought she'd have moved to a big-city paper by now.

"What will are you talking about?" she said without bothering to say hello. "Has somebody stolen one?"

"We don't know," Rhodes said. "We were just talking about the possibility."

"It wouldn't have anything to do with Helen Harris, would it?" Jennifer said.

One of her annoying habits, or at least annoying to Rhodes, was her ability to find out what was going on in town almost as fast as Rhodes did. Sometimes, even faster. He gave Ruth a warning glance, which was probably unnecessary.

"Mrs. Harris had an accident," Rhodes said. "We were wondering about her heirs."

Jennifer took a tiny digital recorder out of her purse and turned it on.

"I don't have anything for the paper," Rhodes said.

Jennifer didn't turn off the recorder. "I heard that there was some suspicion of foul play."

Rhodes thought it was no wonder he found her annoying at times. "Who told you that?"

Jennifer smiled. "You know we reporters never give up our sources."

"I bet you're payin' off somebody with the ambulance service," Hack said. "Either that, or you know the justice of the peace."

Jennifer just smiled.

"Mrs. Harris had an accident," Rhodes said. "But since she was alone in the house, we have to investigate it and make sure. Right, Deputy Grady?"

"Right," Ruth said with a nod.

Jennifer held the recorder a little closer to Rhodes. "So you're willing to go on the record as having determined that Mrs. Harris's death was just a household accident?"

Rhodes wasn't willing to go on the record about anything. "Not yet. But we don't have any reason to suspect that it wasn't."

He wasn't being entirely truthful, but he knew everyone in the office would be happy to back him up.

"I don't believe you, Sheriff," Jennifer said.

"People seldom do. I think it's my dishonest face."

Jennifer stopped smiling. "You and I haven't had any problems before, Sheriff. I hope we're not going to start now."

She had been involved in several of the county's recent cases, not because Rhodes had invited her to be involved but because of her tenacity. Rhodes suppressed a sigh. He figured she'd involve herself this time, too, regardless of what he did or said. Assuming there was anything to be involved in, that is.

"We're not going to have any problems," he said. "I'd never offend the press."

Someone muffled a snort of laughter. Rhodes was pretty sure it was Hack, but the dispatcher had a perfectly straight face when Rhodes looked in his direction.

Jennifer grinned and said she was glad to hear that the sheriff planned on being cooperative with her as the *Herald*'s representative. "So when is the autopsy?"

"How did you know there'd be one?"

"An accident in the home, nobody present, a woman dies. Seems to me something like that would call for an autopsy."

"Maybe you should run for sheriff next election," Hack said. "You know the job already."

Jennifer gave him a skeptical look, raising one eyebrow. Rhodes had always admired that skill.

"Are you joking?" she said.

"Not a bit of it," Hack said with a straight face. "The sheriff needs some competition."

"I've had plenty in the past," Rhodes reminded him. "I don't need any more."

"You don't have to worry about me." Jennifer turned off the recorder. "I don't have any political ambitions. Just remember to let me know if Mrs. Harris's death turns out to be something more than an accident."

Rhodes thought she'd find out anyway. With her sources, she might find out before he did. But he told her he'd let her know. She thanked him and left.

"Now," Rhodes said to Ruth, "you can tell me what else you found out at Mrs. Harris's house."

"Nothing," Ruth said. "I didn't even know the will was missing until I got back here. I dusted for prints in the kitchen, and of course I found some. Some on the back gate, too. They probably all belong to Mrs. Harris, though."

"You can't be sure."

"No. I'll have a closer look later. I'm pretty sure there's more than one set. Right now I need to copy these lists for you."

"The rest are all there?"

Ruth flipped through the folders. "They're all there. Red Hats, OWLS, Rusty Nuggets. Names and phone numbers of all the members."

"Let me have the copies when you're finished," Rhodes said. "Then you can take the originals back to the house. And notify the next of kin. There's a brother in Montana. Hack, see if you can locate a phone number for him. Buddy, you can tell Leonard Thorpe. He's her cousin. Lives at the Tranquility Park."

"Right. Are you going to talk to all the people on these lists?"

"No. You're going to talk to some of them."

"Who gets the Red Hats?" Hack said.

"We'll flip for it," Rhodes told him.

The Clearview city dump, or sanitary landfill as it was called by the more sensitive sorts, wasn't one of the most attractive places in Blacklin County, but it was among the most scenic. More than once Rhodes had even seen seagulls flying around, scavenging for food, an unusual sight so far from the Gulf Coast.

There were no seagulls in sight when he stepped out of the county car that afternoon, however, and he didn't blame them for staying away. The odor was overpowering, and Rhodes imagined that he could see a haze of stink hovering over the dump site, which was a big hole in the ground, surrounded by trash of all descriptions. A big part of the stink seemed to be coming from the carcass of a large animal that Rhodes couldn't identify, partly because he was too far away to have a good look at it and partly because of its advanced decomposition.

The growl of a bulldozer came from behind a mound of trash, and Rhodes saw the pile start to move. A swarm of black flies rose from the carcass and hovered over it like a storm cloud.

After the pile of garbage and trash was pushed into the hole, it would all be covered over, except for the flies, who would no doubt fly away and find some other delicate morsel to feed on. The smell wouldn't be so bad for a while, not until more mounds of trash and garbage had accumulated.

A battered, old black Ford pickup sat not far from where the bulldozer worked, and a man wearing a crumpled straw cowboy hat was picking through some of the trash. Rhodes wondered what he was looking for.

Rhodes hadn't come to the sanitary landfill for pleasure. He'd come to visit Billy Joe Byron, who lived there. Well, not *there,* exactly, but close by in a little, unpainted shotgun house with a dirt yard decorated by things Billy Joe had picked up at the dump: toilet bowls, a couple of broken deck chairs, a piece of a granite countertop, and a couple of lawn flamingos. A bottle tree made of a coatrack stood near the front door, and the red, blue, and green bottles caught the sun and threw it in patches on the bare wood of the house. A weathered picture of some poker-playing dogs was nailed to the wall.

Rhodes breathed through his mouth and walked up to the front door. It was shortly after noon, and he hoped that Billy Joe would be home.

The screen door hung askew in its frame, and Rhodes thought it might fall to the ground when he knocked. It didn't, but a screw came out and fell by his feet. He picked it up and was about to try screwing it back in when Billy Joe came to the door.

"Hey, Billy Joe," Rhodes said.

Billy Joe looked at him for a couple of seconds before he spoke. "Hey . . . Sheriff."

No one knew how old Billy Joe was. He'd been around Clearview for as long as Rhodes could remember, but the only real sign of his age was the gray hair at his temples and in the day-old stubble on his face.

"I need to ask you a few questions," Rhodes said.

". . . what?"

"Questions," Rhodes said, knowing that he'd be lucky to get much information from Billy Joe, who wasn't the world's best communicator.

"O . . . kay."

Rhodes knew he wouldn't be invited inside. The idea would simply never occur to Billy Joe, which was fine with Rhodes. He didn't think he wanted to see what was in there.

"Where have you been today, Billy Joe?"

"Been . . . here."

Rhodes took a deep breath, trying not to smell too much. "Have you been anywhere else?"

". . . yeah."

"Where?"

"Been . . . to town."

Billy Joe went to town just about every day. He spent his time walking all over, and he could be seen on the streets or in the alleys smoking a cigarette and looking as if he might know a secret that no one else had figured out. He checked people's trash for things he might like, such as an old picture of some poker-playing dogs, and he took whatever he wanted. He never took anything that wasn't put out in the alleys, however, and he never intentionally caused any trouble. Billy Joe lived alone, got a small amount of some kind of government assistance money, and cared for himself in a minimal way. The house he lived in wasn't really his, and it was on city property, but no one minded as long as he didn't bother anyone.

"Where in town?"

"All . . . over."

Rhodes didn't think it would do any good to ask about street names. He was sure that Billy Joe had no idea about things like that. He just wandered around without ever seeming to have any goal in mind.

"You know where my house is?"

Billy Joe nodded and felt his shirt pocket. Discovering that he had a package of cigarettes there, he took them out and tapped one out. He stuck it in his mouth and dug in the pocket of his jeans until he found a butane lighter. He lit the cigarette and exhaled a cloud of smoke.

"Were you close to my house today?"

". . . maybe."

"Do you know Mrs. Harris?"

Billy Joe nodded. ". . . nice . . . lady."

"Were you at her house today?"

Billy Joe smiled, showing a few yellow teeth with lots of gaps between them. He exhaled smoke and nodded. As Rhodes knew, this was the way most conversations with Billy Joe went. He said only a couple of words at a time, and sometimes no words at all, using just a nod or a shake of the head to get his meaning across.

"Did anything happen while you were there?"

Billy Joe nodded again and went inside his house. Rhodes waited, since he hadn't been asked to follow. He looked at the poker-playing dogs, who seemed to be having much more fun than Rhodes was. Maybe that was because they couldn't smell the dump. Rhodes wondered if they were playing Texas Hold 'Em, which seemed to be the latest fad. Which reminded Rhodes of Leonard Thorpe, who had more than once been in trouble for illegal gambling. He'd set up some poker tournaments in his trailer, planning to turn a profit on them. An anonymous tipster always turned him in, and Rhodes had raided three of the proposed tournaments.

When Billy Joe came back, he was holding an old electric fan. Rhodes asked what it was, and Billy Joe explained in his roundabout way that he'd found it outside Mrs. Harris's back fence. She'd put it out to be picked up by the trash truck, but Billy Joe had found it first.

Rhodes had no idea what Billy Joe would do with a fan, since his house didn't even have electricity, but Billy Joe seemed quite happy with his find. No matter how many different ways Rhodes approached the topic of Mrs. Harris, however, Billy Joe couldn't, or wouldn't, tell him anything more about what he'd seen in the neighborhood.

After a few fruitless minutes, Rhodes gave up and told Billy Joe that it had been a pleasure to talk with him.

"Me . . . too," Billy Joe said, which Rhodes interpreted to mean that Billy Joe had enjoyed the conversation, no matter how tortured it had been. Probably not too many people took the time to have a conversation with Billy Joe. It was too frustrating for them.

Rhodes walked back to the county car. The smell of the dump was out of his nostrils, and he was thinking about lunch when the radio crackled.

"You anywhere near the trailer park?" Hack said.

"Close enough. Why?"

"You'd better get over there."

"What's the problem?"

"Some fella runnin' around with a chain saw."

Rhodes had already turned the car in the direction of the mobile-home park. "Is his name Leatherface?"

"Nope, but he's actin' like it was, chasin' some other fella around the park and sayin' he's gonna cut him up in pieces and wrap the parts up for sale."

"Call Ruth for backup," Rhodes said.

"She's already on the way. You're the backup. Watch out for your hands and feet."

"I'll try to remember," Rhodes said. "If it's not Leatherface, who is it?"

"Leonard Thorpe," Hack said.

Chapter 7

▼

THE ENTRANCE TO THE TRANQUILITY MOBILE HOME PARK HAD A white brick wall on each side, with flowers planted in front. The brick had recently been cleaned and dazzled in the sunlight.

At the front of the park, the trailers were all new. They had awnings over the doors, with little lawns and flower beds in front. A couple of them even had small fishponds with fountains in them, and several had aboveground pools in the back. But the farther from the entrance Rhodes drove, the more run-down the trailers became.

At the very back of the park were the trailers that had been there from the park's opening, at least thirty years earlier. Some had sides streaked with rust. Others had green and black mildew growing on them. The skirts around many of them were either only partially intact or gone completely. One or two of the trailers had been kept up well, and their small yards and flower beds were the equal of any in the front of the park, but mostly the lawns were scraggly and weedy, more dirt than grass.

Rhodes saw Ruth's county car parked near one of the oldest trailers in the place. Thorpe's trailer. Rhodes stopped behind the county car.

A small crowd had gathered in front of the car, surrounding Ruth. People were talking loud, and some of them were laughing. A couple of dogs barked and frisked around the edges of the group.

When Rhodes got out of his car, he could hear the roar of a gas-powered chain saw above the babble, but he couldn't tell where the sound was coming from. He walked over to join Ruth, who pointed at a small wooded area in back of the mobile-home park. The trees were close together, and vines of wild grapes hung from some of the limbs.

Though he could still hear the saw, Rhodes didn't see either the saw or the man wielding it.

"They're back in the trees," someone said in Rhodes's ear. "They'll show up in a minute."

"Who?" Rhodes said to Ruth.

"I'm not sure," she told him.

"It's that Thorpe fella," said the voice in Rhodes's ear.

Rhodes turned to see who was talking to him. The man must have been around seventy. He was tall, skinny, and his cheeks were as pink as if he'd just shaved, which might have been the case. Rhodes smelled Aqua Velva.

"You sure?" Rhodes said.

"Sure I'm sure." The man pointed. "I live in that trailer right over there."

Rhodes wasn't sure what that was supposed to tell him.

"Next door to Thorpe," the man said. "Name's Sherman, Gid Sherman."

He offered his hand. Rhodes shook it, thinking that the man's voice sounded familiar. He might well be the anonymous caller who had turned Thorpe in for gambling.

While Rhodes was thinking this over, someone yelled, "Here they come!"

A man ran from the cover of the trees. He was old, but he was moving along at a pretty good clip. Rhodes didn't blame him, since Thorpe was right behind with the chain saw, which was getting louder now that it was closer.

"Shoot him, Sheriff!" someone called out. "He's gaining!"

Ruth turned to Rhodes. "Want me to shoot him?"

"I don't think he's gaining, but keep your gun handy," Rhodes said. "Isn't that Alton Brant he's chasing?"

It was, and the Korean War vet was high-stepping it when he passed the little crowd. He was flat of stomach and clear of eye, and he didn't even seem to be breathing hard.

Thorpe wasn't much younger than Brant. He wore cutoff jeans and a Harley-Davidson T-shirt. Rhodes didn't think Thorpe owned a motorcycle, but it was the thought that counted. Thorpe was still muscular enough to fill out the shirt in the right way, with a flat stomach and wide chest. The T-shirt was soaked with sweat from Thorpe's exertions, and his face was red, but he was a handsome man, not movie-star handsome, but rugged. Iron-gray hair showed on the sides of his head not covered by the Houston Astros cap he wore.

When Brant went past, Rhodes moved out from the crowd and

stood in Thorpe's path. Thorpe saw him and came to a shambling stop. His mouth was open, and he took deep, gasping breaths.

"What's the trouble?" Rhodes had to raise his voice to be heard over the roar of the saw.

It took Thorpe a few seconds to catch his breath. When he did, he said, "Get out of my way, Sheriff."

Rhodes didn't move. Thorpe revved the chain saw and made a feint at him. Rhodes smelled gas and hot oil.

"Assault with a deadly weapon," Rhodes said. "You don't need that on your record."

"You can't fool me, Sheriff." Thorpe revved the saw again. "It's too late to keep that off my record."

Rhodes wondered if he should tell Ruth to shoot him, but the crowd was milling around, and some of them were already behind Thorpe. No good would come from firing a pistol in a situation like that.

Thorpe jumped forward, thrusting the saw at Rhodes. Rhodes jumped backward, watching the spinning chain and remembering for some reason a cartoon he'd once seen where a character was sliced in half.

The crowd moved back, too, sucking in a collective breath. Rhodes figured they were having a great day. Nothing like a good chain-saw fight to break the monotony.

He thought of the cartoon again. He had a feeling he wouldn't be nearly as bloodless as the cartoon character had been if he was split in half, and he wouldn't go back together quite so easily, either.

Thorpe raised the saw into the air, and Rhodes thought maybe he was going to give up. Thorpe fooled him, however. He rushed forward.

Rhodes made a clumsy move backward and turned his ankle. He fell to the ground and looked up to see the saw swinging down at him. He rolled away, but the saw took a little of his shirt and scraped some skin off his back before hitting the ground and throwing chunks of dirt into the air all around.

Thorpe lost his balance and almost lost his grip on the saw, but he managed to keep his feet as Rhodes rolled over again and grabbed the bumper of Ruth's county car to pull himself up.

He heard Ruth yell for Thorpe to freeze, but he held up his hand. He didn't want anybody to get killed, not even Thorpe, not if it could be prevented.

The crowd had moved a good distance away now. Rhodes didn't blame them. When there's a man with a chain saw and a deputy with a pistol, the sensible thing to do is get away.

"Listen, Thorpe," Rhodes said. "You're already in enough trouble as it is. Put down the saw and don't make things any worse."

"I've assaulted an officer," Thorpe said. "How could it get any worse?"

"You could kill me."

"I might have to do that unless you'll let me leave."

"Leave?"

"Let me go after Brant. He's the one I want. After I take care of him, I'll let you arrest me. I'm not gonna hurt anybody else."

"You're not going to hurt him, either."

"I am, by God. I'll take care of him one piece at a time. You can't stop me."

Ruth had assumed the shooting stance, feet spread slightly, both hands gripping her pistol. If Rhodes nodded, she'd shoot.

Most likely she'd wound Thorpe, but there was always the chance that she might kill him, and then they'd have a dead body on their hands. Or she might miss and hit one of the bystanders. That would lead to no end of report writing. Thorpe wasn't worth it, although for the moment, Rhodes didn't see any other way to handle him.

"Everybody leave," Rhodes said. "Right now. Get back in your homes and stay there until this is over."

He heard a lot of grumbling, but people began to move away, except for one man. Alton Brant was back, walking calmly through the crowd with a long-handled shovel. Rhodes thought he knew what Brant had in mind, and he decided not to discourage him.

"What's all this about, anyway, Mr. Thorpe?" Rhodes said. "Why are you after Brant?"

"I like that *mister*. Nice and polite. But it doesn't change the fact that what this is about is my business. Now you and your deputy just back off, and we'll call it quits."

Rhodes's skin was stinging a little where the saw had scraped him. He wondered if Thorpe really believed he'd back off.

"You know I can't do that. I have to enforce the laws, and you've broken about ten of them."

"I'm gonna break me a few more before I'm done here."

By that time Brant was directly behind Thorpe and not more than ten feet away. The noise of the saw was more than loud enough to cover his approach as long as Thorpe was concentrating on Rhodes.

"You can't just cut somebody into pieces and then walk away," Rhodes said.

Thorpe grinned. "I don't give a damn what happens after I cut him up. You can lock me in your hoosegow and throw away the key for all I care."

"You wouldn't like it there," Rhodes said, wondering how long it had been since he'd heard the word *hoosegow*.

Thorpe opened his mouth to say something further, but he didn't get a word out before Brant slammed the metal scoop of the shovel into the back of his head. The shovel landed with a satisfactory clang, and Thorpe pitched forward.

As he did, the chain saw flew from his limp fingers, straight at Rhodes.

The saw stopped operating as soon as Thorpe released the trigger, which made it less dangerous but still capable of causing serious damage.

Rhodes dodged aside, and the saw hit the hood of the county car, sliding up to the windshield, removing the white paint and leaving a long, jagged metallic scar.

The scar bothered Rhodes almost as much as Thorpe's lying facedown about four feet away from him. He'd have to explain the scar to the county commissioners, who wouldn't be happy about having to pay for it.

Thorpe moaned, and Rhodes turned to look at him. He twitched a little, moaned again, and lay still.

"I hope I didn't hit him too hard," Alton Brant said.

"Did you dent the shovel?" Rhodes said.

Brant turned the shovel in his hands and looked at the bottom of the scoop. "Nope. Not in the least."

"We'd better call the ambulance, anyway," Ruth Grady said, walking over to stand beside Rhodes. "We don't want to take any chances with him and get sued."

"If anybody gets sued, it'll be me," Brant said. "I'm the one who hit him."

"He's the kind who'll sue anybody that's handy," Rhodes said. "Especially the county."

The commissioners wouldn't like that, either, Rhodes thought, so it was best not to let it happen. He told Ruth to call for the ambulance.

"Want me to get the first-aid kit for your back?"

Rhodes told her that his back would be okay. "Just a scratch." Then he looked around and saw that most of the crowd had left, either to avoid being sued or because all the fun was over. Even the two dogs were gone.

One of the few people still hanging around was the man who'd spoken to Rhodes earlier. He looked at Rhodes but didn't speak. He turned and walked away.

Rhodes didn't have time for him at the moment. He knelt down and checked to make sure that Thorpe was breathing and that he had a pulse. Satisfied that Thorpe was doing all right, Rhodes stood up to talk to Brant.

"What was that all about?" He motioned to the chain saw with his thumb. The saw still lay on the hood of the county car, right next to the windshield at the end of the ugly scratch.

"It was my fault," Brant said, and Rhodes knew he wasn't talking about the scratch.

Brant's gray hair was cut so close to the top of his head that only a bit of stubble showed. He appeared to be almost bald, but Rhodes could see that he actually had a lot of hair, or would if he'd let it grow. His voice had an edge of command that might long ago have ordered soldiers into battle. Or maybe not. Rhodes didn't remember if Brant had been an officer during the war.

"Thorpe was the one with the chain saw," Rhodes pointed out. "That wasn't your fault."

"No, but I'm the one who started it all." Brant's face became mournful. "I came out here and accused him of killing Helen."

"Now why would you do a thing like that?"

"I don't know. It was a stupid stunt. I should have known he wouldn't take it well."

"You probably didn't figure on the chain saw, though."

Brant tried to grin, but it didn't quite work. "No, I didn't figure on that. I'm just glad he didn't have a gun."

"He probably has one somewhere or other in his trailer."

"If he does, I was lucky we were outside when I accused him and it wasn't handy."

"And the chain saw was?"

Brant indicated a small metal toolshed next to Thorpe's trailer. The door was open, and Rhodes could see a rake and a hoe leaning against the back wall. A couple of aluminum chairs with green webbing were folded up and leaning on the hoe and rake.

"The chain saw was in there," Brant said. "I don't think it would be a good place to keep a gun."

Rhodes wondered why Thorpe would need a chain saw at all. Maybe he used it to cut wood in the winter, but there was no fireplace in the trailer.

"You're lucky he didn't cut off your arms," Rhodes said.

"So are you. Thanks for stepping in."

"Just doing my job. Why did you think he might have killed Mrs. Harris?"

"She was about to come into money," Brant said. "Gas money. There were going to be gas wells drilled on her property, and they'd have made her wealthy."

Rhodes wasn't sure what that had to do with anything, but he didn't ask. He just let Brant keep on talking.

"Thorpe bothered Helen a lot. He needed money all the time, and some of the ways he tried to make it weren't legal. But I guess you know that."

"The poker games," Rhodes said.

"Yes, and a few other things that Helen talked him out of. Well, I say she talked him out of them, but it was more the money she gave him that did it."

Rhodes thought they were getting off the track, even if he wasn't sure what the track was.

"If she was giving him money, why would he kill her?" he said.

"That wasn't the reason. He wanted more than she was giving him, and killing her would have been a way to get it. He would have inherited the mineral rights to her property."

"How do you know that?"

"I witnessed her will," Brant said.

Chapter 8

▼

THE AMBULANCE ARRIVED AND TOOK THORPE AWAY. HE'D RE-
gained consciousness, but he wasn't doing any talking. He probably didn't feel like it.

Rhodes took the chain saw off the hood of Ruth's car and put it
in the toolshed. Ruth followed the ambulance to the hospital in the
county car with the intention of taking Thorpe to jail if nothing
was wrong with him. If he was seriously concussed, she'd stay to
watch his room until she was relieved. She would also question
him when he was feeling up to it, if he ever was.

That left Rhodes to finish with Brant and to do any further investigation into Helen Harris's death for a while. Rhodes suggested to Brant that they go to the courthouse to finish their
discussion.

"We'll have more privacy there," Rhodes said.

He could almost feel the stares of the people in the trailers, although he couldn't see anybody at the windows.

Brant agreed that privacy might be a good idea. Rhodes didn't want to go to the jail because he was afraid that Jennifer Loam might come looking for him there, and he didn't want her to find him talking to Brant.

"I'll meet you there in half an hour," Rhodes said, thinking that he needed to get on another shirt. It didn't look good for the sheriff to be walking around in a torn shirt with a bare, scraped back.

At home Rhodes looked for Yancey and found him under the bed. The cat was in the kitchen, lying near the refrigerator.

"He hasn't hurt you has he?" Rhodes asked the dog.

Yancey didn't answer, and he didn't come out from under the bed. Rhodes wondered if the cat might not be useful. It had the ability to keep Yancey quiet for unprecedented lengths of time.

Rhodes left Yancey and went back to the kitchen. He took off the ripped shirt and hid it in the bottom of the kitchen trash can under a couple of plastic wrappers where he hoped Ivy wouldn't find it. He didn't want to worry her unnecessarily.

The cat watched him through slitted eyes, and Rhodes figured it would tattle on him if it could talk.

When the shirt was taken care of, Rhodes got a paper towel and went to the bathroom. He soaked the towel with alcohol and rubbed his back as best he could. The alcohol stung, and Rhodes sucked his breath in between his teeth. Then he went back to the kitchen and hid the towel with the shirt.

"One of these days I'm going to get caught," he told the cat, who didn't seem to care in the least.

Rhodes went to the bedroom and put on a clean shirt. Yancey

slipped out from under the bed. He didn't yip or bounce, but he seemed marginally more chipper.

"Don't let him get the best of you," Rhodes told Yancey, but he was afraid that the advice was too late.

The courthouse was only a couple of blocks from the jail. Rhodes parked in the back and waited for Brant to arrive. When he did, they both got out of their cars and went into the building. It was cool and quiet because the courts weren't in session, and Rhodes's office was on the second floor, away from some of the usual bustle.

Rhodes seldom used the courthouse office, and he'd used it even less often in recent months because someone—he didn't know who—had removed the old Dr Pepper machine, the one that had dispensed real glass bottles, and replaced it with one that gave you a much bigger plastic bottle. It might have been a bigger value for the money, but to Rhodes it didn't add up. He would have paid extra for the glass bottles.

Brant followed Rhodes into the office, and Rhodes was glad to see that things were clean and dusted. He trusted the cleaning staff to take care of things like that even though he didn't show up much, and sometimes they let him down. This time, however, there were no spiderwebs.

Rhodes sat behind his desk and Brant sat in a heavy wooden chair opposite him. Brant sat with his back straight, his feet on the floor, and his hands flat along his thighs.

"You say you witnessed Mrs. Harris's will?" Rhodes said.

"That's right. It couldn't have been more than a couple of months ago."

Rhodes found that hard to believe. Someone who paid as much attention to details as Mrs. Harris would likely have made a will long ago. Rhodes said as much.

Brant nodded. "She did make one a long time ago. This was a new one. She wanted to make some changes after she found out about the gas wells."

Brant's face changed. He struggled to keep it straight and almost managed it. But not quite. He reached into a back pocket of his pants, brought out a handkerchief, and brushed at his eyes.

"I apologize," he said, folding the handkerchief and replacing it. "I used to have much better control of my emotions. I think it has something to do with getting older."

He hadn't really looked old to Rhodes, not until that moment of vulnerability.

"It's not fair, you see," Brant said. "Helen has always gotten by on her teacher retirement, but 'gotten by' is all. She never had any nice things, she never got to travel, she never even got a new car."

Rhodes hadn't looked in the garage, but come to think of it, he remembered that Mrs. Harris drove a very old, but very clean, Chevrolet. Rhodes himself occasionally drove an Edsel, but it wasn't his main car. He'd bought it because it was so ugly that it was attractive to him.

"Thorpe was her only relative," Brant said, "except for her brother up in Montana. He has plenty of money, Helen said, and because Thorpe was so dependent on her, she decided to leave him both the land and the mineral rights. Her earlier will left everything to charity, and I told her to leave it like that. She didn't listen to me, and now she's dead."

"You still think Thorpe killed her?"

"Yes. That's exactly the kind of thing he'd do. To get the money."

"He'd get it eventually. He's younger than she was."

"Not by much. Not enough so that he'd want to wait."

Brant seemed convinced, but Rhodes thought that there must be other possibilities.

"She didn't have any enemies?"

"Helen? Of course not. Everybody loved her. She was in a lot of clubs and groups. Ask anybody."

Rhodes heard a noise in the hallway outside his door. Then someone knocked.

"Who's that?" Brant asked.

"I don't have any idea." But Rhodes did have an idea, or maybe it was a premonition. He stood up and went to the door. He opened it, and Jennifer Loam stood there looking up at him.

"You can run," she said, "but you can't hide."

Rhodes didn't ask how she'd tracked him down. She'd been to the courthouse office before, so it wasn't surprising that she had figured he might be there. She'd probably seen his car parked behind the building.

"Aren't you going to ask me in?" she said.

Rhodes opened the door wider and stepped back so the reporter could come inside. He closed the door behind her and went back to his desk. Brant stood up. Jennifer said hello to him and sat in a chair near his. When she was seated, Brant sat back down.

"You two know each other?" Rhodes said.

"I've interviewed Colonel Brant for the paper," Jennifer said.

Rhodes noticed that she used Brant's military rank, which was probably important to the man, even though he hadn't been in the service for years. Some ex-military people that Rhodes had known always liked to recall their time in the service. Brant was obviously one of those, because he brightened when she used the title.

"She did a fine job of writing up the interview, too." Brant smiled. "Didn't misquote me a single time."

Rhodes thought of asking how many times she *did* misquote him, but this wasn't the time for wisecracks.

"I don't suppose you came here to interview him again."

"No." Jennifer got out her digital recorder. "I came here to ask about the quarrel at the mobile-home park."

"That was just a private misunderstanding," Rhodes said.

"Yes," Brant said. "That's all it was. It wasn't anything your readers would be interested in."

"I'm sure." Jennifer's tone let them know she didn't believe a word of it. "Just a man chasing another man around a mobile-home park with a chain saw. Nothing interesting about that at all." She paused and put on a thoughtful look. "But if that's so, why are you two hiding out in here? Just talking over old times?"

"We're not hiding out," Rhodes said. "We had to straighten out a few things. All it boils down to is that Mr. Thorpe got hit with a shovel."

"My sources tell me there was a little more to it than that, but I'll settle for your telling me how that happened."

"It was an accident. The shovel slipped out of Mr. Brant's hand."

"Wow," Jennifer said with a straight face. Rhodes thought she would have done well in one of Thorpe's Texas Hold 'Em games. "The readers are going to love that one. Are you sure you can't do any better?"

"To be honest," Brant told her, "I thought he'd killed Helen Harris."

Jennifer smiled a thin, meaningless smile at Rhodes. "I thought Mrs. Harris had an accident."

"That's what I think," Rhodes said, not mentioning that Brant didn't feel the same way. For that matter, Rhodes wasn't sure he felt that way, and Jennifer probably knew it. "However, it's still under investigation."

"Right. That's a nice noncommittal phrase, *under investigation.* What does it mean exactly?"

"I'll bet you know."

Jennifer thought it over, then gave Rhodes a grin. "It means that the snoopy girl reporter isn't going to get anything else out of you. Am I right?"

"I always said you were smart."

Jennifer turned in her chair. "What about you, Mr. Brant? Are you feeling any more cooperative than the sheriff."

"Not a lot, I'm afraid. I don't want this to get in the paper. It's an embarrassment to me."

"I'm sorry about that, but it's my job to see that people are informed."

"We don't want to stop you from doing your job," Rhodes said. "But we don't want to cause ourselves any unnecessary problems, either."

"I already know the details of the chain-saw fight," Jennifer said. "I talked to someone at the mobile-home park about it. So it's already going into the paper."

She said it matter-of-factly, as if to let Rhodes know there was nothing he could do about it, not that he'd have tried.

"Fine," he said. "People need to be informed about the things that are going on in their community."

"Even if it embarrasses them?"

Rhodes looked at Brant, who said, "I suppose so."

"I'm glad you feel that way. And I'm glad the sheriff believes in the right of the people to be informed. That means I can interview Leonard Thorpe."

Rhodes tried not to show his surprise. "He's a prisoner. You can't talk to him."

"I was told that he's a patient in the hospital."

"That, too. But he's still a prisoner, and he's under guard."

Jennifer snapped off her recorder and stood up. Brant started to rise as well, but she told him not to bother.

"Thank you for your time, Sheriff," she said. "You, too, Mr. Brant. I hope you like the story in tomorrow's paper."

"I'm sure it will be up to your usual standard," Rhodes said without irony. He did like Jennifer's writing.

Jennifer walked to the door.

"Hang on a minute," Rhodes said. "You wouldn't like to have a cat, would you? Already housebroken. Just needs a good home."

"I have a dog," Jennifer said, and left.

"I have a dog, too," Rhodes told Brant. "Two of them. You know Helen's cat pretty well, I guess."

"That cat and I never did get along. I can't take it, if that's what you mean."

"Don't be too hasty. You might change your mind."

"I might," Brant said, getting Rhodes's hopes up. "But I doubt it. I have a dog, too, a dalmatian."

"Oh."

"Yes." Brant paused. "That reporter's awfully young."

"And good at her job. I'm not sure I want to read her story."

"Maybe I should just have told her the truth."

"If you did that, and if she printed it, some people might think you should be charged with a crime."

"They could be right."

Rhodes nodded. He could think of several charges that might be brought against Brant, but he didn't see any reason for them. Not at the moment.

"It still doesn't make sense to me that Thorpe would have killed Mrs. Harris," he said.

"Why not? You saw how violent he can be."

"There's something you don't know."

"What?"

"There's not a will leaving the money to Thorpe."

"You mean she changed it again? But that can't be. She'd have asked me to witness it."

"I don't mean she changed it again," Rhodes said. "I mean it's gone."

Chapter 9

▼

ACCORDING TO BRANT, HELEN HARRIS HAD WRITTEN HER WILL out by hand, following a form she'd found in some library book.

"She didn't think she needed a lawyer," Brant said. "She didn't want to spend the money, and she didn't have a complicated estate. So she thought a holographic will would be fine. I witnessed her signature."

"As careful as she was, I'd have thought she'd want more than one witness," Rhodes said.

"Naturally. Francine Oates was the other witness. I suppose Helen thought we were both upstanding citizens."

"No question about that. Did Mrs. Harris have a safe-deposit box."

"I'm sure she didn't. You'd be surprised how much the rent on those things can be, even in a small town like Clearview."

"She should have had an extra copy of the will," Rhodes said.

"I'm sure she intended to make one. There's a photocopier at the public library. She might not have gotten around to it, though."

"Where would a copy be if she'd made one?"

"I have no idea. She might have given one to me, but I don't have it. Francine Oates, maybe."

Rhodes thought he'd have to check on that, even though Francine hadn't mentioned having one.

"How does any of this affect Helen's death?" Brant said.

Rhodes didn't know. "We'll find out if it does, eventually."

Brant wasn't too happy with that answer, but he and Rhodes parted on good terms, with Rhodes warning him to stay away from Leo Thorpe.

"I'll stay away from him as long as I know justice is going to be done," Brant said. "Otherwise, I can't promise you anything."

Rhodes didn't like that answer, but he figured it would do.

When Rhodes got back to the jail, Hack and Lawton looked about as happy as he'd ever seen them. He knew that meant trouble.

Even worse, they didn't ask him about the incident at the mobile-home park, about which they would have been abnormally curious at almost any time. Their lack of interest was a sure sign that they were up to something. Rhodes didn't have to wait long to find out what it was.

"There he is," Hack said to Lawton as Rhodes walked to his desk. "Just look at him."

"A fine figure of a man," Lawton said.

"Practically a movie star," Hack went on.

Lawton nodded. "Cary Grant."

"Too sissy. Not any of those little short fellas like you see these days, either. Tom Cruise, Brad Pitt, and like that. John Wayne, maybe."

"Clint Eastwood," Lawton suggested. "Lee Marvin."

Rhodes turned to face them. "All right, you two. What's going on?"

Hack smiled and looked at Lawton. "I never knew anybody famous before, Lawton. Did you?"

"Not like a close friend or anything. I saw Roy Rogers once at the rodeo down in Houston."

"Seein' somebody at a rodeo don't count. I'm talking about somebody you see every day, not knowin' that he's a celebrity."

"Nope," Lawton said. "Never knew anybody like that."

"Till now," Hack said.

"That's right. Not till now."

"Hang on a minute. I forgot somebody. We knew Terry Don Coslin."

"Sure enough. We knew him, all right. I'd forgot all about him."

Terry Don Coslin was a onetime Clearview resident who'd become famous as a model for paperback romance-novel covers. He'd come home for a visit and come to a bad end. But for a little while, he'd been every woman's favorite fantasy.

"Terry Don was pretty famous, all right," Hack said. "Too bad he's not still around. He'd be perfect."

"Perfect for what?" Rhodes said, though he was well aware that asking Hack and Lawton such a question was as likely to extend their routine as to put a stop to it. More likely, as a matter of fact.

"Perfect for the cover," Hack said.

Rhodes tried to resist, but he couldn't. "What cover?"

"The book cover," Lawton said. "That's what."

Rhodes wanted to say, "Oh. Of course. I see what you mean." He knew it would confound them.

But he couldn't say it. He said exactly what they expected. "What book cover?"

"The one that ought to have you on it," Hack said.

Rhodes remembered something like that from his high school English classes. It was called a circular definition. He didn't think it would do any good to remind Hack of that, so he simply repeated his earlier question in a different tone of voice.

"What book cover?"

Hack must have recognized the tone change because he quit smiling. "The cover of the book those two women wrote."

At last something was making sense, of a sort. Rhodes didn't have to ask which two women. "You mean Claudia and Jan."

"Yep, that's the two."

Claudia and Jan had shown up in Blacklin County a couple of times, once at a writers' workshop where Terry Don Coslin had appeared, and once when a set of mammoth bones had been uncovered in a creek bed. Both times, they'd become peripherally involved in murder.

"I thought they were writing a magazine article," Rhodes said.

"Maybe so, but it's not an article they called about. It's a book about . . . now let me be sure I got this exactly right. I don't want to mess it up. You can help me out if I go wrong, Lawton."

Lawton grinned and nodded while Hack picked up a piece of paper from his desk. He looked down at the paper, then looked back at Rhodes. "One of those women, either Claudia or Jan, I'm not sure which one it was, called here and told me that this book of theirs is about 'a handsome, crime-bustin' sheriff.' " Hack looked up from the paper and grinned at Rhodes. "That would be you."

Rhodes's stomach felt as if it had been hollowed out, and he hoped his face wasn't turning red. The last time they'd been in Clearview, Claudia and Jan had mentioned a book like that, using those exact words, but he'd thought they were only kidding. They'd even told him that he would be the model for their main character. That had been a joke, too, or so he'd thought. It was looking as if he'd thought wrong.

"What you got to say about that?" Hack asked. "Cat got your tongue?"

"I didn't know about any book," Rhodes said.

"Course you didn't. They just got the word about it. They're plumb tickled to death about it. They got themselves an 'agent,' and he's the one sold the book for them. It's coming out sometime next year, they say. It'll be in Wal-Mart and all like that. You know. Like Vernell's books. So that's why Lawton and I are so happy. We can tell ever'body we know the handsome, crime-bustin' sheriff in that book up close and personal, and we see him just about ever' day."

Rhodes didn't know what to say. He imagined the sheriff on the book cover looking the way Terry Don had on the romance-novel covers, shirt open to the navel as if it didn't have any buttons, long, black, wavy hair, his chiseled face looking deep into the eyes of a beautiful woman who leaned in the crook of his arm and stared soulfully back at him, his chest ridged with muscle.

Unlike Terry Don, however, the sheriff character would have a couple of Glocks belted to his waist, or maybe an assault rifle under his free arm. Or he'd have Glocks and an assault rifle both.

"Yes, sir, Sheriff," Lawton said. "You'll look real good on that book cover."

The trouble with that idea was that Rhodes didn't look a thing like a cover model. Sure, he tried to exercise now and then on his stationary bike, and, yes, Ivy tried to keep him on a healthy diet. Even at that, however, his chest would never be ridged with muscle, nor would his stomach ever be as flat and rock hard as Terry Don's had been. Those Blizzards Rhodes would occasionally sneak at the Dairy Queen might have something to do with it, he thought.

"I'm not going to be on the book cover," he said, "and Claudia and Jan didn't tell you that I would."

"Well, no," Hack admitted. "They didn't say that in so many words, but I figured that if the book was about you, handsome and crime-bustin' and all that, they'd naturally want your picture on the front of it."

"The book's not about me."

"Sure it is. That's what she said, whichever one of 'em it was."

"No, she didn't."

"Well, maybe not exactly, but that's what she meant, all right. She said you were the 'inspiration' for the book, and she wanted you to be the first one to know about it."

"Seems as if I'm not the first, though," Rhodes said.

"You can't blame us for that," Hack said, trying out his bland-and-innocent look. "It's not our fault you're never here. If you stayed around the office more, you'd be the first to find out stuff."

"Yeah," Lawton said, "but you gotta remember that he has to be out there bustin' crime to protect the good citizens of the county."

"Right," Rhodes said. "From chain-saw killers and the like."

Hack had been ready to say something else about the book, but the words didn't come out. He sat there with his mouth half-open.

Lawton's eyes widened. His mouth worked, and Rhodes could tell he was trying not to ask what he was dying to know. It took a couple of seconds, but his curiosity won out in the end.

"You gonna tell us about that?"

Rhodes looked as if he didn't understand. "About what?"

"The chain-saw killer," Hack said. "Nobody said anything to me on the phone about a killin'."

"That's because there wasn't one," Rhodes said, enjoying himself. It wasn't often he could turn the tables on Hack and Lawton so soon after they'd had their way with him.

"Well, what was there, then?" Hack said. He was no better at keeping quiet than Rhodes had been. "You gonna tell us or not?"

Rhodes could have made them suffer, but it wasn't worth it in the long run, so he told them about the episode at Tranquility. They were disappointed that it hadn't been more exciting, but Lawton said that a picture of the sheriff in a backless shirt might make a good book cover.

Hack agreed and said it was nice that the handsome, crime-bustin' sheriff had taken another hardened criminal off the streets.

"I don't think he was ever on the streets," Rhodes said. "He pretty much stayed around his trailer."

"Shows what you know," Hack said, and that comment gave him back the upper hand because of the implication that he knew something that Rhodes didn't.

"You'd better tell me," Rhodes said, using his no-nonsense voice so it wouldn't take all day to get an answer.

"Leo Thorpe gets around," Hack said. "Ain't that right, Lawton?"

"Why are you pickin' on me?" the jailer said. "You think I hang around with that kind of fella? What is there about me that would give you an idea like that?"

"You're the one told me about it, how Leo owned the place," Hack said. "That's all I'm sayin'. You don't need to get your dandruff up about it."

"I'm not gettin' my dandruff up. I'm just wonderin' if you think I'm some kind of hooligan that hangs out with toughs all the time."

"Lawton," Rhodes said, hoping the no-nonsense voice would work better this time.

Lawton gave Hack a final glare, then said to Rhodes, "You know about the Royal Rack?"

The Royal Rack was a pool hall. Located just inside the city limits, it claimed to be a place that was "fun for the whole family," although Rhodes couldn't imagine the family that would have fun there. The Addams Family, maybe.

"I'm the sheriff," Rhodes said.

"Yeah. So you'd know."

"He's been there a few times himself," Hack said. "In the crime-bustin' line of duty, of course."

"What does this have to do with Thorpe?"

"I guess you don't know as much as you think you do," Lawton said. "Not meanin' any disrespect, you understand."

Rhodes sighed, said he understood, and asked what it was that he didn't know.

"Leo Thorpe owns the Royal Rack."

That was indeed information that Rhodes didn't have. He said, "How do you know?"

"He hangs out there," Hack said.

"Lawton? Or Thorpe?"

"Both of 'em."

"There's nothin' wrong with likin' to shoot a game of pool now and then," Lawton said. "When I get off work, I like to relax, and I don't have a girlfriend like some people."

The reference to Miz McGee made Rhodes smile. She hadn't been a girl in fifty or more years.

"Come to think of it," Lawton said, "you ought to take her for a game of pool now and then. She might enjoy it."

"Sure," Hack said.

"Don't get off the subject," Rhodes said. "How do you know Thorpe owns the pool hall?"

"I heard him say so. It was sort of an accident. He hangs around there a lot, and he was talkin' to somebody about the place. Told him he was the new owner."

"When was this?"

"'Bout a week ago, maybe a little bit more. I just happened to overhear him."

Rhodes wondered how Thorpe had gotten the money to buy the pool hall, but Lawton didn't have the answer to that one. Rhodes didn't know if the pool hall had anything to do with Mrs. Harris's murder, but it was something to check into. He concluded his conversation, if that's what it had been, with Hack and Lawton and started writing a report on the mobile-home-park incident.

He was almost finished when the telephone rang. Hack took the call and listened for a while, occasionally looking over at Rhodes. When he hung up, he said, "You'd better get out to the hospital. Your prisoner's escaped."

Chapter 10

▼

AS HE DROVE TO THE HOSPITAL, RHODES TOLD HIMSELF THAT HE didn't think of Thorpe as "his" prisoner. Thorpe was Ruth Grady's prisoner, or he had been, and Rhodes couldn't imagine a situation in which Ruth would let a prisoner escape. It just wasn't like her to do that. She hadn't been hurt, Hack said, but she hadn't explained anything, either.

Rhodes parked in the hospital visitors' lot and went inside through the front door. The scene in the combination lobby/waiting room was chaotic. The room was crammed with people— men, women, and children—most of them talking loudly and waving their arms. The young receptionist behind the desk looked harried and helpless. A couple of Pink Ladies moved around the edges of the group. Both of them were red-faced and angry. Ruth was there, trying to calm everyone down and not succeeding.

It didn't take Rhodes long to size things up. Most of the people in the room belonged to a single large extended family: the Browns.

Nobody knew for sure just how many Browns there were. They were clannish, few of them had any visible means of support, and they kept their business, whatever it was, to themselves. They were also prolific, and it was hard to say just how many children each of the adults might have had because they didn't often all gather in one place at the same time.

Some of them liked to gather in the hospital waiting room, however, because of its many benefits. It was air-conditioned in summer and warm in winter, it had quite a few seats (uncomfortable ones, to be sure, but seats all the same), it had television, and best of all it had free coffee and doughnuts.

A place like that was made to order for the Browns, who liked anything that was free, and the more of it, the better. There had been a couple of minor disturbances at the hospital during the winter when the Browns had eaten all the doughnuts before eight o'clock, and Rhodes had gone out to quell the impending riots. He'd explained to the Browns that the amenities were for people who had family members in the hospital and that both the ill and the people who cared about them deserved a little respect. If the Browns didn't understand anything else, they understood about family, and Rhodes thought the problem had been solved. As was the case more often than he liked to think about, he'd obviously been wrong.

Ruth saw him come through the door and said, "It's the sheriff."

The sudden quiet surprised Rhodes, and all faces turned to him.

"What's going on?" he said, and everyone began to talk at once again.

Rhodes held up a hand. It took a little longer this time, but the babble subsided.

"This is a hospital," Rhodes said. "There are sick people here. It's a place where you're supposed to be quiet. I don't want to hear any more noise. Understand?"

Heads nodded.

"Deputy Grady, do you want to tell me what's going on?"

"I'll do that, Sheriff," one of the Pink Ladies said, stepping forward. "It's . . . these people."

The Browns mumbled among themselves. They were an oddly assorted crew, Rhodes thought, some tall, some short, some fat, some skinny as broom handles. Some were well-groomed, while others looked as if they'd last had a good bath during the early years of the Clinton administration. But all of them had the distinguishing marks of the Brown clan, big noses and big ears that stuck out from the sides of their heads.

"Quiet," Rhodes said, and the mumbling stopped. He asked the Pink Lady her name.

"Ella Long." She pointed to her name tag, but Rhodes was too far away to read it. "I've volunteered here for two years. We've had trouble with . . . these people before."

"The Browns," Rhodes said.

"That's right, and this was the last straw."

"What happened?"

"They came in here and ate all the doughnuts. They drank all the coffee. It's not the first time."

Rhodes looked at Cal Brown, the oldest member of the family in the room. "Didn't I explain to you a while back that this room and the refreshments were for people who had family in the hospital?"

Cal was one of the skinny Browns, and his nose was more

beaky than large. He wore a dirty, white, short-billed cap, a garish aloha shirt with red, green, and yellow flowers, jeans, and battered Nikes.

"I know what you told us," he said. "We got family in the hospital."

Rhodes looked past him at the receptionist. "Is that right?"

The receptionist threw up her hands and rolled her eyes. Rhodes assumed that was a yes.

"Who?" Rhodes said.

"My nephew Rodney," Cal said. "He's in the ER. Cut off his finger with a band saw, and they're sewin' it back on him right now. We packed it in ice and all, just the way you're s'posed to do, and we got him here quick's we could. While we're waitin' for him to get fixed up, we thought it would be all right if we helped ourselves to the goodies, like you said we could, bein' as how we got family here."

"It was like a plague of locusts," Ella Long said. "You can't imagine."

Rhodes could imagine. "The thing of it is," he said to Cal, "you and yours ate and drank all there was. Nobody else will get anything now. You know that's not right."

"We're here on family business. We got a loved one in the ER. You said that's what the goodies was for. So we partook of 'em."

"I understand that. But you partook so much that there's nothing left for anybody else. That's not right."

"You never said anything about that before."

He's got me there, Rhodes thought. "I'm saying it now."

"Don't seem right to deny us. We got a family member in the ER, and he ain't even got his finger sewed back on yet."

"I sympathize with Rodney. But I think the best thing to do is for one or two of you to stay here and the rest of you to go on home. You don't all have to wait for him. There's nothing left to partake of, anyway."

There was a little more mumbling and grumbling. One of the youngsters punched another in the upper arm and got punched back. Two of the women separated them and shushed them, and when things were calm again, Cal sent most of the bunch home after a little more conversation with Rhodes convinced him that the snacks and coffee wouldn't be replenished. Cal and his wife, Agnes, he said, would stay and wait for Rodney.

Ella Long wasn't entirely happy with that solution, but she seemed at least somewhat mollified by the promised absence of the majority of the Browns.

After things had been sorted out and Cal and Agnes were sitting on the chairs watching *Oprah* on the TV, Ruth and Rhodes had a chance to talk. They went outside, and Ruth explained what had happened to Thorpe.

"It was all my fault," she said. "I got distracted."

"The Browns," Rhodes said.

Ruth nodded. "I thought Thorpe was still out of it. He didn't seem to wake up the whole way here, according to the EMT I talked to, and he was still unconscious when they put him in a room, or so I thought. I guess he faked us out. I was sitting in the hall by his door, but when the ruckus with the Browns started, that Pink Lady you talked to, Ella Long, came running and asked me to help. I thought it would be all right, so I did. Thorpe took advantage of the all the confusion. I went to check on him, and he was gone. By the time I got back here, things had just gotten worse, so I had the receptionist call Hack. I'm sorry about Thorpe."

"I don't blame you," Rhodes told her. "I'd have done the same thing."

"That doesn't make me feel much better. I left the prisoner. I should have guessed he might be faking it, but I didn't think he could fool the trained personnel. Anyway, I should at least have looked in on him before I left the door. I didn't, though. I just got out of the chair and came right to the lobby." Ruth shook her head. "It wouldn't bother me so much if I'd been able to get the situation under control, but I couldn't even do that."

"It's not easy to get the Browns to cooperate."

"Not for me. They shut right up when you came in."

Rhodes grinned. "Cal and I go back a long way. He used to pick fights with me when we were in grade school."

"Who won?"

"They shut up right when I came in."

Ruth looked at him for a second as if wondering why he was repeating her own words. Then she got it and smiled. "So you were a tough kid?"

"Not so much, but I was tougher than Cal. Anyway, we need to find Thorpe. He can't have gotten far if they'd put him in a hospital gown."

"His clothes were in the little closet in the room. He changed back into them."

"That might make it tougher. We need to get started."

"I asked the receptionist to send Buddy out looking while you were coming here."

Rhodes didn't think there were too many places Thorpe could go. "Did you suggest where to look?"

"I thought the mobile-home park would be the best place to start."

That was as good an idea as any. Thorpe might head for home because there was no place else for him to go. His old pickup was there, and if he wanted to leave town, it was likely that he'd need it.

"Let's see where Buddy is," Rhodes said, and they went to the county car to use the radio.

Buddy was prowling the streets and alleys between the hospital and the mobile-home park, and Rhodes told him to check out the Royal Rack.

"I'll drive out to his trailer and wait for him to show up," Rhodes said. "Ruth will take over on the streets. If he's not at the pool hall, you can help her look."

"I'm really sorry about this, Sheriff," Ruth said.

Rhodes told her not to worry. "It's not like Thorpe was a hardened criminal. According to Hack and Lawton, he's a respectable businessman, the new owner of the Royal Rack. He was just upset and lost his temper."

Ruth didn't sound convinced. "It takes quite a temper to make a man want to cut people up with a chainsaw, not to mention to assault the county sheriff."

Rhodes didn't have misgivings about any of that. What bothered him was that Thorpe might somehow be involved in the death of Helen Harris. He didn't tell Ruth what he was thinking because he didn't want her to feel any worse than she did already and because he was confident that they'd have Thorpe back in custody in short order.

Rhodes had been wrong when he thought he'd solved the hospital's problem with the Browns back in the winter.

As it turned out, he was wrong about Thorpe, too.

Chapter 11

▼

RHODES PARKED IN FRONT OF THORPE'S TRAILER, PREPARED TO wait as long as it took. Either Buddy or Ruth would find Thorpe, or he'd show up here. It was as simple as that.

Or it would have been if Thorpe had showed up. Rhodes had been sitting for about five minutes when the tall man who smelled like Aqua Velva came out of a double-wide farther up the white-graveled trailer-park "street" and walked down to Rhodes's car.

"Nice day," the man said when he got there.

"Not for sitting in a car," Rhodes said.

"You could get out. Thorpe's got him a couple of lawn chairs in that little toolshed of his."

Rhodes remembered the chairs. He got out of the car while the man went to fetch them.

"Gid Sherman's the name," the man said when he returned with the chairs.

He handed one chair to Rhodes, who unfolded it and sat down.

Sherman put his own chair nearby. It was getting on to the end of the afternoon, and the mild spring weather was just right for sitting. A bank of dark clouds was building up back to the north, which might mean they'd be in for a rainstorm later in the afternoon or early evening.

"You mind if I smoke?" Sherman said.

Rhodes said he didn't, although he thought the smell of the smoke would spoil the mood. But if it would make Sherman more comfortable and more likely to talk, it would be worth it.

Sherman lit a cigarette. After a few puffs, he said, "I guess you've figured out who I am."

"I think so. I've talked to you on the phone."

"That's right. I called you about Thorpe's little games of chance."

"You didn't give your name."

"Nope. Didn't think you needed it for what you had to do."

"You also didn't say why you wanted the games stopped."

"Nope. Didn't think you needed to know that either."

"Care to tell me now?"

Sherman blew a smoke ring. It hovered in the still air for a couple of seconds, then a breeze whipped by from somewhere to break it apart.

Sherman looked back at the clouds, then turned to Rhodes. "Looks like we're in for some rain."

"That's what I think, too."

"Yeah. Well, I don't like Thorpe. That's about the size of it, I guess. He doesn't like me a whole lot, either."

"So you keep an eye on him."

"Not much of one. I just heard about those poker deals from

somebody and figured I'd put a stop to 'em out of meanness more than anything else."

Rhodes thought there was more to it than that. If that was the case, Sherman would get around to it eventually. They sat in silence while Sherman finished his cigarette. When he was done, he fieldstripped it and stuck the remnants in his pocket.

"You were in the service?" Rhodes said.

"Yep. United States army. I was in Korea, just like Colonel Brant."

"Did you know him then?"

"Nope. Him and me wouldn't've been associatin'. I was just a lowly PFC, not in his class. And anyway, I never served with his unit."

"But you know him now."

"Yep. We've talked a time or two when he's been over here to see Thorpe."

"He visits Thorpe?"

"Comes around right often," Sherman said. "Course he don't stay long, just as long as it takes to cuss him out."

"Why would he be doing that?"

"He don't like Thorpe, which is why I don't like Thorpe. A man like the lieutenant can tell a bad un, and Thorpe's a bad un." Sherman got out another cigarette and lit up. "That's why I've been callin' about him. I got no use for somebody who'd give the lieutenant a hard time."

Rhodes wondered why Thorpe would be giving Brant a hard time. He had an idea, but he'd have to ask Brant about it.

"You waitin' for Thorpe?" Sherman said. "I thought he was in the hospital."

"He got away."

"That's a shame. I wouldn't figure on him coming back here, though. He'll go to ground somewhere."

"You have any idea where?"

Sherman puffed his cigarette, smiled. "Not a one."

The radio on the county car crackled, and Rhodes excused himself to answer the call.

It was Buddy, who said that he was having a problem at the Royal Rack. "You want to come help me out?"

"Let me check on something." Rhodes went to ask Sherman for a favor.

"Sure," Sherman said. "I'll watch the place. If Thorpe shows up, I'll call the jail."

Rhodes thanked him and told Buddy he'd be at the Royal Rack in a few minutes.

"Good," Buddy said. "I think I might have to shoot somebody if you don't come on."

"I'll have to make a stop on the way. Can you control your itchy trigger finger?"

"I'll try," Buddy said.

The Royal Rack was a concrete-block building that had been painted white when it was built, but that had been a long time ago. Now the bottom blocks were heavily coated with dirt kicked up by rain, and the sides of the building were more of a reddish brown than white.

The place's slogan was painted on the front wall twice, on each side of the door: FUN FOR THE WHOLE FAMILY. Rhodes could re-member when the lettering had been bright red, but it had faded now to something almost pink. On one side some clever wag had used spray paint to change *Whole* to *WhoRe*. Someone must have caught him before he could do the other side, or perhaps he'd run out of either paint or inspiration.

Two county cars were in the parking lot, Buddy's and Ruth's. Rhodes was feeling a little tired of bailing his deputies out of bad situations. That was unfair, though, he thought. It had happened twice in one day, but when was the last time it had happened? He couldn't remember, which meant that it wasn't what he could call a common occurrence.

He looked around the parking lot as he walked to the door. Lots of pickups, a couple of older Camaros, a few vans. No SUVs, no family sedans, no luxury cars.

In the north the clouds were getting heavier and darker. As Rhodes looked, the edges were lit up by lightning.

Rhodes went through the door of the Royal Rack. The place was well lighted, or at least the tables were well lighted by the fluorescent bulbs in the fixtures hanging above them. Get away from the tables, however, and the lighting was considerably dimmer.

"Over here, Sheriff," Buddy said.

He was standing off to one side with his back against the wall. A couple of the pool tables were occupied by people who appeared to be completely oblivious of Buddy's presence and who, if they knew that Rhodes had come in, didn't care.

"Ten ball in the side," somebody said, and Rhodes heard the thunk of the cue and the click of the balls.

"What's happening, Buddy?" Rhodes said, walking over to the deputy.

"There's a back room that they won't let me check."

Rhodes looked over the pool hall. It was a sizable place, probably sixty feet across the front and seventy-five feet deep. At the back where the lighting was the dimmest was the office and another room. Both doors were closed.

People stood along the walls, watching Rhodes and Buddy. Some of them were drinking soft drinks in cans or eating candy that they'd bought from the vending machines nearby. Some were even drinking water in plastic bottles from the same machines. No beer was sold in the Royal Rack because it was, after all, a place for the whole family.

A few people continued to shoot pool, playing rotation or nineball. Rhodes heard the sound of a cue ball being struck, followed by the click of its contact with another ball.

As far as Rhodes could tell, however, no families were present. There were a couple of women, but they didn't look like anyone's mother. They wore tight shorts and T-shirts that were equally tight. Possibly tighter. The men wore jeans and work shoes, some of which looked as if they had steel toes. Not something you'd want to be kicked with, Rhodes thought. Both the women and nearly all the men wore some kind of cap. The younger ones had the bills turned to the back, a practice that made absolutely no sense to Rhodes. Ivy had once told him that maybe turning the bill that way kept the sun off the wearer's neck.

"No more rednecks," she'd said.

Rhodes didn't buy it, but he supposed it didn't make much difference if he did or not.

"Who won't let you in the room back there?" he asked Buddy.

"That fella by the door."

That fella was a hefty man that Rhodes had met a time or two on other visits to the Royal Rack. Named Wayne York, he claimed to be the manager.

"You think Thorpe might be in there?" Rhodes said.

"Could be."

"There's a back door," Rhodes said. "Is Ruth out there?"

"Yes. I called her and asked her to cover it, just in case. I didn't want anybody sneaking out."

"I guess we'd better talk to Mr. York, then."

"I already talked to him. Like I said, he's not letting anybody into that room."

"I think he might change his mind now. Come on."

They walked toward the rear of the room, past the pool tables and the vending machines, and Rhodes could almost feel the eyes watching them. He wondered if anybody was hoping a fight would break out. That was a silly thought. Probably everybody was.

Wayne York leaned against the wall by the door with his arms crossed over his chest, showing off muscles Rhodes thought must have been developed by a lot of long hours of working with some kind of weights or a resistance machine. York didn't wear a cap, and his black hair was short and spiky. It glistened as if it had been coated with some kind of oil. He had a toothpick stuck in the corner of his mouth.

"We need to have a look in this room," Rhodes said, indicating the door.

"Can't let you do that."

The toothpick bounced up and down as York spoke, and Rhodes wondered if York had been studying old George Raft movies. No, Raft used the coin-flipping bit. Maybe the toothpick was York's own tough-guy interpretation.

"Why not?" Rhodes said.

"'Cause this is private property. Can't let you in without a search warrant."

"You let us in the front door."

"Hey, it's a pool hall. Everybody's welcome. Want to shoot a game of nine-ball? This is the place."

Rhodes said he didn't want to shoot a game of nine-ball and added, "The room back of that door is part of the pool hall."

"Nope. That's different. That's private property."

York was already beginning to repeat his lines. He needed a better writer, and Rhodes needed a better straight man. He had to do all the work himself.

"Aren't you going to tell me I'd need a search warrant to get inside?"

York grinned, tipping the toothpick upward at a rakish angle. "Yeah, I should've said that. You can't get in without a search warrant."

"That's better." Rhodes pulled the warrant from his back pocket. "I just happen to have one."

He had paid a quick visit to the county judge on his way to the Royal Rack and explained that the place might be harboring a fugitive. It hadn't taken long to get the warrant signed.

York uncrossed his arms. "Lemme see that."

Rhodes handed it to him. "Buddy can read it to you if it gives you any trouble."

York looked confused, as if he thought Rhodes might be messing with him but wasn't quite sure. He took the search warrant, unfolded it, and tried to look as if he understood what he was reading.

"Satisfied?" Rhodes said after a couple of seconds.

"I can't really say."

York looked genuinely perplexed. Behind Rhodes everyone seemed to have stopped breathing, caught up in the suspense of the moment. Would York go ballistic? Would his head pop like a blister? Or would he just open the door? Rhodes couldn't hear a sound other than York's breathing, not even the scrape of a shoe on the rough concrete floor.

"Well?" Rhodes said.

"I'm not supposed to let anybody in there. It's private—"

"Property. I know. I have a search warrant. You're holding it."

"Yeah, but. . . ." York's voice trailed off when he couldn't think of any argument that might work. Then something occurred to him. "I'm not the owner. I'd have to ask him about it."

"See, that's the problem," Buddy said. "We think the owner might be in that room."

York cheered up considerably. "Hey, if that's the problem, then I can set your mind at ease right now. He's not there."

"Yeah," Buddy said. "That would do the trick if we could just believe you."

"You don't believe me?" York sounded honestly hurt.

"We believe you," Rhodes told him, "but it's our job to make sure. Mr. Thorpe might be in there without your knowledge."

"Mr. Thorpe?"

"The owner."

"How did you know about him being the owner?"

"He's the sheriff," Buddy said. "He knows everything."

"Well, you don't know everything if you think he's in that room, because he's not."

"We still have to check," Rhodes said. "Open the door."

York shrugged and handed Rhodes the warrant. "I guess I got to."

Rhodes stuck the warrant back in his pocket, and York pulled out a ring of keys. He fumbled around with them, making what seemed to Rhodes to be an unnecessary amount of noise. Then he turned to the door and kicked against it a few times.

"It sticks," he said by way of explanation as he inserted a key into the lock. He twisted and rattled the handle, kicking the door a couple more times for good measure.

The walls were thick, and so was the door, but Rhodes could hear something on the other side, a noisy scraping on the floor, as if chairs were being shoved around.

"Damn door's stuck," York said.

"Buddy, shoot off the lock," Rhodes said.

Buddy drew his sidearm, and York swung the door open quickly.

"Better than WD-40," Buddy said, putting the pistol back in its holster.

The inside of the room was all confusion. People milled around, some of them trying to get out the back door, others looking for places to hide.

There was nowhere to hide, and Ruth Grady stood in the back doorway smiling at the men who milled around in front of her as if daring them to try to get past.

Rhodes thought they'd be wise not to try it. Ruth was already upset that Thorpe had gotten away from her, and she wasn't going to let anybody else do the same. She held her pistol at her side, pointing toward the ground, but she looked ready to use it if she had to. Nobody tested her resolve.

Five poker tables were in the room. An attempt had been made to clear a couple of them, but without much success. Chips were scattered around the tables, and cigarettes still smoldered in the ashtrays. A thin cloud of smoke hovered near the ceiling.

"I'll be dang," Buddy said. "Looks like we've busted an illegal gambling den."

Nobody but Buddy would have used that phrase, Rhodes thought. He said, "Do you see Leo Thorpe?"

"Nope," Buddy said, "but I see some familiar faces."

So did Rhodes, who recognized a city councilman, a teacher from the local community college, a bank vice president, and the owner of the Dairy Queen.

"This is going to be fun," Rhodes said.

Buddy grinned. "You don't really mean that."

"No," Rhodes said. "I don't."

Chapter 12

▼

IT TOOK OVER TWO HOURS TO GET EVERYTHING SORTED OUT, IN-cluding booking and bonding out and listening to all the threats, excuses, complaints, and tortured explanations.

Adding to the confusion was a phone call from Alton Brant, who'd heard about Thorpe's escape from the hospital.

Brant wasn't pleased. "If you can't hang on to him, maybe you need some help."

Rhodes said that he didn't need or want any help.

"Well, you might get it anyway," Brant said in the voice of an old soldier, and hung up.

Rhodes sighed and looked out at the mob of gamblers who had to be processed. It was turning into a long day.

When the jail was finally cleared, Hack said, "Tell you the truth, I didn't know there was so many innocent men in all of Blacklin County. You'd think just one of 'em might've been guilty of somethin' or other."

"Not a chance," Rhodes said, just before Jennifer Loam came through the door. He wondered what had taken her so long to get there. He'd been expecting her to turn up for at least an hour.

"You must have been covering a big story somewhere," he said.

"I was having dinner if you must know. Even a reporter gets time off for dinner."

"You missed a good story," Rhodes said.

"I didn't miss a thing. I'm sure you keep very accurate records. *Public* records."

"You goin' to name names in the paper?" Hack said.

"That will be an editorial decision."

"I hope you do," Hack told her. "Give a lot of those old boys somethin' to think about."

"I'll need to get the story from you, first," Jennifer said to Rhodes.

"Buddy can fill you in," Rhodes said. "He's already on overtime, but the county can afford it as long as the press is accommodated."

Jennifer was still protesting when Rhodes went out the door.

The dark clouds covered the sky now, and thunder rumbled through them like empty barrels rolling down a wooden stairway. Lightning zigzagged in and out. The wind whipped the legs of Rhodes's pants.

Rhodes didn't really want to spend the evening looking for Leo Thorpe, but somebody had to do it, and he was the one getting the big bucks.

Come to think of it, he wasn't getting the big bucks. But he was the sheriff, and he figured it was his job. Some sheriffs he knew would get their deputies to do it. They believed that a sheriff was nothing more than a county administrator, like the commissioners, and they never left their offices to do any kind of law work. Rhodes didn't fault them for that. It was their choice. His was to get out in the field and do what he could. That was why he'd gotten himself elected in the first place. If he couldn't do it, he might just as well be sitting at home watching *The Last Man on Earth.*

Ivy hadn't been happy when he'd called her with the news.

"It's going to storm," she said. "You'll catch a cold."

"I'll be fine. I never have colds."

"You were sneezing this morning."

"That was the cat."

"I don't believe it. You're not allergic to cats. By the way, I bought some food for Sam, but I see you've already fed him."

"I brought a little food from Mrs. Harris's. I brought a litterbox and a scratching post, too."

"That was very thoughtful of you. You must like Sam better than you're admitting."

"No, I was just being practical. How's Yancey?"

"He's doing fine. I think he and Sam are going to be great friends."

Rhodes didn't like the sound of that. "Lieutenant Brant said that he might want the cat."

That wasn't strictly true, but it could have been true. Or maybe Rhodes just hoped it was true.

Ivy asked about Brant, and Rhodes explained his relationship with Mrs. Harris.

"I knew they were courting, but I didn't know how serious it was," Ivy said. "So it was serious enough for him to want her cat?"

"I hope—think so," Rhodes said.

"You are so transparent."

"I'll bet you say that to all the sheriffs."

"Only the handsome, crime-busting ones."

Uh-oh, Rhodes thought. "Have you been talking to Claudia and Jan?"

"I certainly have. They called the office. When were you planning to tell me the good news?"

"Who says it's good news?"

"I think it's very exciting, and you should, too. They want you to do a signing with them at the Wal-Mart here when the book comes out."

Great, Rhodes thought. "I'll talk to them about it. Right now I have to go out and try to bust some crime."

"I'll wait up for you."

"I don't know when I'll be in."

"That's all right. We need to talk about Sam."

Rhodes knew what he wanted to say about Sam, but he didn't think Ivy wanted to hear it.

"Fine," he said.

"If you're not too tired and if you don't get in too late, maybe we can do more than just talk."

"It's never too late."

"Don't be too sure of that."

Rhodes's first stop was Ballinger's Funeral Home. It was located in an old mansion, left over from Clearview's long-gone oil-boom days. Rhodes hadn't been around for those, but some people said that with the current price of oil, some of the old wells might be able to produce enough to make a bit of money for somebody. That somebody wouldn't be Rhodes, however. He steered the county car into the drive behind the building and parked beside a black Lincoln.

Clyde Ballinger, the owner of the funeral home, lived in a small house that might once have been the servants' quarters. Being a bachelor, Clyde didn't need a big place, and he liked being close to his business. He was waiting at the door when Rhodes got there.

"Fixing to rain," he said as Rhodes came inside.

"Looks that way," Rhodes said. "Is that Dr. White's Lincoln out there?"

Ballinger nodded. "He's been here for a while. He should be able to tell you something before long. Terrible thing about Mrs. Harris."

"It was probably just an accident," Rhodes said, though the way the day's events had unfolded was making that seem ever more unlikely to him.

Ballinger led Rhodes into the little room that served as his office, which looked more like a living room. There was an old couch, a couple of chairs, and even an old color TV set. The newest addition was a computer desk.

As usual, Ballinger's other desk held a couple of old paperback books with gaudy covers, the kind of thing Ballinger preferred over any more modern form of reading material. There was also another book, however, a brand-new hardback. Rhodes didn't remember having ever seen one of those in Ballinger's office. As far as Rhodes knew, Ballinger bought only paperbacks, and he preferred to find them at the local garage sales.

"It's the last one in the Eighty-seventh Precinct series," Ballinger said, putting a finger on the hardback. "Ed McBain. He died last year, so there won't be any more. He'd been writing that series for nearly fifty years, and I'll bet I read them all."

Rhodes recalled that McBain had been one of Ballinger's favorites. The funeral director had often told Rhodes that he should adopt some of the methods of the men of the eight-seven, who, according to Ballinger, always seemed to be doing things better than Rhodes.

"I never met the man," Ballinger said, picking up the book, "but I sort of felt like I knew him. Not *knew* him, but you get the idea."

Rhodes nodded, even though he wasn't really sure he understood.

"He had a lot of different names," Ballinger went on. "Evan Hunter, that was his real one."

They'd had a discussion about that at one time, Rhodes thought, but the details escaped him.

Ballinger put the book back down on the desk, and Rhodes looked at the title. *Fiddlers.* It didn't sound like a cop novel, but what did Rhodes know about that sort of thing? Nothing at all.

"You could learn a lot from a book like this," Ballinger said, putting his hand on it. It seemed to Rhodes that Ballinger felt that in touching the book, he was making some kind of connection with it, or perhaps with its author. "Steve Carella. He works out of the eight-seven. Now that's my idea of a lawman."

"Handsome?" Rhodes said. "Out there on the streets busting crime?"

Ballinger grinned. "Exactly."

"You might be surprised about me, then."

Ballinger gave him a blank look.

"We can talk about it some other time," Rhodes said. "Right now I'd better go over and see what Dr. White's found out."

"He's not ready yet or he'd give me a call. Have a seat."

Rhodes and Ballinger sat down, Ballinger behind the desk and Rhodes in an uncomfortable upholstered chair.

"What do you think happened to Helen Harris," Ballinger said, and Rhodes gave him the accident story.

"I hope that's it," Ballinger said when Rhodes concluded. "But when you get involved, it's not always what it seems to be at first."

Rhodes didn't think he needed to respond to that.

"I have coffee now and then with a couple of men in the metal-detecting club. The Rusty Nuggets. Did you know Helen was a member?"

Rhodes said that he knew.

"I figured. Anyway, they were telling me that there was a . . . I guess you could call it an *incident* with her a few weeks ago."

Rhodes got interested. "What kind of incident?"

"Well, you know how those metal-detecting types are. Very picky about certain things. You can't disturb the ground, you can't—"

"Hold on. How can you dig something up if you can't disturb the ground?"

"Well, I didn't mean it that way. You can disturb the ground, but you have to put it back the way it was. I'm told most of the old-timers can dig something up and replace the divot so you'd never know it had been lifted."

"So Mrs. Harris disturbed the ground?"

"No, no, that's not it. She found something. Everybody knew she did because she got excited about it. Then when it came time for show-and-tell or whatever they call it, she wouldn't let any-

body see it. She even went so far as to deny that she'd found anything in the first place. But they all knew better than that."

"Don't they have rules about that kind of thing?"

"Not for the kind of hunt they were on. Now if they were on
some kind of county-owned site, or a historical site, something
along those lines, everybody'd have to turn in the finds. But this
was on private property. I forget who owned it. Might even have
been her place, come to think of it. So if she found something,
there wasn't much anybody could do about her not showing it."

"These friends of yours," Rhodes said. "Who are they?"

"The Gadney boys. Burl and Truck."

Rhodes knew them, though they were hardly boys. Burl was
about forty-five, and Truck was a little older. Truck, of course, was
a nickname. Truck hadn't done anything to earn it. It had been
given to him because of his size, which was considerable. He was
remembered fondly by fans of the Clearview High football team,
the Catamounts, as the biggest fullback in school history. He
wasn't fast, and he wasn't shifty, but it took nearly every player on
the other team to bring him down if he got up a head of steam.

"Where do you have coffee with them?"

"At Franklin's."

Franklin's was the drugstore across the street from the courthouse. It hadn't been remodeled since the 1950s, and it still had an
old-fashioned soda fountain. Unfortunately, the fountain was out of
commission, which took away from the charm of the place, but
Homer Franklin didn't care. He had about as much interest in charm
as he did in attracting new business, which was no interest at all.

Just as there was no longer a functioning fountain, there was
no pharmacy. Franklin catered to the old-time citizens of
Clearview, the ones who'd been around for years and weren't

looking for any drug more serious than the caffeine they'd get in a bad cup of coffee.

"They're there every morning," Ballinger said. "If you want to ask them about it."

Rhodes remembered the shelf in Mrs. Harris's house and the item that Ruth assured him was missing. Maybe she'd been right about it.

"I'll drop by tomorrow and talk to them," Rhodes said.

The phone rang, and Ballinger answered it. He listened for only a second and hung up.

"Dr. White's ready for you."

"What did he find out?"

"He didn't say."

The rain had started, but it was only a sprinkle. Rhodes walked fast to the back door of the funeral home without getting more than a few drops of water on his shirt and pants.

Ballinger stayed behind. He said he wanted to read some more of *Fiddlers,* and whatever had happened to Helen Harris wasn't his business anyway.

Rhodes entered the back door and brushed the raindrops off his shirtsleeves. Dr. White came into the little hallway through another door, one that Rhodes knew led into the room where White had been working. He was a kindly looking man with only a fringe of hair around his mostly bald head. He had watery blue eyes and big, competent hands.

"Well?" Rhodes said.

"She was murdered."

Chapter 13

▼

"HAVE A LOOK AT THIS," DR. WHITE SAID. HE WAS SITTING ON A stool at a table holding a laptop computer. The computer screen displayed a picture of Helen Harris lying on her kitchen floor. Ruth Grady had taken digital photographs of the crime scene and transferred the pictures to a CD, which Dr. White had put into the computer. As Rhodes leaned over to look at the screen, he thought that maybe *CSI: Blacklin County* wasn't quite as far-fetched as it had seemed.

"See the way her head's lying?"

Rhodes said that he did.

"Fine. Now if she'd twisted her ankle, say, and fallen from the stool, it should have hit her on this side of her head." Dr. White touched the screen with the tip of a ballpoint pen, indicating the side of the head on the floor. "But the impact was here." He touched the temple that was facing up. "Besides that, the impact should have moved the stool. It's on its edge. It should be bottom-side up. I'm just guessing about that part, but I believe it. I think someone hit her with the stool."

Rhodes, who had suspected it all along, now began to have doubts.

"It seems like an awfully elaborate setup. Who'd think to get out the lightbulb and all the rest of it?"

"Why does it have to be a setup?" Dr. White said. "What if Helen was already changing the bulb when someone came in? Everything would be in place, just like you saw it. The stool would have been a handy opportunity, and the rest just happens to fit with the accident theory."

Rhodes was easy to convince. "It would have to be someone she knew."

"I'd say that was a good probability. Do you have any suspects?"

"One, so far." For the moment Rhodes was discounting Billy Joe Bryon. "Leonard Thorpe."

Dr. White nodded. "I know Leo. He's a patient of mine. Not a very nice man."

"That seems to be the general opinion."

"Have you questioned him?"

Rhodes gave White a quick summary of the day's encounter with Thorpe and its result.

"He was running a poker game out at the pool hall?"

"It was the safest place," Rhodes said. "We'd raided him a couple of times at the mobile-home park because we were tipped off. Nobody knew about the pool hall."

"Except the players."

"Right. Except them. And they weren't going to tell anybody about it."

"I heard something about his leaving the hospital, but I didn't realize he was a murder suspect. I just thought he'd been in a fight."

"He wasn't a suspect at the time," Rhodes said.

"Maybe you could arrest all the Browns. Charge them with aiding and abetting a fugitive or something along those lines."

Rhodes grinned. "We couldn't afford to keep them in the jail. The county would go broke feeding them."

"True. Too bad."

"Are you willing to go on record about Mrs. Harris's murder?"

"Of course. There's more to it than I told you, such as the way the neck is twisted and a couple of other little things. But I don't have any doubt that someone hit her with the stool."

"I don't know yet about prints," Rhodes said. "Ruth will be working on that tomorrow."

"In the picture the legs of that stool look like unfinished wood. Might not take good prints. Might have been wiped, too. Everybody watches television these days."

"All too true," Rhodes said.

"I hope you catch whoever killed Helen. Everybody liked her."

"Not everybody."

"Almost everybody, then. Do you have any idea where Thorpe might be?"

"He could be in Mexico for all I know."

"Knowing you, that won't stop you from looking for him."

"No," Rhodes said. "That won't stop me."

Rhodes spent several hours driving around town and looking for Thorpe. He went by the Royal Rack, which was closed and dark, rain running down its sides and kicking up more dirt to stick to the concrete blocks at the bottom.

Thorpe's trailer was dark as well, so Rhodes stopped to ask Gid Sherman if he'd seen anything of Thorpe. The rain was coming down hard, and Rhodes got soaked in the short distance between the car and Sherman's trailer.

"Haven't seen hide nor hair of him," Sherman said after he'd opened his door and invited Rhodes inside. "You'd best believe I've been watching that trailer of his mighty close, too. If he was in there, he'd have to show a light, and there hasn't been a sign of one. He didn't come back before dark, either. I sat out in his yard till after sundown, just in case he showed up."

Rhodes thanked Sherman for the help and the information. "Do you have any idea where else he might've gone?"

Sherman shook his head. "Never talked to him about any place he might hide out in. Didn't talk to him much at all. Didn't like him enough to talk to him. Even if I had, it wouldn't make much difference. He wasn't around much."

That was interesting, Rhodes thought, wondering where Thorpe had spent his time.

"Maybe someone else around here could tell you," Sherman said, "but I doubt it. Didn't anybody socialize with Thorpe. Didn't anybody like him any better'n I did."

Rhodes thanked him again and dashed back to his car through the rain. Sometimes in the spring the rain would last all night. In the morning, water would be running in ditches along the sides of all the county roads and the fields would be full of mud. It was just such a rain that had rushed along the banks of Pittman Creek the previous year and uncovered the bones of a Columbian mammoth. Rhodes wouldn't have thought that a few bones from a prehistoric animal could cause so much trouble, but that was another time he'd been wrong. That seemed to be happening a lot lately.

The lights of the county car made a bright path through the raindrops. Rhodes saw that water was already beginning to pool in the yards in front of the trailers. If Thorpe wasn't somewhere safe and dry, he'd catch a cold.

Rhodes grinned as the idea occurred to him. Now he was thinking like Ivy. When he started doing that, it was time to go home for a hot bath and a cold supper.

He got the cold supper first. Ivy had made a meat loaf that had actual meat in it, for which Rhodes was grateful. She'd recently tried a meatless meat loaf that she'd made with some veggie burgers she'd bought at the grocery store. While Ivy considered the dish a big success, Rhodes had been a lot less enthusiastic. He'd thought he'd concealed his lack of excitement well, but evidently he hadn't succeeded. Which was fine with him as long as it resulted in a real meat loaf.

"I can put a slice in the microwave if you want me to," Ivy told him.

Rhodes said he'd prefer to have a cold meat-loaf sandwich with a slice of American cheese on it. He knew Ivy wouldn't approve of the cheese, but he couldn't resist cheese on a cold meat-loaf sandwich. He put salad dressing on it, too, which was a further sin, but he tried to make up for it by using 100 percent wholewheat bread. Not that there was any choice. Ivy never bought any other kind.

Rhodes sat at the table in the kitchen and put his sandwich together from the things that Ivy set on the table. Rhodes tried to ignore the cat, which lay over by the refrigerator and watched.

Yancey was in the room, too, sitting quietly by Rhodes's chair. Rhodes looked down at him. "Has he been this quiet all day?"

Ivy smiled. "I can't say about that, but he's been quiet ever since I got home."

"Maybe the cat is a good influence on him."

"Sam," Ivy said to remind him of the cat's name yet again. "So you think we should keep him?"

"I didn't say that."

Rhodes took a bite of his sandwich to avoid further conversation about the cat, but Ivy didn't give up that easily.

"Sam's behaved himself perfectly. He's used the litterbox, and he hasn't attacked Yancey. I don't think it would be a good idea to give him away to strangers. He might be unhappy. Cats are easily upset."

What about me? Rhodes thought. "We're strangers."

"Not exactly. Sam remembers me from the times I've seen him at Helen's house, and you're a notorious soft touch when it comes to animals."

"Not all animals. Dogs."

"If you really don't want Sam, maybe Leonard Thorpe would. Something to remember his cousin by."

If she thought that idea would perk Rhodes up, she was wrong. He set the sandwich in the plate in front of him and finished chewing his current bite. He said, "We don't allow cats in the jail, and I don't think they allow them in the prisons, either."

"You don't know for sure that he's guilty of anything."

"I know several things he's guilty of." Rhodes told Ivy about some of the day's events while he ate the rest of his sandwich.

"You're right," she said when he finished. "He won't be wanting Sam."

As if he'd heard his name, the cat stood up and stretched carefully, walked over to Rhodes's chair, and lay down beside Yancey.

To Rhodes's surprise, Yancey didn't object. He didn't look happy, but he didn't run, either.

"See?" Ivy said. "They've getting to be friends. It would be wrong to separate them."

Rhodes sneezed.

"Don't start that again," Ivy said. "You and I both know you aren't allergic to cats."

"Maybe I have a cold from being out in the rain."

"You know better than that, too. You tell me all the time that a little rain can't give somebody a cold."

"But you tell me that it can."

"You never listen, though, do you. You go take your bath, and I'll clean up in here."

"What about after that?"

"After that," Ivy said, "we'll see what develops."

That was good enough for Rhodes.

Rhodes dreamed that he was trapped inside a burning building. The flames danced all around him, and the heat was intense. He couldn't escape from it, no matter which way he turned because the walls were closing in on him and there was no doorway in any of them.

As he stumbled around in the heat, he tripped, landing on the floor. A burning timber dropped from somewhere above. Rhodes tried to squirm out of the way, but for some reason he could no longer move. He seemed to be tied to the floor somehow, and the timber landed right beside him, pressing into his back, growing hotter and hotter until Rhodes thought his clothes would burst into flame.

Rhodes came awake, clawing at the covers and throwing them off. He struggled out of the bed and stood up.

Ivy turned over. "What's the matter?"

"I was having a bad dream." Rhodes looked at the bed and saw some kind of dark lump in the middle, right about where his back had been. "Is that cat in our bed?"

Ivy sat up and turned on her reading light. The cat was indeed in the bed, curled into a ball, sound asleep. The movement, the talking, and the light didn't seem to have bothered him in the least.

"That's it," Rhodes said. "I'm going to feed him to Speedo."

"You're not going to do anything to him. He probably slept in Helen's bed, and now you're taking her place."

"I don't want to take her place. I want to get a good night's rest, without a cat sticking to my back."

Ivy picked up the cat. Rhodes heard it purring as she set it on the floor on her side of the bed. It walked out of the room, its tail high, and Rhodes shut the door.

"That's mean," Ivy said.

Rhodes didn't think it was mean. He thought it was something more like self-preservation. "He can sleep with Yancey. I don't want to be Helen. Let Yancey do it."

"Yancey might not want to."

"That's too bad for Yancey. He'll have to do the job until we find a home for the cat."

"I think Sam has already found a home."

Rhodes didn't want to argue, so he kept quiet and lay back down. The bed was still warm where the cat had been lying, and Rhodes scrooched over to get to a cool spot. He didn't find one, however.

Outside, wind and rain lashed the house. It was a long time before Rhodes could go back to sleep.

Chapter 14

▼

THE NEXT MORNING THE CAT WATCHED WHILE RHODES WAS GO-
ing out to feed Speedo, but it made no attempt to leave the house.
Rhodes had heard that cats didn't like water, and the backyard
was full of puddles. Some of them were hidden by the grass, but
the cat probably sensed them. It was dry and comfortable, and
Rhodes had already fed it. It seemed perfectly content.

When Rhodes opened the door, Yancey came bounding and
yipping into the kitchen. He was his old self again, and Rhodes
wondered if the dog and the cat had entered into some sort of
agreement. Rhodes let Yancey out and followed him into the yard.
Yancey ran over to Speedo, splashing through the grass, and the
two dogs stood nose to nose and looked at each other silently. As
if, thought Rhodes, some kind of telepathic communication were
going on and Yancey were telling the bigger dog about his new
pal. After a few seconds, the dogs broke apart and started running
around the yard, paying no attention at all to their getting wet.

While the dogs were playing, Rhodes put out food and water for Speedo. Then he stood on the back steps and watched Yancey chase Speedo around as if he were the big dog and Speedo the tiny one. They tired each other out after a few minutes, and Speedo shook himself, flinging water drops all around. Yancey did the same, though not as effectively. When he was satisfactorily dry, Speedo went to his food dish and started to eat. Yancey and Rhodes went back inside.

Ivy was in the kitchen talking to the cat. Yancey bounced around making wet pawprints on the floor while Rhodes poured some orange juice.

"Just one big happy family," he said after he'd drunk a couple of swallows.

"Absolutely," Ivy said. "Sam is fitting right in."

Rhodes felt something tickling the inside of his nose and knew he was about to sneeze. He made an effort to control it, but that proved impossible.

"You're just trying to make Sam feel bad," Ivy told him when he sneezed.

"No, he's making *me* feel bad."

"Then you'd better get used to it. He seems perfectly at home here, and I think we should let him stay."

"We'll talk about it later. I need to get to the jail."

"I got a call while you were out in the yard," Ivy said before he could leave. "The OWLS will be meeting today at two o'clock in the library. I can't go, but I told Thelma Rice that you might like to talk to them. I told her I'd call her back and let her know."

"Thanks. Tell her I'll be there."

"She's also in the Red Hats. They're meeting at noon at the Round-Up."

The Round-Up was a local restaurant with a limited menu: most items were guaranteed to clog your arteries. Naturally it was popular.

"I guess I could make both meetings," Rhodes said, though he'd been hoping to put one or both of those groups off on Ruth Grady. This way, however, would be easier than going through the membership lists and calling everybody on the phone and setting up a time to talk to each of them.

"I'll let Thelma know you'll be there," Ivy said, and Rhodes thought she might be enjoying this a little too much.

"Women like me," he said. "I'll be just fine."

"I know. I never doubted it."

Rhodes didn't reply to that. He looked at the cat and Yancey. They were lying side by side on the floor near the refrigerator. Yancey was still wet, so the cat was keeping a safe distance from him. Rhodes took that as a good sign and left to go to the jail.

Not much had gone on in Clearview overnight, a couple of kids drag racing on a residential street after midnight, an attempted burglary at the hardware store, a report of a dead animal on the road, a fight in the Dairy Queen parking lot. Even Hack and Lawton couldn't make anything from any of that, or not enough to tease Rhodes with.

Rhodes asked if there'd been any calls related to something that might lead them to Leonard Thorpe.

"Not a thing," Hack said. "You can sift through the reports for yourself, but you won't find anything. It's like he just vanished off the face of the earth."

"He didn't, though," Lawton said. "He's hiding out somewhere."

"How'd he get wherever he is, then?" Rhodes said. "That's what I'd like to know."

"He had to have some help," Hack said. "But who'd help him?"

"Somebody would," Lawton said. "That's how he got away."

Rhodes thought the circular reasoning was coming into play again, and it wasn't helping.

"I'm going to see Francine Oates about Helen Harris's will," he said. "Call me if anything comes up."

"I always do," Hack said.

"If Jennifer Loam calls or comes by, tell her I'm on the way to Canada."

"I always do," Hack said.

Francine didn't appear too happy to see Rhodes again, but she was hospitable, as a lady would be. They were in Francine's kitchen again, and Rhodes was drinking another Dublin Dr Pepper. He knew he shouldn't, but he couldn't resist. It wasn't as if the drink was a bribe or anything like that.

"I didn't even look at the will, of course." Francine was dressed as she had been the day before, in a long-sleeved shirt and jeans. "I think I told you that."

Rhodes agreed that she had.

"Whatever she did with her land was none of my concern," Francine went on. "I believe in minding my own business and not other people's."

"I didn't mean to imply that you'd pry. The problem is that the will seems to be missing. Do you have any idea if she made a copy?"

"It would have been easy if she had a computer and scanner,

but I don't think she did. She probably didn't make a copy. If she did, I haven't seen it."

Rhodes had been afraid of that. He supposed it didn't really matter that the will was missing, since Brant had seen it and had told him the contents, but this loose end bothered Rhodes. And what if Brant wasn't telling the truth? Not that there was any reason to doubt him, unless there was some truth to the notion that Francine had advanced about Brant's having killed Mrs. Harris for the gas wells. After all, Rhodes had only Brant's word about the contents of the will.

Rhodes finished his Dr Pepper and told Francine he'd be seeing her at the meeting of the OWLS.

"I'm looking forward to that," Francine said.

She was just being polite. Rhodes could tell she didn't mean it.

Franklin's Drug was old and shadowy. If you wanted a pack of Beemans pepsin chewing gum or a tube of Brylcreem, it was the place to come.

It was also the place to come if you wanted to drink a cup of coffee in the company of the county's older male citizens. In the back there were four tables and a big coffeemaker. Rhodes made his way past shelves of toothpaste, razors and shaving cream, and aids to digestion.

The Gadney brothers sat at a table by themselves, and they looked up at Rhodes as if they were expecting him. Clyde Ballinger was at one of the other tables, and he raised his coffee cup to Rhodes.

Rhodes pulled out a chair at the Gadneys' table and sat down. Both brothers looked as if they might actually use Brylcreem on their hair, which was slicked back and combed down close to their heads. Burl was about Rhodes's size, but Truck seemed to overflow the chair where he sat.

"Hey, Sheriff," he said, and Burl echoed him. Both had deep voices like bass singers in a church choir.

"Hey, Truck. Hey, Burl."

"Clyde says you need to talk to us about the Rusty Nuggets," Truck said. "Something about Helen Harris."

"I heard she found something on one of your outings," Rhodes said. "Something she didn't want to tell anybody about."

"That's right," Burl said. "We don't have any hard-and-fast rules about that kind of thing, but the idea is that we all share stories about what we've found. It's kind of like an unwritten rule. Helen flat out refused, and that was after she'd got us all excited."

"Yeah," Truck said. "She found something good because we heard her hooting when she did. She was laughing like somebody'd tickled her near 'bout to death. She shut up right quick, though, and then she wouldn't say another word on the subject."

"Clyde told me you have a kind of show-and-tell," Rhodes said.

"That's right," Burl said. "At every meeting we have a little display of the finds. They're divided into categories. There's a category for U.S. coins, one for buttons, one for foreign coins, one for jewelry. Like that. You get points for a find, and if you have the top find in your category, you get more points. They're totaled up at the end of the year."

"And there's a prize?" Rhodes said.

"Yeah. There's a prize for the find of the month, too."

"Helen Harris wouldn't show or tell, either one," Truck said. "Not that time. It takes the fun out of it when somebody acts like that." He paused. "We couldn't force her to show us."

Truck sounded as if it had been left up to him, things would have been different.

"We couldn't legally make her give it up, either," Burl said. "If we'd been on somebody else's land, we could have, but this was on her place out near the county line to the east, where they're drilling those gas wells. Since it was her own property, we couldn't very well tell her she had to give whatever she found to the owner."

"Everybody always shares, though," Truck said. "That's part of the fun of finding stuff. If somebody holds out, it takes away from the fun. She made a lot of the members pretty mad. Couple of 'em wanted to throw her out of the club."

"Who?"

Truck looked down at the table and mumbled something about how people ought to follow the rules.

"He was one of 'em that wanted to kick her out," Burl said. "He was really mad about it."

Rhodes thought that Truck could have killed Helen Harris with that stool without half trying if he'd been mad enough.

"Have you seen her since that day?" Rhodes said.

Truck continued to look at the table. "Nope. Why do you want to know?"

"Just wondering. Do you have any idea at all what she found?"

"Not the least," Burl said. "Must've been pretty little, though, little enough for her to stick it in her pocket. Or she might have hidden it in the house."

"Her house?" Rhodes said.

"Well, sure. But that's not what I meant. We were hunting around the old Tumlinson place. You know where that is?"

Rhodes said that he didn't.

"It's an old house on Helen's land. It's been vacant for probably fifty years now, but it's still in decent shape. A fella could live there if he had to and didn't mind going without plumbing and air-conditioning and the like. There's even an old water well. Places like that, you can find some good stuff now and then. Old coins and things."

"You think Helen found a coin or something like that?"

"Don't know. I wish I did."

Rhodes talked to the brothers for a while longer, but he didn't get any more out of them. Truck wouldn't say much, and Burl didn't know any more than he'd already told.

The only thing Rhodes was sure of was that the more he learned about Helen Harris, the less he knew.

He told the brothers he appreciated their help, spoke to Clyde Ballinger, and left.

Chapter 15

▼

THE SIGN IN FRONT OF THE ROUND-UP MADE THE RESTAURANT'S mission clear: ABSOLUTELY NO CHICKEN, FISH, OR VEGETARIAN DISHES CAN BE FOUND ON OUR MENU!

If you liked beef, you were in for a treat. If you didn't, you were out of luck. Or you could order TODAY'S SPECIAL: GIANT BAKED POTATO STUFFED WITH BBQ BEEF, CHEESE, SOUR CREAM, BACON, AND GREEN ONIONS and then try removing the beef. Rhodes didn't think that had ever been done, however.

The asphalt parking lot was crowded with cars, and Rhodes had to park a good distance from the door. The open spots in the lot were dotted with puddles from the previous night's rain. Rhodes watched where he was going because he didn't want to get his shoes wet.

He negotiated the distance successfully, and when he went inside the restaurant, he was greeted by Mary Jo Colley, who said, "I hope you're not here to start a riot, Sheriff."

Mary Jo was a waitress at the Round-Up, and she'd been on the edges of the investigation Rhodes had made when the mammoth had been found. That investigation had involved a little fracas at the Round-Up.

"I'm just here to see the Red Hat ladies," Rhodes said.

Mary Jo rolled her eyes. "That bunch. They're in the party room, and they're about as rowdy as those Bigfoot hunters you tangled with a while back."

"Let's hope not." Rhodes remembered the night he and the Bigfoot hunters had gotten into it.

Mary Jo laughed and led him through the noisy restaurant to the party room. She opened one of the double doors, and Rhodes could hear all the loud talk. Mary Jo turned to him with an I-told-you-so look, and he went inside.

He'd never seen so many red hats and purple dresses in one place, and Mary Jo had been right in comparing the Red Hats with the Bigfoot hunters as to the noise they made. The women were laughing, talking, and gesturing, and Rhodes was pretty sure an elephant could have strolled into the room without attracting much notice. Someone as insignificant as the county sheriff attracted no notice at all. Mary Jo closed the door and left Rhodes to do whatever he could.

Rhodes looked around until he spotted Thelma Rice. Her round hat was among the largest in the room. It looked a little bit as if a red flying saucer had landed on her head. Rhodes tried to get her attention by waving, but she was so involved in her conversation with the other women at her table that she didn't even glance his way. He felt like an invisible man, which made him a little uncomfortable. He shook off the feeling, walked over to the table, and tapped Thelma on the shoulder.

"Look out, Thelma," one of the other women said when she saw who was standing there. "The law's finally caught up with you."

The rest of the room was so full of chatter that Rhodes had to strain to make out the words. He smiled at Thelma to show that he wasn't there to arrest her and said that he'd like to talk to the group about Helen Harris.

"You'll have to get their attention," Thelma said. She was short and wore big glasses with round lenses.

Hearing the dull roar of the conversation and laughter all around, Rhodes thought that firing a shotgun into the ceiling might be the only way, but he didn't think the Round-Up's owner would approve.

Seeing that he was helpless, Thelma said, "I'll do it."

She stood up and gave Rhodes her hand. He didn't know why, but he took it anyway. Taking a firm grip on his fingers, Thelma pulled her purple dress up a bit and stepped on the chair where she'd been sitting. Even when she straightened to her full height on the chair seat, she wasn't more than a couple of inches taller than Rhodes, and that was including the hat.

Thelma let go of Rhodes's hand and put the thumb and index finger of her right hand to the corners of her mouth. She took a deep breath and then whistled so shrilly that Rhodes thought half the dogs in Clearview must have heard her. He wished he could whistle like that. He'd tried to learn the skill, but he'd never had much success. The talk and laughter stopped at once, and everyone looked at Thelma.

"The sheriff has something to say," she told them, and reached for Rhodes's hand again.

He stuck it out, and she grabbed it. She stepped down and sat at the table, leaving Rhodes the center of attention.

"Most of you know that Helen Harris died yesterday," he said, and all the nods set red hats bobbing all over the room. "I'm investigating her death, and there are a few things that need clearing up. I'd like to talk to anyone who knew her well."

Everyone started babbling again. Thelma Rice reached out and tugged at Rhodes's shirt. "I knew her better than anybody here. Where can we talk?"

"Follow me," Rhodes said.

They went out into the main section of the restaurant, where people were actually eating instead of visiting. Rhodes looked around at all the stuffed animal heads on the walls. Those had given more than a little trouble in the past, but they seemed to be anchored safely enough now.

Rhodes led Thelma into the office of the restaurant's owner. He was out making the rounds of the tables, chatting up the regulars and welcoming the newcomers, and he wouldn't mind if Rhodes used the office.

"What do you want to know?" Thelma asked when Rhodes had closed the door and shut out some of the restaurant clamor.

"I'd like to know if Mrs. Harris had any enemies," Rhodes said. "Or if she'd had trouble with anybody in your group."

"Why the Red Hats? Helen was in a lot of organizations. If you could call us organized. Are you going to ask the same thing at the OWLS meeting?"

"Yes. I'm not picking on anybody."

"Well, I can tell you right now that Helen was well liked in both groups. For the most part. Like anybody, she had her detractors, but she wasn't ever in any big arguments, if you don't count the one with Lily Gadney."

Lily Gadney was Truck's wife. Rhodes hadn't seen her among the Red Hats.

"She's in the OWLS," Thelma told him. "Not the Red Hats. Schoolteachers prefer a reading group. She and Helen had quite a fuss at the last meeting. I thought it might get nasty, but we got them calmed down."

"They were arguing about the book selection?"

Thelma gave Rhodes a coquettish look from under the brim of her red hat. "I think you know better than that, Sheriff. You're the kind of man who always knows more than he's letting on."

Rhodes wished that were the case. The truth of the matter was that most of the time he felt as if he knew a lot less than he was letting on. In this case, however, he was acting a little more naive than he actually was.

"Could it have been about something Mrs. Harris found?"

"See? You knew all a long."

"Tell me about the fuss," Rhodes said without acknowledging that he'd known a thing.

"It got a little loud." Thelma touched her hat brim. "I know what you're thinking. We're a noisy bunch, but that's the Red Hats. The OWLS aren't like that, though. We meet in the library, and we're very well behaved. We don't want to disturb anybody, but Helen and Lily certainly did. I was worried that we might get kicked out and told not to come back. So was Francine Oates. I thought she was going to have a stroke."

Francine hadn't mentioned the argument to Rhodes, but he could understand why she'd be upset. Loud arguments in the library wouldn't fit into her ladylike view of the world. Rhodes was sorry that Ivy hadn't been at that meeting to tell him about the argument.

"Do you remember anything specific that was said?"

"Not really." Thelma grinned as if thinking about the little tiff was a pleasant memory. "Well, I remember a little, I guess. I think it was about something that Helen found at the old Tumlinson place."

Rhodes would really have liked to know what it was that Helen had found. "You didn't happen to hear what it was, I suppose."

"No. Is that important?"

"It might be."

"Lily was upset, whatever it was. It was a real fracas, and it bothered all of us, especially Francine. I thought she was going to cry. Anyway, Helen said something like 'finders, keepers' and Lily called her a name, and that started it all. I had to stand between them because I thought it might get rough."

Rhodes wished more than ever that he had some idea what Mrs. Harris had found. He also wished he knew why Lily Gadney would be so upset by whatever it was, and he wondered even more why Truck hadn't mentioned anything about the little set-to. He promised himself that he'd find out after he'd finished talking to the members of the OWLS.

"You're definitely coming to the meeting of the OWLS?" Thelma said.

"I'll be there."

"Good. We're all really looking forward to seeing you."

Rhodes couldn't figure out why, and Thelma wouldn't tell him. He had an uncomfortable feeling that he'd find the answer all too soon.

Chapter 16

▼

THE CLEARVIEW LIBRARY WAS AN IMPRESSIVE WHITE STONE building built with money donated by a Houston philanthropist. Neither the city nor the county would have been able to afford such a place, and most readers in Clearview were quite pleased to have it in their town.

Rhodes remembered an earlier building that had been almost as nice, but the shifting clay soil of Blacklin County had caused the foundation to crack during a prolonged drought. The walls had soon cracked like the foundation, and the new building had been constructed to take its place. Rhodes hoped it was going to prove sturdier than the old one had been.

Being warm in winter and cool in summer, the library was almost as popular with the Browns as the hospital, but because it didn't offer free food or television, they had to content themselves with the computers. The library had instituted a policy limiting its patrons to thirty minutes of computer use, unless no one was waiting. The policy had worked out well enough. The Browns were happy with thirty minutes. They'd just get back in line for another turn. Rhodes had no idea what they used the computers for, and he thought that was no doubt just as well.

Rhodes saw a couple of the Browns tapping away on the keyboards when he entered the library that afternoon. He was uncomfortably full, having taken advantage of the Round-Up's lunch special. The baked potato had not been appreciably smaller than an official NFL football. Rhodes didn't plan to mention to Ivy that he'd eaten it, which he had. Most of it, anyway. And he certainly hadn't tried to remove the beef.

The OWLS were in one of the library's meeting rooms. On his way there, Rhodes passed the circulation desk and waved to Karen Sandstrom, someone else who had been involved in the case of the mammoth bones. One thing about being sheriff in a small county, Rhodes thought, was that you never stopped running into people you'd met in your line of work. That wasn't always a good thing, though in this case it was.

As Thelma Rice had said, the OWLS weren't as noisy as the Red Hats. There weren't as many of them, for one thing, though several still wore the same outfits they'd had on in the Round-Up.

Thelma got up and crossed the room to meet Rhodes at the door. "We're really pleased that you're here, Sheriff. Come on in."

Rhodes allowed himself to be led to a table in the front of the room. A small lectern sat on the table, and when Thelma stood behind it, no one in the room could see her.

Rhodes was a little disappointed at the near silence. He had hoped that Thelma would have to whistle again. He thought about asking her to teach him how to whistle like that but rejected the idea as hopeless. Some people just weren't musically talented, and he was one of them.

Thelma shoved the lectern aside. The sound of it scraping on the table was enough to bring complete silence to the room. Looking out over the women sitting at the tables in front of her, Thelma said, "Good afternoon, OWLS."

The women smiled and said, "Good afternoon, Thelma," in polite voices.

Rhodes saw Francine Oates sitting at a table near the back of the room. She didn't look as happy as the others. She was no doubt getting tired of seeing Rhodes.

Lily Gadney was there, too. She was a large woman, but nowhere nearly as big as Truck. Her face was round and smiling, most of the time, but she wasn't smiling now.

"We have a very special literary guest today," Thelma said, grabbing Rhodes's attention.

He looked around to see if Vernell Lindsey was in the room. She was the only literary person in Clearview as far as he knew, but she was nowhere around. In fact, Thelma was looking at Rhodes.

"It's our very own handsome, crime-busting sheriff, Mr. Dan Rhodes," Thelma said.

Rhodes wondered if it was legal for the sheriff to shoot his own wife for telling tales. He was an officer of the law, after all. Surely the jury would see things his way, especially after he explained the circumstances.

"That's right," Thelma continued. "I've heard that our own county sheriff is going to be the star of a novel that you can be sure we'll put on our reading list as soon as it's available."

Thelma clapped her hands. The other OWLS looked a little baffled, but they all applauded dutifully.

When the applause died down, which didn't take long, Thelma explained about Claudia and Jan and the book they'd written. "Wouldn't it be wonderful if Hollywood bought the movie rights and Sheriff Rhodes became a big movie star?"

Everyone oohed and aahed about that for a couple of seconds. Thelma waited until it was quiet again. "Sheriff Rhodes isn't here today to tell us about his literary debut, though. He's here to grill us about a crime. Who knows? Maybe we'll be in the next book!"

She clapped again, and the applause was more enthusiastic than previously. Rhodes wished he'd sent Ruth Grady to do this job, but he'd called Hack and asked him to have her talk to Alton Brant to see if he had any idea what Mrs. Harris had found while out hunting with the metal-detecting club.

Rhodes also wished Ivy weren't such a blabbermouth, though he admitted to himself that he hadn't asked her to keep the book a secret.

Thelma moved aside and motioned for Rhodes to step behind the table. He did, and he pulled the lectern in front of him. He didn't have any notes to put on it, but he felt an obscure need for some kind of protection.

"Tell us about the book, Sheriff," a woman seated at the front table said. Pearl Long, Rhodes thought. She taught English at Clearview High.

"I don't know anything about the book," Rhodes said. "I think maybe the whole thing's a practical joke. I came here to ask about Helen Harris."

He saw Pearl's look of disappointment, but it didn't bother him. He wasn't about to talk about the book, and he didn't know anything about it, anyway. He didn't like the idea of addressing the OWLS formally. He was pretty sure Steve Carella and the boys of the eight-seven wouldn't approve. Rhodes didn't think it was entirely his fault, however. It hadn't been his intention, but the OWLS seemed to expect it. He'd wanted to interview individuals, the way he'd done with Thelma at the Round-Up. He'd have to try for the same kind of arrangement.

"I've already talked to some of you," Rhodes said, looking at Francine, who gave him a halfhearted smile. "Now I want to have a conversation with some of the rest of you. Especially anybody who knew Mrs. Harris well. There are a couple things I'd like to clear up before we close our investigation."

"Was she murdered, Sheriff?" Pearl Long said, with not quite as much interest as she'd shown in the book.

Rhodes didn't see any reason to keep things a secret now. Jennifer Loam would be publishing the story in the paper within a day or two.

"Yes," Rhodes said. "It looks that way. Maybe some of you can help me catch whoever did it."

A little titter of excitement rippled through the room. Several women raised their hands and said that they'd be glad to help.

Lily Gadney wasn't one of them.

"Why didn't you want to talk to me?" Rhodes asked Lily Gadney.

They were alone in the head librarian's office. Rhodes had already talked to the women who'd volunteered, but they hadn't been much help, even though they'd all known about the argument between Lily and Helen. They didn't have anything to add to what Rhodes had found out from Thelma.

Lily's lips made a thin line across her round face. She shook her head but said nothing.

Rhodes waited a couple of seconds to give her a chance to speak. When she didn't, he said, "I hear that you and Mrs. Harris had quite a quarrel during the last meeting."

After another pause, Lily said, "Maybe. I don't see what that has to do with anything."

She clutched a large purse with a yellow-and-orange butterfly on the side. She looked away from Rhodes and squirmed in the chair. It wasn't easy. Because of her size, she didn't have much squirming room.

"It might not mean a thing," Rhodes said. "What I'm interested in is what Mrs. Harris found at the Tumlinson place."

Lily drew herself up straight. "I'm sure I wouldn't know."

"That's what the quarrel was about, though, right?"

"What if it was?"

"If it was, then you must know what she found," Rhodes said, knowing that wasn't the case but wanting to draw her out.

Lily was insulted. "Are you accusing me of being a liar?"

"I'm not accusing you of anything. I'm just trying fo find out something that might help me solve a crime."

"I'm not involved in any crime, and neither is Truck."

Rhodes wondered why she'd mentioned her husband, who hadn't been a part of the questioning at all. It seemed worth pursuing, so he said, "I'm not so sure of that."

"You've got a lot of nerve!"

"Sometimes that's what it takes when people are hiding things from me."

"I'm not hiding anything. I know you talked to Truck this morning. He told me."

"It's a funny thing, but he didn't mention that you and Mrs. Harris had had a falling-out."

"He didn't think it was important."

That could have been true, but Rhodes didn't believe it. "Everything's important in a case like this."

"Maybe to you. But the rest of us just want to stay out of it."

"You can't. You're involved because you knew Mrs. Harris and because you had a confrontation with her."

Lily looked away. "Does that mean I'm a suspect?"

"It means I think you know something you're not telling me."

"Are you going to arrest me?" Lily's voice quivered just the least bit, and her chin trembled. "I haven't done anything."

That was true, but it was becoming clear to Rhodes that there was more to what had happened between her and Mrs. Harris than she was letting on.

"Nobody's going to arrest you," Rhodes said. "Yet. But it might come to that if you don't tell me the truth."

"I've *been* telling you the truth," Lily said in a tone that was totally lacking in conviction.

"Not the whole truth. We both know that. I think it's time that you did."

Tears gathered in the corners of Lily's eyes, and she dug around in her purse until she found a tissue. After she blotted her eyes, she put the tissue back in the purse and clasped her hands around it.

"Well? Are you going to tell me?"

"It wasn't me," she said. "It was Truck."

*   *   *

Rhodes hadn't been expecting a confession, which was just as well, because he didn't get one.

"He went over there," Lily said. "To Helen's house, I mean. To talk to her, that's all. Just talk. She said some mean things to me, and he didn't like that. She wouldn't tell what she found, and he didn't like that, either. So he went over there."

Rhodes knew that the OWLS met only once a month, so it didn't seem likely that Truck had waited all this time to pay a visit to Mrs. Harris. He had, however.

"I tried to talk him out of it," Lily said. "I told him that it didn't matter, so he didn't do anything at first. The more he thought about it, though, the madder he got."

Rhodes stopped her at that point. He wanted to know more about the argument that had started it all.

"I'm sorry that happened. It was my fault. I told Helen that some of the Rusty Nuggets didn't think much of the way she'd behaved, and she told me it was none of my business, which it wasn't, since I'm not even in the club. Truck got mad about it, though, which is the only reason I mentioned it. She got really mad about it, and some of the ladies were upset by our little tiff."

"Francine Oates was," Rhodes said.

He'd talked to Francine just before bringing Lily in, but she'd claimed that she'd forgotten all about the quarrel. "Now that you bring it up again, it was upsetting to see such bad behavior in the library," she'd told him. "Ladies shouldn't behave any such way."

"She wasn't the only one," Lily said. "I don't blame them. I should never have acted like that. I don't know what got into me."

"Maybe it was because Truck was so angry."

"Oh, he was. He thought Helen was ruining the club. I guess some of that rubbed off on me."

"You said he was so upset that eventually he went to see Helen. Just exactly when was that?"

"It wasn't yesterday, if that's what you're thinking." Lily paused. "Or even the day before."

Rhodes looked around the librarian's office. Shelves were on three walls, and all of them held books. Most of the books had pieces of paper stuck in them. Rhodes didn't think anybody would be reading that many books all at once, and he wondered what the pieces of paper were for.

"I'd like to know just which day he went," Rhodes said.

Lily looked down at her clasped hands. "I'm not sure."

"I'll bet you can remember if you think about it for a second."

Lily looked up. "I can try."

Rhodes thought she knew very well when Truck had paid the visit, but he gave Lily a few seconds to gather her thoughts. Then he said, "Well?"

"It must have been on Tuesday."

Mrs. Harris hadn't been dead then, so it was a safe thing to say.

"What happened when he went to see her?" Rhodes asked.

"Nothing. She wouldn't talk about it. That made Truck even madder, but he didn't do anything about it. I know he didn't."

"Did he tell you he didn't?"

"Yes. He said Helen wouldn't talk to him, so he got mad and left. That's what he'd do. Truck's got a temper, but he doesn't like to hurt people."

That wasn't precisely the way Rhodes remembered things. He'd heard that when Truck was playing football, he'd much rather run over the opposing players than run around them. Rhodes thought he was going to have to talk to Truck again.

"You're sure you don't know what Mrs. Harris found?" Rhodes said.

"I'm positive. Truck didn't know, either."

Rhodes believed her, at least for her part. He still wasn't convinced about Truck.

"Does anybody else know that Truck went by to see Mrs. Harris?"

"I don't know. I didn't tell anybody, but I can't speak for Truck."

Rhodes thought that Truck had kept it a secret, too. Burl would have mentioned it if he'd known.

"Can I go now?" Lily said. "I've told you all I know. You won't do anything to Truck, will you?"

Rhodes didn't make her any promises.

Truck's Trucks was located on the highway coming into Clearview from the south. Truck had opened it after he'd flunked out of college during his senior year. The way Rhodes had heard the story, Truck might have been an excellent college fullback if he'd just gone to class occasionally and tried to do well on the playing field. Instead he'd barely managed to stay eligible, never seemed to learn the playbook, and spent the majority of his time having fun, if you considered drinking and drugging fun. Truck had, and it had cost him any chance he might have had of making football a career beyond college.

So he'd come home, straightened out, and started selling used cars and trucks. The name of his car lot was written on a full-size plywood cutout of a pickup nailed up about twelve feet above the ground between a couple of poles. The paint on the plywood was so faded that the words could hardly be read, but that didn't matter, either. Everyone in Clearview knew where Truck's Trucks was.

It started to rain again just as Rhodes drove into the place and parked. Not a heavy rain, just a thin drizzle that turned the sky a dull shade of gray.

Everywhere Rhodes looked there were old cars and pickups, some of them in great condition, some of them missing wheels and windshields and in such dire need of repair that Rhodes was sure they'd never leave the lot. Truck must have been cannibalizing them for parts.

Truck's office was in a little shack that looked almost as bad as the one Billy Joe Byron lived in, the major difference being that it had electricity.

The car lot wasn't paved, and there were holes all over it, all of them filled with water from the rain. The ground was slick, muddy, and treacherous. The drizzle didn't help things. Rhodes tried not to slip and fall as he went toward the office. He was almost there when he heard the gunshot.

Chapter 17

▼

THE SOUND CAME FROM SOMEWHERE NEAR THE BACK OF THE CAR lot. Rhodes went to the county car and called Hack.

"Send me some backup to Truck's Trucks," he said when the dispatcher came on.

"You started another fight?"

"I guess so. Shots fired."

"I'm sendin' Ruth."

Rhodes told him that was fine, then started down the muddy, rutted track that served as a road through the cars and pickups that Truck had accumulated over the years.

The farther from the front of the lot that Rhodes went, the older and more decrepit the automobiles became, until the place resembled a junkyard more than a car lot.

It started to rain a little harder, and Rhodes stopped to wipe the water. off his face, looking around to see if he could spot the source of the shot. He bent down, pulled up his pants leg, and removed his pistol from the ankle holster. He'd switched to the holster a while back, and he still wasn't sure he liked it.

When he straightened, he heard another shot and broke into a trot. His shoes slipped on the muddy track, but he managed to keep his balance.

Near the back of the lot, he saw a man crouching down behind the rusted hulk of an old Buick, one of the really big, long ones from the 1970s. Rhodes stopped and looked for some cover of his own, moving off the track and standing beside what was left of a Plymouth Duster. He could easily see over the roof because the wheels and axles had been removed at some point. The window glass was also missing, and, as Rhodes saw when he glanced inside, so were the seats. The headliner was gone as well. The Duster was nothing more than a skeleton.

The crouching man stood up, and Rhodes could tell from his size that he couldn't be anyone but Truck. As Rhodes watched, he fired another shot. The bullet whined off the top of a car near the back fence.

The fence itself was quite a piece of work, easily ten feet tall and made of rusting sheet metal that was now slick and wet with rain. It went around three-quarters of the lot, and nobody was going to climb it. If anybody was back there, he was going to have to come by Truck to get out, and whoever tried that was likely to get shot.

Rhodes wasn't interested in seeing Truck shoot anybody, however.

"Truck," he called. "This is Sheriff Rhodes. What's going on here."

Truck turned around as if to be sure that Rhodes was really the one doing the talking. He must have been satisfied that it was because he said, "There's a son of a bitch back there that wants to kill me, that's what."

It didn't look that way to Rhodes, who pointed out that Truck was the one doing the shooting.

"Hell, yes. I keep this gun in the office in case any robbers come by. Good thing I had it, too."

Truck turned back around and fired off another shot. This one spanged into the fence and went right on through.

"That's reckless endangerment. You don't know what's back there, Truck. You might kill somebody if you don't stop shooting right now."

This time Truck didn't look back. "I'm gonna kill me somebody, all right. Alton Brant."

Rhodes had heard enough. "I'm putting you under arrest, Truck. Put the pistol down on the ground, clasp your hands on your head, and come here."

By way of an answer, Truck turned and fired a shot at Rhodes. The bullet whipped through the skeleton of the Duster and broke out a side window in an old Dodge Dart behind Rhodes, who thought that Truck's temper probably wasn't anywhere near as mild as Lily had implied.

"The charges against you are piling up, Truck, and they're getting a lot worse. You'd better put down the pistol like I told you."

"You want to make me?"

"I guess I'll have to."

"You and what army?"

"Well, all I have is my deputy," Rhodes said as Ruth Grady walked up to stand beside him. "But that's two against one."

"Damn," Truck said. "That's not fair."

"What's all the shooting about?" Ruth asked Rhodes.

Rhodes told her that he wasn't sure. "Truck said something about Alton Brant trying to kill him. Did you talk to Alton today?"

"I haven't been able to find him. He hasn't been at home."

"If Truck's right, he's hunkered down back by the fence somewhere, I guess."

"No wonder I couldn't find him. You think he's really there?"

Rhodes said that he did and called out to Truck. "You ready to put down the pistol?"

The rain clouds were so thick and black by this time that it was almost like night, making it more difficult to tell what Truck was doing, but he did bend down and put something on the ground.

"Is that his pistol?" Rhodes said.

"I think so," Ruth said.

Rhodes nodded and repeated his instructions to Truck, who clasped his hands on his head and started toward them. When he did, a head popped up above the roofline of a car near the fence. It looked a lot like Alton Brant's head, but Rhodes couldn't be sure with the rain. He didn't say anything because he didn't want to call Truck's attention to Brant.

When Truck reached them, Ruth told him to turn around and put his hands behind his back. She used plastic cuffs on him, and Rhodes told her to take him to Truck's office while he went to retrieve the pistol.

Truck trudged off through the rain with Ruth behind him. Rhodes headed for the pistol, keeping an eye out for Brant.

"Are you back there, Mr. Brant?" Rhodes said when he got to where the pistol lay. He picked it up and stuck it in a pants pocket.

"Is he gone?" Brant said from behind a car.

"He's gone. You seem to have turned into a serious menace. I should have locked you up for that fight with Leo Thorpe."

"He was the one with the chain saw," Brant said, coming out from behind the car and walking toward Rhodes. "Not me."

"Be sure I can see your hands," Rhodes said, not a bit sure that he trusted Brant any longer. He might have served his country with honor in a long-gone war, but that didn't mean he hadn't changed over the years.

"I don't have a weapon," Brant said, but he kept his hands in plain sight, or as plain a sight as Rhodes could have through the curtain of rain.

"We ought to get inside," Rhodes said as Brant approached him. "You just walk on by. I'll be right behind you."

"You're not going to arrest me?"

"Not yet. We'll go have a talk with Truck and see if we can get this straightened out some way."

Brant passed Rhodes by and continued walking through the rain. Rhodes returned his pistol to the ankle holster and fell in behind him. They followed the little road back to the front of the lot. By the time they got to the building that served as Truck's office, Rhodes was thoroughly soaked, and his shoes were caked with mud.

Brant climbed up on the little porch and went inside. Rhodes followed him, glad to get under a roof. He stopped on the porch and scraped his shoes on the edge, trying to remove some of the mud. He didn't have much success, so he went on inside. It was Truck's own fault if the floor got muddy.

The building had only one room. Its walls were covered with calendars, most of them years old, given to Truck by various auto-parts and tool companies. Truck sat at his desk, an old rolltop that might have been an antique but that was in such bad shape that no antique dealer would touch it. Truck's well-oiled hair was plastered flat to his head, and he was wetter than Rhodes if that was possible.

For that matter all of them were wet. Water dripped from their clothes to the muddy floor and created little puddles. Rhodes looked around for something to dry off with, but there was nothing. He wiped water from his face with his hand and wiped his hand on his wet pants without much effect.

"Well?" He looked at Brant. "Let's hear your side of it first."

"He doesn't have a side," Truck said. "Son of a bitch wanted to kill me."

Rhodes looked at Brant. "Well?"

"He's right. I was upset."

"You seem to get upset awfully easily," Ruth said.

"Only when I think someone's killed a woman I cared about."

"You think Truck killed Mrs. Harris?" Rhodes said.

"I know he was at her house. I was going to ask him about it nicely, but he got upset. The next thing I knew he'd grabbed a pistol out of a drawer and was pointing it at me."

"Man comes in here accusing me of murder," Truck said, "you better believe I'm getting my hands on a gun."

"I didn't have one," Brant pointed out.

"How was I to know that?"

Truck could have killed Brant with his bare hands without breaking a sweat, but Rhodes wasn't interested in hearing them argue. He said, "Truck went to Mrs. Harris's house to get her to tell him what she'd found on an outing with the Rusty Nuggets. Isn't that right, Truck?"

Truck nodded, and water ran out of his hair and down his face. He couldn't brush it off because his hands were cuffed behind him.

"So what I want to know," Rhodes said to Brant, "is if she told you what she found."

"No. I wasn't interested in metal detecting, so we never talked about it much."

"She seemed awfully proud of that find," Rhodes said. "I thought she might have mentioned it."

"She didn't, though." Brant paused. "She did seem pretty pleased about something lately. I didn't know what it was, and when I asked her, she just said it was the gas wells and the money she'd be getting."

"What she found wasn't any gas well," Truck said. "It was something little enough for her to stick in a pocket."

Brant shrugged. "I wouldn't know. She never said a thing about it to me."

Rhodes didn't know whether to believe him or not, but he was inclining toward the *not*. He didn't get to think any further about it because Truck lurched up out of his chair, knocked Ruth to one side with his shoulder, hit Brant and spun him around with the other shoulder, and ran right over Rhodes, flattening him to the floor.

Truck was out the door and off the porch by the time Rhodes recovered. He jumped up and went outside, where Truck was running awkwardly toward the highway.

Rhodes went after him.

A slight incline led up from the car lot to the highway. Truck slipped going up it, and his feet slid out from under him. He fell face forward onto the slick mud.

Rhodes reached him and pulled him up. Mud covered his shirt and stuck to his face. Rhodes had almost as much on himself, having picked it up from the floor when Truck had knocked him down.

"That wasn't very smart, Truck. What did you plan to do, hitch a ride?"

Truck didn't say anything.

"You didn't have a free thumb. You'd just have gotten run over."

"Might be the best thing," Truck said in a sorrowful voice. "I've really screwed up this time."

Rhodes turned him around and marched him back toward the office. "Maybe not so much. It's your first offense, so you'll probably get off light. All you've done is assault an officer, resist arrest, attempt murder, and for all I know engage in mopery."

"What the hell is mopery?"

"I never figured that out, myself." Rhodes told him, helping him up on the porch. "But even if you're guilty of it, it's better than running out on the highway and getting flattened by an eighteen-wheeler."

Instead of taking him back inside, Rhodes put him into the backseat of Ruth's car. Ruth was standing on the porch, and he asked if she was all right.

"Sure. I bounced off the wall, but I wasn't hurt. Mr. Brant's okay, too. He's inside."

"You take Truck to the jail and book him," Rhodes said. "I'll have a few more words with Mr. Brant."

"What if he tries to escape again?"

She was probably thinking of Thorpe. "Shoot him."

"How about if I just pistol-whip him?"

"I guess that would be all right," Rhodes said.

Ruth came down off the porch. "All this because of one murder. I wish I knew what was going on."

"You're not the only one," Rhodes told her.

Brant was sitting in the chair when Rhodes went back into the office. He was a lot drier than Rhodes now, and a lot less muddy, but there wasn't anything Rhodes could do about his appearance.

"I think you know more than you've been letting on," Rhodes said.

"I wish I did, and I wish I didn't let my temper get the best of me."

"You don't think things through," Rhodes said. "First Thorpe and now Truck. Truck wouldn't kill anybody over something dug up on a metal-detecting trip."

"He sure acts like someone who would."

"So do you."

"I don't mind confrontations, if that's what you mean. Some people avoid them, but I'm not like that."

"Maybe you should be."

"That's what Helen used to tell me. She didn't like confrontations. She was more the sly type when it came to getting back at people."

This was another side of Mrs. Harris that Rhodes hadn't heard about. "She liked to get back at people?"

"Doesn't everybody?"

Rhodes nodded. "Not everybody. Too many, though. That's one reason I'll always have a job."

"Did you ever find Thorpe?"

"No. Buddy's been looking for him all day. We don't know where he's gotten to."

"And you don't have any ideas?"

"No," Rhodes repeated, but it wasn't true. He thought he might know where Thorpe had gone, and he planned to have a look as soon as he got a chance, but he certainly didn't want Brant getting in the way. Or doing something even worse.

"Are you going to charge me with anything?" Brant said.

"No. As far as I can tell, you were obnoxious, but there's no law against that."

"Truck might have other ideas."

"If he says you threatened him, we might have to file on you. Otherwise, you're free to go. The next time you get after somebody, though, I'm going to lock you up for a month."

"Thanks. I'll be careful not to let my temper get the best of me."

Brant got up and walked out of the little office, leaving Rhodes behind to wonder how he was going to lock the place up for the night.

Chapter 18

▼

RHODES WENT BY THE JAIL BEFORE GOING HOME TO BATHE AND change. It was late afternoon, and the rain had finally stopped for good. Off in the west the sun was going down behind the black clouds, edging them with orange and red. In the distance a train was passing through town, and Rhodes heard the whistle when it came to a crossing.

"Jennifer Loam didn't believe you were in Canada," Hack said when Rhodes entered the jail. He looked the sheriff over. "Neither do I. You look like you've been to some place really muddy. The Amazon jungle, maybe. I bet the inside of the car looks bad, too."

The county didn't like it when Rhodes or his deputies made a mess of the cars. Rhodes wondered if Ruth had filed her report on the chain-saw damages.

"You should see the other fella," Rhodes said.

Hack grinned. "I saw him, all right. He don't look much worse than you do. We got him locked up, and he's not happy about it."

"He didn't make bond?"

"Didn't even try. He says he belongs in jail. His wife came by, madder'n a wet hen. If I was him, I'd stay in jail, too."

Rhodes thought it was a good idea, himself. He asked if Buddy had found Leo Thorpe.

"Nope, not a sign of him, not hide nor hair. Buddy says he's just dropped off the edge of the world."

"We'll find him. Sooner or later. Have there been any calls I should know about?"

"Just one that might interest you. From some fella named Sherman." Hack looked through his call log. "Gid Sherman. He says somebody's been at Thorpe's trailer."

"Who?"

"He didn't know. Said he wanted to talk to you about it. You want to call him?"

Rhodes was wet, muddy, and tired. He wanted a bath and a hot supper. But he wanted to talk to Sherman, and he preferred face-to-face visits to phone calls. He could pay Sherman a visit on the way home.

"Call him and let him know I'm on the way to see him," Rhodes said.

"You look like somebody drug you through a mudhole." Sherman stood in the doorway of his trailer, looking out at Rhodes, who felt even worse than he looked. All around him in the mobile-home park, lights were on behind the windows, and he knew that the people inside the trailers were warm and dry, eating dinner and watching television, little realizing that the crime-busting sheriff was still on the job. They'd never even think about that when it came time to vote in the next election.

"I'd ask you to come in, but I just cleaned the place up today. No offense."

Rhodes told Sherman that none was taken. "You told the dispatcher that you saw somebody at Thorpe's trailer."

"Yep. I'm pretty sure it wasn't Thorpe, though."

"Do you know who it was?"

"Couldn't tell. It was raining too hard. I would've gone out and looked, but I didn't want to get wet." Sherman gave Rhodes an up-and-down look. "Getting wet doesn't seem to bother you much, though."

"Just doing my job. What else can you tell me about whoever was over there?"

"Not much. He went in and didn't stay long. Left in some kind of old car."

"How old?"

"Couldn't say."

The old car made Rhodes think of Truck and the car lot, but he knew Truck couldn't have been there. He was too busy chasing Alton Brant with intent to kill. Or at least to hurt badly.

"How big was the person you saw?"

"Like I said, it was raining, and it was dark, too. My eyes ain't what they used to be. Best I can tell you is that it was just some normal-sized fella. Could've been a woman, far as that goes. He was wearing rain gear. Or she was. Couldn't say one way or the other."

"Did Thorpe ever have women visit him?"

"Now that you mention it, he was quite a hand with the ladies for an old fella. Me, I don't mess around with the ladies anymore. Maybe I oughta try some of that Viagra."

Rhodes thought that was a little more information than he'd asked for.

Sherman shook his head regretfully. "Anyway, Thorpe was different from me. Either that or he had a prescription. He had him a woman somewhere or other. I know that cousin of his didn't like it."

"Mrs. Harris."

"Yeah, that's the one. She came out here with Colonel Brant a time or two and I heard 'em arguing about it."

"I don't guess you heard any names mentioned."

"Not a one. Don't even know for sure that's what all the fuss was about, but it sounded like it was."

"Did any women ever visit him here?"

"If they did, I didn't see 'em. He liked the ladies, though. You could ask around the park. People know that about him because he liked to talk. Never named any names that I know of. He was a gentleman that way. You can bet that's the only way he was."

Rhodes talked to Sherman for another couple of minutes without finding out anything else useful, so he thanked him for the call and drove home.

On the way he thought things over, trying to sort out all he'd heard and to see what he was overlooking. Experience had taught him that he always overlooked something that didn't seem significant at the time he heard it or saw it but that later turned out to be important. This time, however, he couldn't think of a thing.

* * *

"You're scaring Sam," Ivy said.

Rhodes looked over at the cat, who didn't look scared at all. He lay near the refrigerator, so relaxed that he looked boneless.

"I don't think so."

"Well, you're scaring me. Are you going to tell me about it, or are you going to clean up first?"

"I need to feed Speedo."

"I've already done it. Yancey, too."

Rhodes glanced around the kitchen, but Yancey was nowhere in sight.

"He's in the bedroom," Ivy said. "Under the bed. He and Sam had a falling-out."

Rhodes glanced over at the cat, which twitched its tail and didn't appear to be the least sorrowful or guilty. "The cat doesn't seem to be any the worse for wear. What about Yancey?"

"His feelings are hurt, but other than that, he's fine."

"I've been trying to find the cat a home," Rhodes said. "I can't find anybody who wants him."

"We want him. Just look at him. You can see how much he likes it here."

Rhodes could see it all right. He couldn't understand why the cat had adopted them, but then there were lots of things about cats that he didn't understand.

"You need to get out of those clothes," Ivy said.

"Would it lead to anything if I did?"

"Not unless you're a lot cleaner under them than I think you are."

"I can take a bath."

"Now there's a fine idea. You do that, and I'll get dinner ready.

I'll warm the meat loaf in the oven, and we'll have mashed pota-
toes with it."

That sounded fine to Rhodes, and he went off to bathe.

The warmed-up meat loaf was excellent, and while they were eating, Yancey came out of hiding. He peered around the kitchen
from the safety of the hall. Rhodes expected him to flee when he
caught sight of the cat, but he walked over to it and sniffed its
nose.

"See?" Ivy said. "They're still friends. Even friends fall out
sometimes."

Rhodes thought about all the friends who'd fallen out in the last
couple of days: Thorpe and Brant, Truck and Brant, Helen Harris
and someone as yet unknown. Most of them weren't really
friends, more like acquaintances, and they weren't getting along
anywhere nearly as well as the cat and Yancey.

Alton Brant seemed to be the instigator of a lot of the trouble,
which bothered Rhodes a bit. Brant had even at one point said that
he had trouble controlling his emotions, and he'd lost his temper
with both Truck Gadney and Leo Thorpe. Rhodes wondered if
Brant had ever lost his temper with Helen Harris, and what he
might have done if it had happened. Would he have picked up a
stool and hit her with it?

He mentioned the idea to Ivy.

"He might have," she said, "but I don't think so. He seems like
such an upright person."

Rhodes had known a great many upright people who'd done
things a lot worse than hitting someone with a stool. Sometimes

they didn't even intend any harm, or so they said after the fact. Rhodes had a hard time believing them.

He thought about Billy Joe Bryon, who had once upon a time done what he might have thought was a good thing and a harmless one, but it had turned out to be exactly the wrong thing and all too harmful. Could it have happened again? Rhodes didn't think so, but it wasn't out of the question.

Leo Thorpe was another problem. He had the best motive of anyone to kill Helen Harris since he was her heir. Or he was supposed to be, according to Brant. Now, however, there was no will to prove it, and no Leo Thorpe.

The missing will bothered Rhodes. If Thorpe had killed Mrs. Harris, he wouldn't have taken the will. He'd have wanted it found. So where was the will?

"You're not eating," Ivy said, giving him a pointed look.

"I'm thinking," Rhodes told her, applying himself to the meat loaf again.

When they'd finished eating, he helped Ivy clean off the table. Then he said, "I have to go out for a while."

Early in their marriage, Ivy hadn't wanted him to go out in the evenings, but she'd grown used to it, and she seemed to understand that his job required him to keep irregular hours and to put himself at risk now and then.

"Where?" she said.

"Looking for Leo Thorpe."

"Couldn't you look for him in the morning?"

"I could. But I don't want to wait. If he's hiding where I think he is, he might leave if I wait too long. I don't want him to get away again."

"If he's not where you think he is, you'll just be wasting your time."

"I do that a lot. It's part of the job."

"What if you do find him? Is he dangerous?"

"He doesn't have his chain saw," Rhodes said. "So he's probably harmless."

"Chain saw?"

"Never mind. Just a joke."

Ivy didn't look as if she believed him. "You could send one of the deputies."

"I know, but this is something I want to do myself."

"That's the way you always feel, but now and then you should let someone else have the fun."

"It might not be any fun." In fact, Rhodes was pretty sure it wouldn't be.

"It'll be fun for you. I know how you feel."

She knew him all too well, Rhodes thought.

"You'll stay out of trouble, won't you?" she said.

Rhodes said that he didn't plan to get into anything he couldn't handle.

Ivy looked skeptical. "That's not much of an answer. Will you try not to get all muddied up again?"

Rhodes was glad for the qualifier. "I'll try," he promised.

Chapter 19

▼

THE ROAD TO SHELDON WAS AS STRAIGHT AS A RAILROAD TRACK, which made sense because it was built on an old railbed. Long ago, before Rhodes was born, before anybody in Clearview was born for that matter, there had been a coal mine near Sheldon, an open-pit mine of which no trace now remained.

At one time, however, it must have produced a good bit of coal. Otherwise there wouldn't have been any need for the railroad.

Unlike most of the highways in Blacklin and the surrounding counties, the road had been cut straight through the little hills instead of going over them, and the bed had been built up in all the low places. It was flat and level all the way. Rhodes assumed this had been done to make things easier for the locomotives pulling the coal trains, now as forgotten as the mine itself.

Coal mining had returned to the county in recent years, but it was now done more efficiently. Huge cranes bigger than dinosaurs scooped the coal out of the earth, and it was hauled only a short distance to the big lignite-burning power plant that was a major source of employment for the county. After the coal was mined, the earth that had been dug away was replaced and the grass was replanted. It didn't take long for things to return to a semblance of what they'd been, except there were no trees.

The lignite plant had come along too late to be of any help to Sheldon, which had gone the way of the mine and the railroad. It had disappeared long ago. Rhodes could remember a time when there had been a store at a crossroads where the town had once been, but nothing was left of the store except an empty building.

All that remained of Sheldon itself was a state historical marker affixed to a concrete stand by the side of the road, and Rhodes figured that few people pulled over to read it.

Rhodes wondered if in fifty or sixty years the big cranes would be gone and the lignite plant vacant, as forgotten as the coal cars and the town of Sheldon.

If the town itself was gone, however, a good many people still lived in the country between Clearview and where Sheldon had been. Some of them still farmed in a small way, raising corn, tomatoes, and watermelons that they sold in little tin-roofed roadside stands. There were a couple of peach orchards, and Rhodes knew of one man who still grew a little cotton every year, though that was more for nostalgic reasons than for any profit that he might make.

Rhodes drove past the scattered houses and wondered how many people living in them had mineral rights that would make them rich in the coming years. He knew that at least some of them did, and they'd be building new homes sooner or later, maybe where the old homes were or maybe in town, leaving the country around Sheldon even more deserted than it already was.

He wondered what Helen Harris would have done with her money if she'd lived to get any of it. Maybe she'd have built a new house or, as Brant had implied, bought herself a new car or traveled to some place far from Clearview and Blacklin County. Or she might just have stayed home and watched TV.

A mile or so before he came to the historical marker, Rhodes turned off onto an unpaved county road. It was mostly clay, and it wasn't even graveled. Rhodes hoped the mudholes wouldn't be too bad. He'd hate to get stuck and have to call for help. The car's traction control system might help, but he didn't want to have to depend on it.

Things went fine for about a hundred yards. Then Rhodes saw a bad hole in front of him. The key to driving in the mud, Rhodes believed, was to keep moving. If you ever stopped, you wouldn't be able to start again.

The county car wallowed and slid a bit, and muddy water sloshed up on the sides, but Rhodes got past the hole without any serious trouble. Maybe the traction control was the key. He thought he'd be able to get to the Tumlinson house without any major problems.

He rounded a curve and drove past some old clay pits that had been dug out forty or fifty years earlier by a brick company in a neighboring county. There hadn't been any environmental rules in place in those days, and the land still looked a little like the surface of the moon with only a few straggling trees and weeds growing on the white soil.

There was a long hill after he passed the pits, but it was all sand rather than clay. The sand got treacherous in the summer if it had been dry for a long time, but when it was wet, the hill was easy to climb.

After a couple more turns, Rhodes drove down another clay road, more like a lane, lined with trees that grew close along the sides and made a canopy overhead, cutting out almost all the moonlight.

Driving up a little hill, Rhodes turned onto Helen Harris's property and went across a brand-new cattle guard installed on the new road. There was no gate because the trucks would be coming and going to the drilling rig all the time. The rig stood about a quarter of a mile away, lighted from top to bottom. Rhodes could hear the sound of drilling even inside the closed car.

Not far away from the rig was the slush pit that Rhodes knew contained the drilling fluid, mud, and water. What else might be mixed in with those things, Rhodes didn't know, and he didn't think he wanted to know.

The Tumlinson house sat near a little copse of trees about fifty yards from the new road. The house was completely dark.

Rhodes didn't want to take a chance of getting the car stuck, so he parked on the road. He didn't mind walking, but he'd have to be careful of the mud, and of whatever else there might be to step in. Rhodes thought that Mrs. Harris had been running a few cattle on the place to get an agricultural exemption and keep her tax rate at a reasonable level.

He got out of the car and transferred his pistol from the ankle holster to his waist at the middle of his back. Then he got the heavy, four-cell flashlight from the trunk.

The night was cool but not cold, even though the stars looked icy in the black sky. The moon was just past full, pale and white. The drilling rig hummed.

Rhodes shone the flashlight on the ground, looking for car tracks. There would be no use in looking on the road, since trucks from the rig would have been in and out all day. He didn't see any tracks, but if a car had been there, it could have parked on the road as Rhodes had done.

He walked to within about twenty yards of the house and shone the light around, looking for footprints in the mud. His own shoes were coated with it, and he knew that anyone who'd been outside the house since the rain would have left traces. Unfortunately, a cow or two had been walking around the area, and the ground was churned up with hoofprints.

Shining the light on the house, Rhodes saw that all the window panes were missing. The front door was still there, sagging on one hinge. Some of the wood in the porch was rotten, and in some of the walls as well. If Thorpe was staying inside, he couldn't have been very comfortable.

"Leo Thorpe! If you're in the house, this would be a good time to come on out."

Rhodes didn't get a response, other than the sound of the drilling rig and the hooting of an owl in a tree somewhere not far away.

Rhodes waited. Called out again. Still no response, but Rhodes thought he heard something rustling in the back of the house. It might have been his imagination, or it might have been a possum or an armadillo. It might even have been Thorpe.

Rhodes went right up to the front porch, shining the light on the ground. He was pretty sure there were footprints there, human ones, though shapeless.

Rhodes had walked up to a lot of houses, some of them at night, and at times he could actually sense the danger inside. He couldn't get any sense of this one at all.

He thought about knocking on the door just to see what would happen, shook his head, and started around the house. Its bare boards had weathered to gray, but they looked almost black in the moonlight.

Two windows were in the back wall, probably both of them for bedrooms. The old water well stood a few yards away, but there was no way of getting water out of it, no pump or bucket that Rhodes could see. Even if there had been, the water wouldn't have been drinkable.

"Are you in there, Thorpe?" Rhodes said, standing well away from the windows with the flashlight turned off.

He heard the rustling noise again. This time he was sure it wasn't his imagination or an animal. It sounded to him as if somebody was making a stealthy move to the front of the house, so he went back around.

When he got to the porch, he heard a louder noise, something scrabbling around in the back. The movement toward the front had been a feint. Someone, probably Thorpe, was going out the back window.

Rhodes ran around the house again, arriving in time to see Thorpe—it had to be Thorpe—running toward the drilling rig. He couldn't hope to get away on foot, but when Rhodes saw all the workers' cars and pickups, he knew what Thorpe had in mind. He'd try to find one with the keys in it, and there'd almost certainly be one. Nobody expected his ride to be stolen out in the middle of a pasture, which meant somebody was in for quite a surprise.

Thorpe stopped, turned, and saw that Rhodes was behind him. He pulled something from his belt, and Rhodes decided it might be a good idea to drop to the ground.

It was. Thorpe fired off a couple of shots in Rhodes's general direction before turning back toward the area where the cars were parked.

Rhodes didn't bother shooting back. Thorpe was too far away, and Rhodes didn't want to kill him by accident. Sticking his pistol back in his waistband, Rhodes made straight for the county car. By the time he got it started, a black pickup was pulling away from the drilling rig. Instead of coming up the road toward Rhodes, it turned in the opposite direction.

Rhodes went after it, though he had no idea where the road led or even what kind of road it was. The one he was on now, built for easy access to the rig, was hard-packed and topped with gravel. Rhodes knew that wouldn't last. The drilling company wouldn't have done any work past their own rig.

Thorpe didn't turn on the lights of the pickup he'd taken, so he must have had an idea of where he was going. That put him one up on Rhodes, who didn't have a clue. Rhodes figured he could just follow the road. What he wondered about was its condition. It was bound to be muddy and treacherous.

If it was, that didn't bother Thorpe, who was driving much faster than was safe. Rhodes saw the black pickup bounce as it hit a bump, and he slowed to avoid banging his head on the county car's roof. As it was, he got a good shaking. The beams from the headlights bounced up and down, and by the time they'd steadied, Rhodes saw Thorpe plow into a shallow creek branch that crossed the road.

Most of the time the creek was likely to be dry, but the recent rains had put a little water into it, and it splashed up on both sides nearly as high as the roof of the pickup as Thorpe sailed into it. Then he was through it and climbing the hill on the other side.

It was one thing to run through water like that in a pickup that sat high off the ground and was built for rough travel. It was quite another thing to do it in a car. In the headlight beams Rhodes could see that the edge of the branch was lined with gravel and pieces of brick. Someone had tried to make the bottom solid enough for crossing in rainy weather, for which Rhodes was grateful. He wasn't worried about getting stuck, however. He was worried about the car engine drowning out in the water. Which was no doubt just what Thorpe was hoping for.

Rhodes braked the car as best he could, and it slid along the muddy ruts of the road. He had to fight the wheel to keep from skidding out across the pasture, which would have made Thorpe almost as happy as having the engine drowned.

Somehow Rhodes kept the car more or less in the ruts and slowed it almost to a crawl by the time he arrived at the water. He drove through it slowly, not making any splashes. It came up to the bottom of the undercarriage, but no higher. Of course the brakes were now wet and just about useless. Rhodes decided he'd just have to forget about using them, even if he needed them.

He followed Thorpe up the hill. He'd lost ground, but he could see the truck ahead. It had crossed the top of the hill, which was cleared pastureland, scattering some sleepy cattle, and was on its way down the other side, into a wooded area.

Rhodes went after it.

At the bottom of the hill, a barbed-wire fence seemed to stretch right across the road. Thorpe didn't slow down. The pickup hit the fence and kept right on going as wires twanged and fence posts flew up on both sides.

When Rhodes got to the hole, he saw that Thorpe had run through a gate, the kind people called a gap, made of barbed wire, instead of crashing through the fence itself, not that there was much difference.

Thick spring weeds grew along both sides of the road, so close that they brushed against the county car as Rhodes drove along. The road entered a long line of trees, and Thorpe drove straight toward them. Rhodes had no idea how Thorpe planned to make his way out to a main road, but he seemed to know what he was doing. Rhodes could only follow him.

Thorpe knew what he was doing, all right. The brake lights on the truck glowed red, and he turned sharply to the left in front of the trees, throwing up a shower of mud as he did a complete one-eighty.

Rhodes stepped on his own brakes. There was plenty of resistance, and not much give. They were too wet, and they weren't going to hold.

Uh-oh, Rhodes thought.

The county car's headlights showed Rhodes that the road went straight ahead, through the line of trees and right into a creek. Not a shallow branch like the one he'd crossed a little while earlier, but the real thing, at least six feet deep and three times as wide.

Once a wooden bridge had crossed it, though not much of one, judging from the little that was left of it now. Rhodes remembered he'd promised Ivy he'd try not to get muddied up. He hadn't promised he wouldn't drown, but he didn't regard that as an option.

Fortunately he hadn't been going as fast as Thorpe. He cranked the steering wheel to the left as fast as he could, and the car responded. The tires held their grip for about a second, then Rhodes felt the car begin to slide through the mud. He fought the wheel and tried to get the car pointed back toward the road as Thorpe had done with the truck.

It wasn't going to work. The car hit a bump and threw Rhodes to the right, causing him to lose his grip on the wheel. The car leaned over, too far over, Rhodes thought, sure the car would roll. It didn't, and he grabbed the wheel again, steadied it, and stepped on the gas. Over the engine noise he heard the whir of the heavy-duty tires as they spun in the mud, digging deeper and deeper, and he hoped they'd find something solid before the car sank in up to the axle.

He'd just about given up hoping when the tires grabbed some traction. They stopped spinning, took hold, and the car surged forward. Rhodes whipped the wheel to the left and somehow got back on the road, headed back the way he'd come. He could see the pickup topping the hill, and he went after it.

Confident this time that he wasn't going to get stuck and having a better idea of where he was going, Rhodes sped up. Thorpe had a good head start, but Rhodes hoped to be able to keep him in sight. He might not be able to stop him before he got off the Harris property and onto the road leading to the highway, however, and then Thorpe would have two directions to choose from. Rhodes grabbed the radio mike and called for backup.

He had to slow down again at the creek branch, and Thorpe gained some more ground. He might have gotten away completely, but he wasn't counting on what happened when he started past the drilling rig.

Rhodes hadn't counted on it, either. He'd never even thought about it.

As Thorpe sped toward the rig, a man ran out into the middle of the road, waving his arms.

The owner of the truck, Rhodes thought. Rhodes wondered if the man could possibly believe that Thorpe would stop, because it was evident that he wouldn't.

The man didn't seem surprised when Thorpe continued to bear down on him. He jumped to the side of the road and produced a pistol from somewhere.

It didn't come as a shock that the man was armed. Rhodes suspected that several of the men working on the rig were licensed to carry and that they had sidearms in their cars or trucks. The man whose pickup Thorpe had stolen must have borrowed one of them.

Thorpe kept right on going. The man raised the pistol and started shooting when Thorpe passed him.

Rhodes saw flame from the barrel and then heard the shot. The man fired again.

Rhodes thought the man was crazy. Thorpe had no intention of stopping, and all the man could do was damage his truck and maybe kill Thorpe.

Come to think of it, killing Thorpe might be his intention. A lot of people in Blacklin County looked on car thieves the way their ancestors had looked on horse thieves.

Rhodes took his foot off the gas pedal, hoping the county car would coast to a stop near enough to the man for Rhodes to put a stop to the shooting. Better for Thorpe to get away than for him to be killed for something like stealing a pickup.

Rhodes pumped the brakes, but the car slowed only a little. It was still rolling along when he came alongside the man with the pistol.

Rhodes opened the door and jumped out. He staggered, tried to retain his balance, couldn't, and fell. He somersaulted to his feet and threw himself at the man, who had time to get off one more shot.

The bullet struck one of the truck's tires, and Thorpe swerved off the road.

Rhodes barreled into the shooter, knocking him to the ground, and kicked the pistol out of his hand. Then he looked to see what was happening to Thorpe.

The pickup ran off the road and over a mound of dirt. It bounced high in the air. Then it rolled over on its right side in the air and sailed out over the slush pit.

It got almost to the middle before it fell, landing with a muddy splash.

Rhodes looked down at the man on the ground. He started to say something, couldn't think of anything, and just shook his head. He looked for the county car. It had gone off the road, too, and it sat in a little ditch with its engine running. Rhodes shook his head again and ran to the slush pit to see what was left of Leo Thorpe.

Chapter 20

▼

THE PICKUP WAS ON ITS SIDE, ABOUT HALF-SUBMERGED IN THE slimy mixture of mud, water, drilling fluid, and who knew what else. Rhodes didn't want to go into the pit, but he didn't see any way out of it. Ivy was going to be disappointed in him.

He slid down the side of the pit and into the water, which was cold and opaque. The bottom of the pit was thick, soft mud, and it sucked at Rhodes's shoes as he waded toward the pickup. All he needed to do was lose a shoe, he thought, to make the day complete. Or to lose both shoes. That would be perfect. His shoes, however, stayed on.

He reached the pickup and slogged around to where he was facing the roof. He banged on the part that was sticking out of the water and called Thorpe's name.

He didn't get an answer, so he tried again. No answer that time, either.

Rhodes didn't want to look in for fear that Thorpe was lying inside with the gun in his hand. Getting shot in the head would be a lot worse than losing a shoe or two.

It was possible, though, or even likely, that Thorpe was too badly injured to do any shooting. Rhodes leaned over and looked inside.

Thorpe was there, lying over on the passenger door, which was on the bottom of the pit. Water was seeping in, and Thorpe was facedown in it, not moving. Not a good sign, Rhodes thought.

Rhodes wriggled over the top of the pickup until he was hanging into the open window. He groped around until he had a hand on Thorpe's head. Taking hold of a handful of hair, Rhodes dragged Thorpe out of the water.

Thorpe wasn't breathing. Rhodes propped him up against the dashboard, climbed up on the side of the truck bed, opened the door, and let it fall toward the windshield. Then he lay down, reached in, and pulled Thorpe along the seat, past the steering wheel, and into the water.

Dragging Thorpe along behind him, Rhodes waded back to the bank of the pit as fast as he could, which wasn't fast. The mud made it heavy going. When he got to the bank, he pushed Thorpe up the slope and started CPR, making sure that the airway was clear and positioning Thorpe's head before beginning the rescue breathing.

They could call it *rescue breathing* all they wanted, Rhodes thought, but it was still mouth-to-mouth, and it wasn't pleasant by any name, least of all when you were doing it for someone like Leo Thorpe. Whether Rhodes liked it or not, it had to be done, so he did it, forcing the air into Thorpe's mouth and checking for vital signs at the proper intervals.

Thorpe still wasn't breathing when Rhodes began the chest

compressions, but he kept them up, alternating with the rescue breathing. After what seemed like a long time, Thorpe coughed, sputtered, spit out water and mud, and breathed.

Rhodes sat back, relieved. He'd been afraid he was going to have a dead murder suspect on his hands, never a good thing. Thorpe wasn't in great shape, but at least he was alive.

Because Thorpe had been unconscious when Rhodes had found him, Rhodes suspected that he had sustained some kind of injury when the pickup had hit the water, if not before. There hadn't been any blood, so Rhodes didn't think Thorpe had been hit by one of the bullets, but now he had a look to make sure.

He found a large knot on the side of Thorpe's head, some blood still oozing from it. Thorpe hadn't been wearing his seat belt, which had made it easier to get him out of the pickup. If he'd been wearing it, though, he might not have hit his head on whatever it had smacked into. Or the knot might have come from a bullet that grazed his skull.

Not that it mattered at the moment.

Rhodes took hold of Thorpe's collar and dragged him up the bank, which was so slick that Rhodes had trouble climbing it. Water and mud squished out of his shoes with every step, but no one offered to help him.

Dragging Thorpe just made things harder, but at least he slid easily on the mud. When Rhodes got to the top of the bank, the man who'd been shooting at Thorpe was standing there watching.

"Is he gonna be okay?" he said.

"I don't know," Rhodes told him. "Why don't you make yourself useful and call 911."

The man held up a cell phone. "Already did." He put the phone into the pocket of his filthy jeans. "You gonna arrest me?"

180

"Yeah. I am."

The man shook his head. "Damn. I was afraid of that."

It was after midnight, and Rhodes was sitting at the kitchen table, cleaning his pistol, a short-barreled .38 Police Special. Other people preferred automatics, but Rhodes was old-fashioned. Give him a good revolver any day.

He hadn't had to use it, however. It was just wet and muddy from his soak in the slush pit. Leo Thorpe hadn't given any trouble. He'd still been unconscious when he was put in the ambulance summoned by the 911 call, and he hadn't regained consciousness by the time Rhodes had gone by the hospital on the way home.

The doctor on duty told Rhodes that Thorpe had been struck by a bullet and had a serious concussion. He added that Thorpe might even have memory loss when he did awaken. When Rhodes asked if there could be any chance that Thorpe was faking it, the doctor hadn't even bothered to answer him. The doctor did answer when Rhodes asked how long Thorpe might remain in a coma. He said that he had no idea.

The man who'd shot Thorpe hadn't given any trouble, either. His defense was that he was just trying to stop Thorpe from getting away with his truck, and Rhodes thought he might even be able to convince a grand jury of that. He'd arrested him anyway, however, and booked him in at the jail.

With all that taken care of, all Rhodes had to do before taking a bath and going to bed was clean his gun.

The smell of gun oil didn't seem to bother the cat, which was asleep in its usual spot by the refrigerator. It bothered Rhodes that he'd thought in terms of *the usual spot,* but he was too tired to worry about it.

Ivy had gone back to bed after Rhodes had come in and told her about his evening. She hadn't even said anything about his appearance. Well, that was a slight exaggeration. She'd said something, all right, but not as much as Rhodes had thought she might.

"You said you'd try not to get muddy," she told him, but without sounding too accusatory.

"*Try* is the important word there," he said. "I tried. I just didn't succeed."

"You surely didn't. You look like the Swamp Thing."

Ivy wasn't a comic book fan. Rhodes had watched the movie version of *Swamp Thing* one night, and she'd watched it with him. She hadn't liked it as much as Rhodes, nor had she appreciated the acting ability of Adrienne Barbeau as much as he had. She'd liked Louis Jourdan, however.

"I don't look like him yet," Rhodes said. "When you think about what might have been in that slush pit, though, I might look like Swamp Thing by tomorrow."

"It would be better if you looked like Louis Jourdan."

"Not a chance."

"You could get a face-lift."

Rhodes grinned. "Even less of a chance."

Ivy shrugged. "Maybe they could use Louis Jourdan on the cover of the crime-bustin'-sheriff book. Or books. I'm sure there'll be a whole series."

"Better Louis Jourdan than somebody who looks like me."

Ivy gave him the once-over, not for the first time that evening.

"With all that pollution you've absorbed, maybe you'll have spider powers."

"I wasn't bitten by a radioactive spider. I was just wading around in a slush pit. It's not the same."

"Oh." Ivy looked even more disappointed than she had about the face-lift. "I was sort of hoping for spider powers."

At times Rhodes had hoped for the same thing, but it had never happened. He just had to muddle along as an ordinary person. One who didn't even look like Louis Jourdan.

"You're going to make a mess in the bathroom," Ivy said.

Rhodes told her that he'd clean up after himself.

"Don't bother. And don't worry about it. I'll take care of it tomorrow."

Rhodes said he'd help her.

"You'll probably be too busy."

Rhodes had a feeling she was right.

The only good thing about the rest of the night, what little was left of it after Rhodes got to bed, was that the cat didn't come in and plaster himself to Rhodes's back.

Even without the cat, Rhodes didn't sleep well. His mind refused to shut down, and he worried about things like the pistol Thorpe had used. Thorpe's gun was taken before he was hospitalized. The owner of the pickup swore that there had been no gun in his vehicle, and Thorpe had shot at Rhodes before he even got into the truck. So where had the pistol come from?

For that matter, how had Thorpe gotten to the Tumlinson house? It was logical enough that he'd know about it. He'd been on the property because it belonged to his cousin. When he escaped from the hospital, however, he'd been on foot. It was possible that he'd walked nearly to Sheldon, a distance of about ten miles, but Rhodes didn't think Thorpe was much of a walker. He was more likely to have gotten a ride. But from whom? He might have hitchhiked, but most people were wary of hitchhikers these days.

There hadn't been any clues in the house when Rhodes had searched it, just some canned food and a change of clothing. Rhodes hadn't been expecting a piece of paper with a phone number on it, but it would have been nice to find one.

Gid Sherman bothered Rhodes almost as much as the pistol and the question of how Thorpe had gotten out of town. Sherman was likable enough, but Rhodes wondered if he'd been telling the whole truth about things. Did Sherman really dislike Thorpe because Thorpe and Alton Brant didn't get along, or was there more to it? Sherman had turned Thorpe in for arranging the poker games, but what if that wasn't the whole story? Could there be a connection to Helen Harris, for example?

For that matter, where had Thorpe gotten the money to buy the Royal Rack and move his poker games there? As far as Rhodes knew, Thorpe didn't have a steady income. He did odd jobs, mowed lawns, repaired roofs and soffits, mended fences, painted a little. Nothing he did would generate enough money to buy a pool hall. It would have been hard for him to get any kind of loan without a steady job or something to put up for security, and Thorpe had neither, at least not that Rhodes knew about.

When he got up the next morning, he didn't feel as if he'd slept at all.

*   *   *

The first place Rhodes went the next day was the courthouse. He looked up the deeds for the Royal Rack and saw that Thorpe had bought it one month previously from someone named Rodney Jackson, who lived in Dallas.

Up in his office, Rhodes called Jackson, who wasn't particularly interested in talking to him.

"All I can tell you is that he made the down payment in cash," Jackson said. "And before you ask, I didn't care where he got it. The deal's all legal, and if he makes his payments on time, the place is his."

Rhodes didn't mention that Thorpe might have trouble making the payments, considering his current situation. He said, "Who managed the place for you?"

"A guy named Wayne York. He did a good job. I hardly ever had to come down there. You need anything else?"

"Not at the moment."

Jackson hung up. He wasn't the most congenial person Rhodes had ever talked to, but he wasn't as bad as some.

Rhodes called Hack and asked him about things at the jail.

"If you mean Truck, he's fine. He's just sorry he caused so much trouble. The fella who shot Thorpe bonded out first thing this mornin'."

"Any calls last night that I need to hear about?"

"You were the one responsible for most of the excitement. Nothin' else happened worth a mention."

"I'll be in when I get a chance then," Rhodes said. "I need to talk to a few people."

"Who?"

"I'm not sure yet."

"You're just sayin' that 'cause you don't think it's any of my business."

"Would I do that?"

"Yep."

Rhodes grinned, though Hack couldn't see him. "Maybe I would, at that."

Chapter 21

▼

GID SHERMAN SAT IN FRONT OF HIS TRAILER ON A METAL LAWN chair, smoking a cigarette. It was a fine morning, Rhodes thought. The front that had brought the rain was past, leaving only a few clouds. It was about seventy degrees and the humidity was low. No wind to speak of. The smoke from Sherman's cigarette hovered around his head for a while and then just disappeared rather than being blown away.

"Mornin', Sheriff," Sherman said when Rhodes got out of the county car. "You'll excuse me if I don't get up. I got a bad case of the dropsy and the heart disease this morning."

Rhodes looked concerned, and Sherman grinned.

"Nothing to worry about. Just means I drop down on my butt and don't have the heart to get up. What can I do for you, Sheriff?"

"You could answer a few questions. If you have the heart for it."

"I think I can handle a question or two. Sorry I can't offer you a chair. This one's all I got. You could borrow one from Thorpe's shed, though, if you were of a mind to."

Rhodes said that he'd stand. "I don't want to sit down and find out I've caught that disease from you."

"I don't know that it's contagious. Anyway, what can I tell you?"

"How long have you known Leo Thorpe?"

Sherman finished his smoke and field-stripped it before he answered. "Just since I've been living here in this lovely mobile-home park."

Sherman's trailer was as old as Thorpe's, but it was in much better condition.

"How long would that be?"

"Let me see." Sherman thought it over. "It's been about five years now."

"I guess you and Thorpe never got along."

Sherman squinted up at Rhodes. "We got along. I just didn't like him."

"Did he know you were the one who'd called about his poker games?"

"I never told him, if that's what you mean."

"So he didn't know."

"He might've guessed."

"You never mentioned how you knew about them."

"Hell," Sherman said. "He asked me if I wanted to play. I always told him I did, and then I'd call you. It could just as well have been anybody else."

"He didn't invite you to play at the Royal Rack?"

"Nope. I heard about that game you busted up there. Who'd think Thorpe could buy a place like that?"

"He didn't have much money?"

Sherman waved a hand in the general direction of Thorpe's trailer. "If you had money, would you be living in a place like that?"

"Maybe he spent the money on the pool hall. So he couldn't afford to move out."

"Where'd he get the money, then, all of a sudden the way he did?"

Rhodes didn't have an answer for that. "You didn't say why Thorpe never invited you to the games at the pool hall."

"Okay, maybe he did know it was me who turned him in. I couldn't say."

Sherman wasn't looking at Rhodes now. Rhodes thought he was lying.

"You might as well tell me about it," Rhodes said.

Sherman gave an involuntary twitch, and his head turned slowly back to Rhodes. "I don't want you to get the wrong idea."

Rhodes said he'd try not to.

"I had a talk with his cousin about him," Sherman said.

"Mrs. Harris?"

"Yeah, her. She seemed nice enough. I thought maybe she'd help me out."

"With what?"

"With Thorpe. He was making threats to me. He knew I'd turned him in. It couldn't have been anybody else. He knew the others didn't do it."

"Did you call Mrs. Harris, or did you go by to see her?"

"I went by. I didn't kill her, though. I haven't been to see her in a good while."

"You liked her, didn't you."

"Yeah, but she liked the Colonel, and he liked her. I couldn't try to cut him out."

People tended to think that nobody over fifty or sixty could have a serious romance. Rhodes had long ago learned better. Certain passions might not have burned as hotly, but that didn't mean there was no fire at all. There was, in fact, often more than enough fire to bring about murder.

"You're sure you haven't seen her lately?" Rhodes said.

"That's what I told you."

"All right. I have one other question. Who should I talk to about Thorpe's liking for the ladies?"

"You could try Miz Gomez. She lives over there."

Sherman pointed to a trailer with a neat yard and a small flower bed.

"Is she home?"

"I'd say so. Her husband works at the lumberyard, and she cleans houses. But she usually doesn't go out until afternoon."

"I'll have a talk with her, then. If you think of anything else I might need to know, give me a call."

Sherman said he would and got out a cigarette. He lit it, and Rhodes walked over to the Gomez trailer.

His knock on the door was answered by a short woman with black eyes and black hair streaked with gray.

"Mrs. Gomez?" Rhodes said.

"Yes. Can I help you?"

Rhodes explained that he was asking questions about Leo Thorpe and that he hoped she might be able to help him.

"I did not like him," she said with only a trace of an accent.

"Why not?"

"He was not a nice man. He made, I think, bad remarks. I am not a young woman, and even if I were, he should not say such things to me."

Rhodes asked her to be a little more specific.

"He was very flattering. He told me how nice I looked, how pretty my hair was. How I was graceful when I walked."

In other words, Rhodes thought, nothing insulting. Flattering, in fact, as Mrs. Gomez had said. It might work with some women, but not her.

"Did he ever make advances?" Rhodes said.

"Oh, no. He was most careful. It may be that he knew Carlos, my husband, would not like it if he became insulting. Carlos is a quiet man, but he is big. Strong."

Rhodes thanked her for her help and went back to his car. Sherman was still sitting in his lawn chair. He didn't wave good-bye when Rhodes drove away.

Jennifer Loam was waiting for Rhodes when he arrived at the jail.

"I told her you were in Canada," Hack said. "For some reason or other she didn't believe me."

Hack sounded out of sorts, and Rhodes wondered if he'd actually expected the reporter to believe him. For that matter, Rhodes wondered if Hack had really told her that.

"We need to talk, Sheriff," she said.

"Sure. I have a report to write about what happened with Leo Thorpe last night, and I'll tell you about it while I work."

"This isn't about Thorpe."

Rhodes was a little surprised. He'd thought she was there to find out about the events of the previous evening. "It's not about Thorpe?"

"No, and I don't want to talk about it here."

No wonder Hack had been upset, Rhodes thought. He looked over at the dispatcher, who was looking at his computer monitor as if he had no idea that a conversation was going on behind his back. Rhodes knew he was listening, though.

"Why not here?" Rhodes said.

"Never mind that. Are you going to talk to me or not?"

Rhodes knew whatever she had to say must be important. Not to mention too sensitive to mention in front of Hack. That was unusual because Jennifer knew Hack, and she knew that he could be trusted not to pass on anything he heard in the office.

"Well?" she said.

"All right. Where do you want to go?"

"I'll meet you in the courthouse."

Rhodes said he'd be there, and she walked out. Hack said, "Must be a mighty big secret. You gonna tell me what it is?"

"I'll think about it."

Rhodes could hear Hack muttering as he left the jail.

Jennifer was waiting at the door of Rhodes's courthouse office when he got there. He unlocked the door, and they went inside. Rhodes went behind his desk and told Jennifer to have a seat. She did, but she didn't relax. She sat on the edge of the chair and tapped the tip of one shoe on the floor. She didn't get out her recorder or even a notebook.

"You must have uncovered something big," Rhodes said. "Have you solved my case for me?"

"I'm not sure. I just know this is important."

There was a long pause. The tapping continued, but more slowly than before.

"Are you going to tell me what it is?"

"I'm thinking it over."

Rhodes thought about the report that he had to write. "If you're not going to tell me, we're wasting a lot of time."

"I know. It's just that I'm not sure if this is something I should tell you, even if it does have a bearing on your murder case."

"It's pretty simple. If it has a bearing, you should tell me."

"I know that. I'm just having to work up to it. I'm usually more straightforward than this."

Rhodes didn't say anything in response. He'd just let her get to it in her own time. Or not.

Jennifer looked down at her foot. The toe stopped tapping, and she looked up at Rhodes. "It's about Colonel Brant. Except that's not his name."

"Not his name? You mean he's living under an alias?"

"No. I didn't mean it that way. His name is Brant, all right, but he's no colonel. He was in the army, but he wasn't promoted but once. He got to be corporal, and that was as high as he went."

Rhodes found it hard to believe. Everybody knew Brant was a colonel. "Are you sure about that?"

Jennifer nodded. "Of course I'm sure. I'd never say something like that if I weren't."

"How did you find out?"

"Doing my job." Jennifer looked embarrassed, and Rhodes could have sworn that she blushed. He wasn't used to seeing people blush. It seemed to have gone out of style. "It's something I should have done a long time ago."

She hadn't been in Clearview for a long time, so Rhodes asked what she meant.

"I did a story on him, remember?"

Rhodes said that he did. "We talked about it with him."

"Yes. I should have done some research at the time I wrote that story, but I made a rookie mistake."

"You were a rookie," Rhodes said, remembering that the story she'd done on Brant had been printed not long after she'd come to Clearview. "You were entitled."

"I was no rookie. This might be my first paying job, but I was a reporter for the college paper at Sam Houston State. A good one."

Rhodes nodded.

"The *Houstonian*," she added in case Rhodes hadn't heard of the paper. "We were taught all about the importance of research, but everybody told me, 'Go interview Colonel Brant. He's a veteran, and he has some good stories.' So I did, and I didn't even think about checking his credentials."

The toe started to tap again.

"You checked them recently, though."

"Yesterday. I thought I should know something about the people involved in the murder, especially someone who's caused a little trouble. I checked Brant's military records and found out that he did serve in Korea, and he even did some of the things he says he did, but there's no record that he ever held a higher rank than corporal."

That made Brant a liar, if it was true, which of course made Rhodes wonder what else the self-styled colonel might have lied about.

"You can see why I didn't want to talk about this in front of anyone, can't you?" Jennifer said.

"I think so."

She put a hand on her knee as if to stop the toe-tapping by applying pressure. It worked.

"Because if I'm wrong," she said, "it would be terrible to start a rumor like that. Even if I'm right, I'm not sure anybody needs to know that Brant's a fraud. He's not really hurting anybody by exaggerating his accomplishments. Look at that man who was Elvis Presley's manager."

"Colonel Tom Parker," Rhodes said.

"That's him. He wasn't even from this country. That didn't stop him from calling himself a colonel, though, and nobody seemed to mind."

She had a point, Rhodes supposed, but then Colonel Parker had never been mixed up in a murder. Not that Rhodes knew about, anyway.

"People have a right to know the truth," he said.

"I know that, but Colonel Brant seems like such a nice man that I hate to hurt him."

Rhodes thought that might be a commendable attitude in most people, but he wasn't sure it was a virtue in a journalist who was supposed to be devoted to objectivity and truth. On the other hand, Brant's impersonation might not qualify as news.

Rhodes stood up. "I appreciate your telling me about this. I'll have a talk with Brant about it and see if there's any connection with what happened to Mrs. Harris."

Jennifer stood up as well. "I'm going with you."

"I don't think that would be a good idea."

"I wouldn't expect you to. I'm going anyway. I want to know why he lied. Maybe what he has to say will help me decide what to do."

Rhodes could have prevented her, but he didn't think Brant was dangerous. On the other hand, Brant might not be so willing to talk if a reporter was present. He started to tell Jennifer that, but he didn't get the chance.

"I'm going," she said, as if that settled it.

Rhodes supposed that it did.

Chapter 22

▼

THE LAWN AT BRANT'S HOUSE WAS JUST AS NEAT AS THE ONE AT
Helen Harris's. The grass along the front sidewalk was trimmed
so precisely that Brant might have used a ruler to check his work.
The white paint on the wooden sections of the house looked as
fresh as if it had been applied within the last month. For all
Rhodes knew that might have been the case.

He parked the county car at the curb and waited until Jennifer
pulled up behind him. They both got out and started up the walk,
with Rhodes in the lead.

"You'd better let me do the talking," Rhodes said.

"Gladly," Jennifer said. "I'll just be the demure girl reporter,
sitting quietly with my hands folded in my lap."

Rhodes grinned. "You're going to have trouble acting the part."

"I'll do my best."

Rhodes didn't believe her for a second.

* * *

Brant answered the doorbell and seemed taken aback to see the sheriff and a reporter standing there. Rhodes didn't blame him.

"This is a surprise," Brant said. "I've behaved myself all day, so I hope you're not here to arrest me."

"No," Rhodes said. "That's not it. Can we go inside?"

Brant nodded and led them to his den, a paneled room right out of the 1970s, which was probably when the house had been built. There were bookshelves on one wall, but there were books on only one shelf. The others held what Rhodes thought must be paperweights, all neatly in line. He walked over and picked one up. It was made of bright red glass with floral designs embedded in it.

"Millefiori," Brant said when Rhodes asked. "It means 'a thousand flowers.' It's a very old glass-blowing technique. It's been around since the Renaissance, although paperweights themselves are a relatively new invention. That one comes from England. I collect them."

Rhodes said he could see that. "They must be expensive."

"Some of them are. Now and then I get lucky and find one at a flea market that's not too costly."

Rhodes put the paperweight down. The shelf was entirely free of dust.

"You probably didn't come here to talk about my collection." Brant looked at Jennifer. "It would make a nice article for the paper, but I'd rather you not write about it. If the wrong person read about it, I might get robbed. Not that you wouldn't track him down, Sheriff, but it would be inconvenient for both of us."

"Yes," Rhodes said. "It would."

"Well, then. Have a seat."

"Maybe we'd better just stand," Rhodes said, looking at an old couch that appeared much too soft to suit him.

"That sounds ominous."

"It's not ominous," Jennifer said. "We just want to ask you something about your background."

So much for the demure girl reporter with folded hands, Rhodes thought.

Rhodes heard a dog bark outside. "Your dalmatian?"

"Yes. He's been with me about ten years. A fine dog. He's not really a full-blood dalmatian, but that's all to the good. He's not as sensitive as they are. You don't want to know about my dog, though."

"No," Jennifer said. "It's a little more serious than that."

"Then maybe I'd better sit down, even if you don't." Brant moved to a platform rocker and dropped into it in a way that made Rhodes think about Gid Sherman's condition, although Brant retained his military bearing.

"You know what the question is?" Jennifer said.

"Judging from your disapproving looks, I think I might."

"You're not a real colonel, are you?" Jennifer said.

Brant looked uncomfortable. "That depends on what you mean by *real.*"

"I'd hoped we wouldn't get into definitions. They're usually just a way of evading the subject."

"Why don't you just tell us straight out," Rhodes said.

Brant slumped just a little. "That's not as easy as you think."

"Try it," Rhodes said.

"I haven't committed any crimes. I've never impersonated an

officer, at least not when I was in the service. Not now, either, not really."

He was still evading, but Rhodes thought he'd eventually get to the point.

Jennifer wasn't quite so patient. "Yes, you really did. You let people think you held a rank you didn't earn."

"It wasn't my fault."

Rhodes had heard that excuse so many times in his career that it was all he could do not to sigh.

Brant must have sensed. Rhodes's skepticism. "I don't mean that I'm not to blame. It all started a long time ago, not long after I first moved here. I came to work at the cotton mill, if you re-member it."

Rhodes did, but he was sure Jennifer didn't. The mill was still there, though it no longer made cotton ducking and canvas. It had been closed for years, but it had recently reopened. Rhodes wasn't sure exactly what went on there now, but he could remember that when he was a small child, the mill whistle could be heard all over town.

"I was the last manager before the place closed down," Brant went on. "Some of the employees, most of them, thought I was a true autocrat, and they took to calling me *colonel*. The title sort of stuck, and then someone from the paper interviewed me one Vet-erans Day. I don't remember who it was, even, but I do know he called me *Colonel Brant*. I should have corrected him, but it never occurred to me to do it. I never even thought about it. So when the article came out in the paper, there I was with a promotion I'd never earned and certainly never asked for."

"You could have said something then," Jennifer told him. "You could have written a letter to the paper or asked the reporter to print a correction."

"I should have. I knew it then, and I know it now. I didn't, though."

He didn't offer any excuses, and Rhodes thought that he'd probably liked the idea of being thought of as a colonel.

"You earned medals," Jennifer said. "You got a Purple Heart."

"I did, indeed. I still have the scar to prove I earned it honorably. I nearly died, in fact, and by the time I recovered, the war was over. I like to think I'd have become a colonel in reality if I hadn't been wounded. I might have stayed in the service, too. As it was, I was discharged from the service at about the same time I was discharged from the hospital."

Rhodes didn't know what to think of the story. He supposed it was true, but he was beginning to wonder about Brant's veracity.

"I never meant to deceive people," Brant said. "I never meant to hurt anyone. It seemed harmless enough to let people use the title if they wanted to."

That, at least, seemed true enough to Rhodes. Brant had never used the title himself. He'd just failed to discourage others from using it.

Jennifer seemed to have come to the same conclusion. "I'm not going to print anything in the paper about this. I just hope that the next time the editor calls you about an interview, you'll refuse."

"I will. I've caused enough trouble already. I don't want to cause any more."

Brant wasn't talking about the trouble with Truck Gadney and Leo Thorpe, and Rhodes wondered about those two. Brant had goaded both of them into fights, and he'd come close to getting killed both times. Rhodes didn't know much about psychology, but he wondered if Brant's reasons for provoking the two men hadn't come from something more than just a desire to avenge the murder of Mrs. Harris.

Or maybe the impulse was something left over from the days when Brant had been in charge of the mill. If he'd been a dictator, and Rhodes had no reason to doubt it, he'd have been in complete control. He could be one of those people who always had to be in control of events, and his provocation of Truck and Thorpe would have been his attempt to bring them to some kind of vigilante justice.

Except that Brant hadn't been armed in either case, and both the other men had been. It was possible that Brant wouldn't have expected that, but surely he hadn't thought his accusations would cause the men to go to Rhodes and confess. There was something else about Brant's accusations that Rhodes couldn't quite put his finger on, but it would come to him sooner or later. He hoped.

A the moment it was all too complicated for Rhodes, but he knew that more was going on with Brant than anybody could see on the surface.

Brant and Jennifer were talking, but Rhodes heard only the buzz, not the words, because he was wondering what Brant might have done if Mrs. Harris had somehow found out that he wasn't a colonel. And if she'd confronted him with his imposture. Judging from the way he'd gone after Truck and Thorpe, he might have reacted violently.

Why face up to Truck and Thorpe, then? To prove to Rhodes that he couldn't possibly have killed Mrs. Harris because of his high regard for her?

While Rhodes was thinking it over, the conversation began to register with him again.

"I'm not ashamed of what I did or didn't do about the rank," Brant said, "but it wouldn't happen again the way it did, not if I could do it over."

"Nobody gets do-overs," Jennifer told him. "It doesn't work like that."

Brant said he knew it didn't and that Jennifer could interview him again on the next Veterans Day. "I'll come clean about it. I'll say I made a mistake and that I just let it go on and on."

Jennifer told him that there wasn't any real need for that, but she'd think it over.

"What's your opinion, Sheriff?" Brant said. "Should I apologize to the community?"

"It might not be a bad idea. Sometimes people are quick to forgive things."

"And sometimes they're not," Jennifer said, as if she knew what she was talking about.

"That's a discussion for another time," Rhodes said. "I think we'd better leave now and let Mr. Brant think things over."

If Brant noticed the omission of his title, he didn't show any sign of it. He stood up and apologized for any trouble he'd caused Jennifer and Rhodes.

"You didn't cause any trouble for us," Rhodes said. "You might have caused it for yourself."

"I'm afraid you're right," Brant said.

Rhodes left it at that, but he figured he wasn't through with Brant. Not yet.

Chapter 23

▼

RHODES KNEW THAT IF HE WENT BACK TO THE JAIL, HACK WOULD try to find out what Jennifer had told him. Rhodes wasn't ready to face that interrogation yet, so to put off the inevitable he decided to do some more investigating.

First, however, he got on the radio to Hack and asked if there'd been a report from the hospital about Leo Thorpe's condition.

"Sure has. You can bet he's not fakin' this time. You don't have to worry about him gettin' away, either. He might not ever be leavin' at all. They didn't come right out and say it, but Thorpe's about as likely to die as to live. Even if he lives, he might not wake up. That bullet did some real damage. His brain's swelled up."

That didn't sound good. Rhodes wanted Thorpe alive even if he was guilty.

"You through with Miz Loam?" Hack said, getting to the subject he had a personal interest in.

"Yes. I'm going to talk to somebody else now."

"You gonna tell me who, or is that another big secret? We're supposed to kind of keep up with you. Part of the job."

"It's no secret. I'll be at Thelma Rice's place."

"I'm glad you trust me enough to let me in on things like that."

Rhodes didn't bother to answer. He signed off and drove to Thelma Rice's house, located on a quiet street in an old neighborhood not too far from the cemetery where Helen Harris would soon be buried.

Thelma didn't have on her red hat or purple dress. She was sitting on a stool in her front yard, working in a flower bed, digging out early weeds. She'd pull them up and toss them into a galvanized bucket by her side, and she was so intent on her work that she didn't hear Rhodes park at the curb, get out of the car, and walk up to her.

She was talking to herself as she yanked out the weeds.

"One more of you sorry suckers gone," Rhodes heard her say as his shadow fell across her. She jerked a little in surprise, then looked up at him from beneath the brim of the blue-and-white sunbonnet she wore.

"You ought not to sneak up on innocent women in their yards, Sheriff. You might scare them to death. You wouldn't want that on your conscience."

"I wasn't trying to scare you. I just didn't want to interrupt."

She took off the cotton work gloves she was wearing and hung them on the side of the bucket. "You must think I'm crazy, talking to the weeds."

Rhodes grinned. "They probably listen better than some people I know."

"You and I must know some of the same people." Thelma stood

up. She wasn't much taller than she'd been while sitting down. "I need a drink."

In Clearview, that comment didn't mean the same thing as it might have in a bigger city. It just meant that Thelma was thirsty. She walked to the end of the flower bed near the driveway where a bright yellow hose lay coiled on the ground. She turned the handle of a faucet that protruded from the wall of the house, then picked up the end of the hose. When the water flowed from it, she put it up to her mouth and drank.

"Not very elegant," she said when she'd finished. She offered the hose to Rhodes. "You need a drink?"

"No, thanks. What I need is to talk to you a little more."

"About Helen?"

"Yes. I don't seem to be getting anywhere with finding out who killed her, and I need to know more."

"Can't help you there. I told you all I know already."

"I'm not asking for facts this time. I'll settle for gossip. It might even be preferable."

Thelma walked back to her stool and sat down. She took her gloves off the bucket and put them back on, pulling them tight and stretching her fingers.

"A lot of people prefer gossip to the truth," she said. "It's a lot more fun, but it can also get people in a lot of trouble. Most of the time, they don't deserve it."

She started to pull the weeds again, but this time she did it in silence.

"You sound like someone who knows the effects."

"I've never married, Sheriff. I inherited a little money from my grandparents, so I've never had to work."

Rhodes remembered that she'd had a job for a while as a secretary at the elementary school, but that had been quite a few years ago.

"I tried working," she said when he mentioned it. "I found out that a single woman with no interest in marriage, or even in dating, was in a precarious position." She threw a handful of weeds into the bucket. If she'd been throwing a baseball, the Houston Astros might have considered giving her a tryout. "People talk about her. They don't really want her working around their children. Do you know what I'm saying?"

Rhodes said that he thought he got the idea.

"You might get the idea, but you don't know how devastating it can be. It was all untrue, of course. Gossip usually is. I'm as straight-arrow as anybody in this town, but I quit the school job anyway. The truth of the matter is that men simply never interested me except as friends or someone to talk to. I never even considered the idea of marriage. I like reading, sewing, and taking care of myself. I don't have any interest in taking on a 'life partner' of either sex. I'm happy right where I am, doing what I like to do." She pulled some weeds and threw them in the bucket. "Even if it's just doing this."

Rhodes said there was nothing wrong with that.

"There certainly isn't, but not everyone sees it that way. Or they didn't when I was young. They had to make more of it than it was. Now that I'm older, though, I'm not considered much of a risk. Old people aren't supposed to be interested in sex, you know."

Rhodes knew. He'd been thinking along those lines not too long ago, himself. He remembered Francine Oates and her romance novel. Even Francine, lady that she considered herself, needed some romance in her life.

"I've aged a little," Thelma went on, "and people don't mind associating with me, maybe because they don't think I'm dangerous anymore. It could be that they've forgotten the gossip, too. I've managed to make quite a few friends in the Red Hats and the OWLS."

"Or maybe they're a little more enlightened now."

"I wouldn't bet on it. Anyway, I don't like talking about people. I know how hurtful that can be."

Rhodes was beginning to get the idea. "That means you're not going to tell me anything."

"You catch on quick, Sheriff."

Rhodes didn't think so. It had taken him longer than it should have, and even though he'd caught on, he wasn't going to give up.

"Wasn't Helen Harris your friend?"

Thelma pulled a few more weeds and put them in the bucket before she looked up at Rhodes again. "Now, that's not fair."

Rhodes could look innocent when it served his purposes. "Just asking."

"I'm sure. You know that Helen was my friend, and I'd like to help. If I can do it without being hurtful. What do you want to know about? Specifically."

"Leonard Thorpe. I've heard he's a romantic kind of guy, but I can't seem to locate anybody he's romanced."

Not counting Mrs. Gomez, Rhodes thought, and she truly didn't count because Thorpe had gotten nowhere with her.

"Do you mean recently? Or just any old time?"

Rhodes hadn't given it any thought. "Any old time will do."

"I did hear a few things about him years ago, when I worked at the school. He cut a wide swath there, so they said."

"Any names?"

"I can't remember any, to tell the truth. That was a long time ago." She paused to reflect. "Well, maybe one name, but I hate to say."

"It could help me find out who killed Mrs. Harris. You never know."

"It's nothing but gossip. Nothing factual about it. You remember when Lily Gadney was teaching at the elementary school?"

Rhodes said that he didn't.

"She was younger than most everybody there. You know how this school system is. The pay is the state minimum. Either you leave after a year or two for a better job, or you stay forever for whatever reason you might have. That means a lot of young teachers coming in every year as the others leave. Lily was one of them, and Leo tried to move in on her."

"He was a good bit older, though."

Thelma made a noise that was somewhere between a laugh and a snort of derision. "When did that ever make a difference to a man?"

She had a point. Rhodes said, "Did he put the moves on anybody else?"

"Several, or so I heard, but I'm not sure of the names. You could find out who was teaching there then. Helen could tell you, I'm sure, if only she were alive. Leonard's behavior was humiliating to her. I remember that much."

Rhodes spent five more minutes trying to get Thelma to remember something more, but Thelma insisted she'd told him all she knew. "And more. I don't really know about Lily. It's gossip, but that's what you said you wanted."

It wasn't that he wanted it so much, Rhodes thought, as that he didn't have anything else.

"You say you like living alone?" Rhodes said.

"Yes. It suits me. I've always been very self-sufficient."

"Have you ever thought about a pet? I know a nice housebroken cat that needs a good home."

Thelma stopped pulling weeds. She smiled under the brim of the bonnet. "I like cats. I've had two living with me for years. Frankie and Johnny. Like the song. They never come outside." She went back to her weeding. "I couldn't possibly take in another one. They'd hate that. They're very spoiled."

Well, Rhodes thought, *at least I tried.*

He left Thelma working in the flower bed and started back to the jail.

On the way he pulled off into the drive-through lane at McDonald's and got a Quarter Pounder with cheese. He told himself that he needed some nourishment and that he'd eat a light supper to make up for his indulgence.

While he sat in his car and ate the burger, he thought about the connection between Lily Gadney and Leo Thorpe and wondered what it meant, if anything. The connection to Helen Harris was tenuous at best, other than that Thorpe's antics had humiliated her. That was something Rhodes needed to know more about. After he finished the burger, he put all the paper and cardboard into the bag it had come in and put everything into the big trash can in the McDonald's parking lot.

If he went back to the jail, he'd have to talk to Hack, and he still wasn't ready for that. He thought it might be a good idea to have another talk with Alton Brant.

*   *   *

Brant wasn't happy to see Rhodes again, but he was polite, inviting him in and offering him a seat in the den. "That is, if you don't mind sitting this time. I wouldn't want to force anything on you."

Rhodes sat on the couch, which was just as uncomfortable as he'd thought it would be.

"I hate to bother you again."

"Right," Brant said.

"I wouldn't have come back if I hadn't heard a few things I hoped you could help me with. You really seemed to have it in for Leonard Thorpe, and it started before he got after you with that chain saw."

"I've already told you that."

Rhodes looked over at the heavy glass paperweights. Put one of those things in a sock, he thought, and you could hit a person in the head with it and cause a lot more damage than you could with a wooden stool.

"I don't think you did tell me," Rhodes said, looking back at Brant. "It doesn't matter. I want to know what the problem was between you and Thorpe."

"It wasn't just me who had a problem. It was Helen."

"It was mainly you, though, wasn't it."

It wasn't a question, and Brant didn't bother with a denial. "Thorpe seemed to have it in for me. I don't know why. He goaded me and tried to make my life miserable."

"Why would he do that?"

"He didn't want me going out with Helen. He hated the idea of it. I don't know why. I asked him about it, but he wouldn't even talk rationally. He took every opportunity to cuss me out and tell me what he thought of me, though. None of it was flattering, believe me."

"You went over to his trailer now and then to get cussed out."

"I was just trying to be friendly. I'd go by to see how he was doing, mainly because Helen asked me to check on him. They didn't get along all that well, but she felt responsible for him, in a way. All I ever got out of it was a good cussing. It was almost as if he was trying to force me to do something to him, get into a fight or insult him. Up until lately, I was able to overlook things like that. Now I seem to get mad about nearly anything. I think it could be some kind of chemical imbalance. The 'grumpy old man syndrome,' I guess. I'm not getting any younger. I'll ask the doctor at my next checkup."

"When Thorpe was younger, his womanizing bothered Mrs. Harris. It still did. Was he seeing anybody in particular these days?"

"I don't know."

Rhodes didn't believe him. He said so.

Brant bristled. "I'm telling you the truth, Sheriff. I don't know who he was seeing. Oh, he was seeing somebody, all right. Helen told me. I don't know how she found out, because Thorpe and whoever it was managed to keep it a big secret. Helen wouldn't say who the woman was, but you're right about the way she felt. She was bothered. A lot." Brant paused and his eyes took on a distant look as he recollected something. "And then she wasn't upset anymore. She was more cheerful than she'd been for a good while. I didn't know why because she wouldn't tell me, so I decided the smart thing to do was to enjoy her good mood. I assumed that it came about because she and Thorpe had worked things out, but now I don't believe that."

"Why not?"

"Because she cheered up right after that metal-detecting trip. Thorpe didn't have anything to do with that."

It occurred to Rhodes that Brant hadn't heard about Thorpe's recent adventures and their result. He explained the situation.

"Thorpe was out there at the Tumlinson place," Rhodes said after he'd finished sketching in the events of the previous night. "Maybe that metal-detecting trip did have something to do with him."

Brant said he couldn't imagine what because Mrs. Harris hadn't mentioned Thorpe lately. "Whether that metal detecting had anything to do with him or not won't make any difference anyway. Not if he's as bad off as you tell me he is. I can't say that I feel sorry for him, and I don't even feel bad about it."

"Why do you say that?"

"Because I think he might have killed Helen. If he didn't kill her, why did he run?"

There was the little matter of assaulting the sheriff with a chain saw, Rhodes thought, among other things.

"You never know about people," Rhodes said. "You thought Truck Gadney was guilty, too. Did Helen ever mention his wife, Lily?"

Brant thought about it and said that he recalled something about how they'd taught school together. "Helen didn't seem too fond of her, if that's what you're looking for. I got the impression that they weren't friendly. What does Lily have to do with all this?"

Rhodes said that he wasn't sure.

"If Thorpe's guilty, you can quit investigating, can't you?"

"I could if Thorpe were guilty, but I don't know that he is, and he can't tell me."

"Then I hope he recovers soon, so he can confess."

Rhodes agreed that would make things much easier. He talked to Brant a while longer without finding out anything more, so he left again. This time he was going to have to go to the jail and face Hack. Probably Lawton, too. He wondered what he was going to tell them about Brant.

Chapter 24

▼

LUCKILY RHODES THOUGHT OF SOMETHING ELSE TO DO BEFORE he'd gotten even a block away from Brant's house. He called Hack and asked about Truck.

"He's doin' fine. Lawton says he seems to like it here."

"It's about time we got a prisoner who appreciated how hard we work to make people feel at home. What I want to know is, who's taking care of Truck's Trucks."

"That would be Lily. She worked out there for a couple of years after she quit teaching school, and she still goes in about once a week to work on the books. Truck says she might not know as much about the business as he does, but she can do all right."

"I'm going out there to talk to her."

Before Rhodes could sign off, Hack said, "When're you comin' back here?"

"As soon as I can," Rhodes said, not meaning a word of it.

"Ruth's been in the lab all day. She's got some stuff for you."

It could have been a ruse, but Rhodes didn't think so. "Tell her to write up a report in case she's gone when I get back."

"She always does her reports. You better come hear what she has to say."

"I'll be there. Later."

Rhodes mulled over what he knew, or thought he knew, about Thorpe. He'd escaped from the hospital, and when he did, he must have had someplace in mind to go. He got clothes, he got a gun, and someone took him to the Tumlinson place. It had to be someone who liked him, someone who'd do him a real favor, knowing it was breaking the law.

Maybe an old girlfriend would do something like that. Maybe someone with whom he'd revived an old romance. Lily and Truck seemed to Rhodes to have problems. If Truck was willing to stay in jail rather than bonding out, something was wrong.

Rhodes also wondered about Thelma Rice. If she was telling the truth, she wasn't really much of a suspect. But what if she wasn't? She'd worked with Helen Harris, she'd known Thorpe, and she'd been aware of his romances. It wasn't impossible that her dislike of men might stem from a bad experience, and judging from everything he knew about Thorpe, a relationship with him would most likely be a bad experience. That didn't explain why Thelma would want to kill anyone other than Thorpe, however. Besides, to hit someone in the head with a stool, Thelma would have had to stand on a stool herself. Rhodes couldn't rule her out completely, but she didn't seem to be one of the better suspects.

Then there was Alton Brant, who seemed a less likely suspect than some of the others. Nevertheless, Rhodes couldn't get past the idea of Brant losing his temper with Mrs. Harris when confronted with his lie about his military rank. Rhodes didn't know that anything like that had happened, but he didn't know that it hadn't.

There were other mysteries aside from who had killed Mrs. Harris, too. The mysterious object she'd found during the metal-detecting trip was one of them. Her refusal to tell what it was rankled a lot of people.

And what about the financing for the Royal Rack? Where did Thorpe get the money for that? Rhodes was convinced that Thorpe hadn't come by it on his own. He'd had help, no question about it. So who had helped him?

The missing will was another piece of the puzzle that didn't fit anywhere. Who took it? Why?

Rhodes was still worrying over all those things when he pulled into the lot at Truck's Trucks. A Ford Explorer was parked next to the little office building, and Rhodes assumed it belonged to Lily.

The car lot was full of mud puddles from the rain, and Rhodes watched his step when he got out of the car, which was already a mess on the inside. Most of the mud had dried, but he'd put towels over the seat before leaving home to keep his clothes clean.

Lily was inside the office, dressed for work in a blue shirt and jeans. Her purse with the big butterfly on the side looked a little incongruous sitting on the rolltop desk. She was wearing some kind of perfume that Rhodes didn't recognize, which didn't make it unique. Rhodes thought that the perfume, whatever it was, was like the purse. It didn't belong in the little office.

"Oh," Lily said when Rhodes walked in. "It's you. What do you want?"

Rhodes wondered if there'd ever been a time when people were glad to see him show up anywhere. At one time there had been, he was sure. But if that was the case, those times were few and far between since he'd been elected sheriff. Even fewer lately, it seemed.

Well, if people wanted to be unfriendly and suspicious of him, then Rhodes might as well give them a reason.

"Leo Thorpe. Your old boyfriend."

Lily's face turned red. "You bastard." She grabbed the handle of her big purse.

Before Rhodes quite knew what was happening, she'd swung the purse in a short arc and smashed it against the left side of his head.

Rhodes might have been able to block the blow if he'd been expecting something, but he was taken completely off guard, which he figured was what he deserved for not easing into things as he usually preferred.

The purse was heavy, as if Lily had put a couple of pistons from an old car in it. Rhodes staggered sideways and fell against a wooden, four-drawer filing cabinet that stood by the wall. It was evidently full of important papers because it didn't move so much as an eighth of an inch when he hit it.

He propped himself up with one arm on a stack of papers on top of the cabinet just before Lily hit him again, on top of his head this time. His arm slipped off the cabinet, and he slid down to the floor, half turning to get his back against the cabinet.

Lily swung the purse at him again. Rhodes ducked almost all the way to the floor, and the purse hit the side of the filing cabinet with a resounding thud. Lily moved the cabinet farther than Rhodes had. The papers on top sailed in all directions and floated around the room like paper airplanes.

Rhodes tried to get up, using the cabinet for support. His foot slipped, and he slid back down, giving Lily an opening. She tried a new tactic, an uppercut swing, with the purse coming from about floor level to smack into his chin.

Or that's what it would have done if Rhodes hadn't turned his head slightly to the side so that the purse hit his jaw on the side instead. As his head bounced off the wooden cabinet, he thought he'd be wearing a butterfly tattoo on that jaw for a while to match the other one.

All the hard work she was doing began to take a toll on Lily. She had to slow down and get her breath, giving Rhodes a chance to try to stand up again. This time he was successful, and he moved away from her. He hoped nobody found out that he was getting beaten half to death by a woman with a purse. Hack and Lawton in particular would never let him live it down. He couldn't even imagine what Ivy would have to say, but he knew it wouldn't be complimentary.

It didn't take Lily long to recover, and she came at Rhodes again. This time he was ready for her, and when she swung the purse at him, he grabbed hold of it with both hands. Lily had a death grip on the handles, and he couldn't jerk it away from her, so he just stepped to the side and kept on pulling as hard as he could, letting first the purse and then Lily go right on past him. When they did, he released his grip.

As Rhodes let go of the purse, Lily's momentum carried her out the door and across the narrow porch. She leaned forward and her arms windmilled as she tried to keep her balance. The purse flew out of her hand. She missed the porch steps with her foot and went sprawling in front of them. The purse landed in a puddle not far from her. Rhodes figured the butterfly would never be the same.

He followed Lily outside and sat on the porch with his feet on the steps. He was a bit winded and thought that it might be a good idea to put in a few more hours, or at least minutes, on his stationary bike every week.

After a minute or so Lily pushed herself up, squirmed around, and sat on the ground, facing away from Rhodes. She looked around and saw her purse, but she didn't make any attempt to get it. Her shoulders shook, and Rhodes thought she might be crying. She could also have been laughing, but Rhodes didn't think so. Whatever she was doing, he didn't intend to interrupt. Since he never knew what to say to someone who was crying, or laughing, for that matter, he sat and waited for her to finish.

It took a while, but that was fine with Rhodes. It gave him time to catch his breath. When he was sure that Lily was finished doing whatever it was she'd been doing, he went and picked up her purse, brushing off the mud and water as best he could. He wiped his hand on his pants, which didn't do them any good. Then he walked to where Lily sat, looking dejected and filthy. She didn't have anything to say. Rhodes offered her his hand.

She glanced up at him and took it. He pulled her to her feet. She had mud all down the front of her shirt and jeans, but she didn't make any move to brush herself off. Rhodes didn't give her the purse. He thought it might be safer if he held on to it for a while. Safer for him.

"Want to go back inside now?"

Lily nodded, and they started back, Rhodes keeping a firm grip on her elbow. When they were inside, Rhodes let her sit at the desk in a wooden chair with rollers. He sat in one of the other two chairs in the office, a straight-backed wooden one with a woven seat.

Rhodes held the big purse in his lap and looked inside it. Lily didn't say anything or try to stop him. He found all kinds of things inside: a checkbook; a zippered makeup bag that held a couple of lipstick tubes and a compact; a key ring heavy with house keys, car keys, and others that Rhodes didn't recognize; a hairbrush; two combs; tissues, some of them stained with lipstick; reading glasses; sunglasses with a broken lens, probably broken when the purse had been used as a weapon against Rhodes; and a well-stuffed wallet. No pistons. Maybe it was the keys that were so heavy. Or the billfold. Or all of it together.

Rhodes set the purse on the floor. "You pack quite a punch."

Lily just looked at the floor.

"I know you don't feel like talking. I don't blame you. Maybe if I read you your rights, you'd feel better about it."

Lily shook her head to let him know that hearing the Miranda rights wouldn't have much effect on how she felt.

"I have to do it anyway if I'm going to arrest you."

Lily's head jerked up. "Arrest me?"

"Assaulting an officer, for starters." Rhodes ran though the Miranda list while Lily looked at him incredulously.

"You're really going to arrest me, put me in the jail with Truck?"

"Not with Truck. We don't let men share cells with women."

"That's not what I meant."

"Just a little lawman joke."

"It wasn't funny. Anyway, you can't arrest me for an assault you provoked. It wasn't my fault."

"I don't think a judge would see it that way. He'd want to know why you reacted so violently to the mention of Leo Thorpe's name. To tell you the truth, I'm interested in that myself."

"That's my business."

"No, it's not. There's been a murder, remember? You're involved in it, whether you like it or not, since you had an argument with the victim. Now it turns out that you have a bad reaction to the mention of her cousin's name, and it also happens that you had an affair with him years ago."

Lily's face reddened. She wasn't blushing, however. She was angry. Rhodes was glad she didn't have the purse in her hands. "Who told you that?"

"No one you'd know," Rhodes lied. "I just found it out by digging around."

"I never had an affair with anybody," Lily said, but her voice lacked conviction.

"Have you heard what happened to Thorpe last night?"

Lily looked blank, and Rhodes realized that she didn't know about Thorpe's condition.

"I hate to have to be the one to tell you." Rhodes went through the story with her.

Before he was finished, Lily had tears in her eyes. Rhodes didn't give her the purse, but he handed her a couple of tissues from it. She dabbed at her eyes and asked if Thorpe was going to live.

"I don't know. Even if he does, he might be in a coma for a long time."

As soon as he said it, he knew it had been a mistake. Now Lily could keep her mouth shut, and he might never prove anything against her.

Unless he could make her think he knew more than he actually did. Several things had occurred to him while he was getting knocked around and later when they'd been outside. He thought he might as well give them a try.

"You and Truck have been having problems, haven't you."

Lily didn't answer.

"It's easy enough to see. He'd rather stay in jail than be at home with you. That says a lot, right there. If you were getting along, he wouldn't do that, and you wouldn't stand for it."

"You don't know anything about me and Truck," Lily told him, evading his eyes.

"I know more than you think." Rhodes stretched the truth a little. "I know you're the one who took Thorpe a pistol and some clothes the other day when he escaped from custody at the hospital. You drove him to the Tumlinson place, too."

Lily twitched as if someone were pinching her at every other word, but she didn't admit anything.

"I'll have to check with Truck," Rhodes said, "but I'm betting he can confirm that you were out of the house when someone was seen at Thorpe's trailer getting the pistol and clothing. There's a witness, too, someone who lives in the trailer next to Thorpe's. You might as well go ahead and tell me about it."

He hadn't really expected Lily to be that easy, and she wasn't. She didn't say a thing.

"I know something else, too."

Lily gave no sign that she'd even heard him.

"I know you stole from Truck, from the business here. You were the bookkeeper, so it would've been easy for you. I know you gave the money to Thorpe. Truck must know it too, or he'd be here now."

Lily started to cry.

Chapter 25

▼

RHODES HANDED LILY A FEW MORE TISSUES, THINKING THAT HE
had made a lucky guess, even though it had been based on the
facts at hand.

It should have been evident to just about anybody that Lily and
Truck were having problems of some kind. When there are trou-
bles in a marriage, Rhodes knew that money was more than likely
to be one of the causes, if not the major one. Hack had just told
Rhodes that Lily worked on the books for Truck. What if she'd
been taking a little of the money for herself all along, squirreling
it away for a rainy day or in case an old lover came calling and
needed a little help? That would explain the trouble, if Truck had
found out what she'd done. Thorpe had gotten the money for the
Royal Rack from somewhere, and the way Rhodes saw it, Lily
was the best bet.

"We'll check out your car, too," Rhodes told her, ignoring her occasional sobs as best he could. "If you drove to the Tumlinson place, there'll still be traces of the soil from there on your car's undercarriage and on the tires. If you've watched *CSI,* you know how easy it is to get a match on that sort of thing."

Rhodes himself had no idea, really, how easy it would be, but he figured that if Lily was a television watcher, the mere mention of the *CSI* magic would be enough to throw a scare into her.

"If Thorpe does recover," Rhodes went on, "he'll be able to corroborate everything for us. He'll be glad to cooperate to make it easier on himself."

"He'd never do that." Lily's voice was muffled because her face was buried in the tissues Rhodes had given her.

"Maybe not. It won't matter. We'll check Truck's books, and I think there'll be plenty of evidence there to prove what we suspect about the money."

"Leo never had a chance in life," Lily said, lifting her face and crumpling the tissues in one hand. Her eyes were red. "If that Helen Harris had ever helped him out, he could have done big things."

Rhodes didn't believe that. He considered Thorpe a smooth-talking con man who got by as best he could without ever exerting himself too much, doing odd jobs to earn a little money and mooching off others, probably the Harrises and any gullible women he could find, to get more.

"The Royal Rack was his big chance," Lily said. "He knew the place was a gold mine, and he'd be set up for the first time in his life with a real moneymaker."

"An illegal moneymaker. Illegal gambling in the back room isn't a good way to get a start on running a legitimate business."

"I didn't know about the gambling. Not until . . ." Lily stopped herself and clamped her mouth shut, pinching her lips into a straight line.

"Until you drove him to the Tumlinson place?"

"You don't know what Truck was like," Lily said, veering off onto another path entirely. "Look at this place."

She waved a hand in an arc that took in the entirety of the office. Rhodes had to admit that it was shabby.

"He could have done so much better," Lily continued, "but all he could do was talk about how great high school had been, how he'd been a big football star and how everyone had cheered him week after week."

That's how it was in Texas, Rhodes thought. Once you'd had the kind of adulation a really good high school player received, it was hard to forget it. For some it was impossible. Rhodes had plenty of reason to know about high school football, both as a player, though not nearly as successful as Truck had been, and as a lawman, having investigated the murder of a popular coach. Lots of people still blamed Rhodes for the team's losing the state championship that year.

"We got married not long after he came back from college," Lily said. "We were young, and we thought life would be wonderful forever." She looked around the office again. "You can see how wrong we were."

Rhodes didn't think Truck would see it quite that way. By all accounts, Truck loved his business, buying and selling, making deals, setting his own hours, having coffee at Franklin's when he pleased and just leaving a note on the door. He could regale his customers and his friends at the drugstore with the tales of his football prowess, and they'd always listen. Rhodes didn't see the Royal Rack as a big step up from that.

"Leo was going to pay me back the money as soon as he got established. He promised."

Oh, Rhodes thought. *Of course a man like Thorpe would never tell a lie about a little thing like that.*

"I could have put it back in the accounts, and Truck would never have known. It would all have worked out if you hadn't interfered."

Rhodes wasn't so sure of that.

"I would never have married Truck if Leo hadn't dumped me. He regretted it later, though."

Rhodes wondered how she knew that. His skepticism must have shown on his face because Lily said, "He told me himself."

Just like he promised to repay the money, Rhodes thought. *Who could doubt him?*

"Why did he dump you?" he asked.

"Another woman, I'm sure." Lily smiled reminiscently. "He does like the women. He knows how to treat us."

That was a side of Thorpe that Rhodes had never seen, though he'd heard enough about it lately. Mrs. Gomez might not agree, however.

"Who was the other woman?"

"I have no idea. He never told me. He likes to keep things like that a secret." She frowned. "Do you think he'll be all right?"

"The doctors don't really know yet."

"I'm sure he'll recover. He has so much to live for."

She must have meant herself, and maybe the Royal Rack, but Rhodes didn't want to ask.

"So your argument with Helen Harris wasn't really about what she found on the metal-detecting club's trip to the Tumlinson place," he said.

"Of course it was. What else could it have been about?"

"Thorpe."

"She didn't know about me and Leo. We kept it a secret from everybody. Leo was good at keeping secrets. So was I. We couldn't have a scandal."

Lily's face changed after she said it, and Rhodes thought she was going to start to cry again. No doubt she was thinking that there was going to be a scandal now, for sure, and she was absolutely right. Things were going to be even worse when she admitted that she'd killed Helen Harris.

Later at the jail, Rhodes didn't have to worry about Hack and Lawton's questions about what Jennifer Loam had to tell him. They forgot all about it when Rhodes brought in Lily Gadney. Brant's secret was safe for the time being.

Ruth Grady served as the matron and got Lily booked, printed, and locked up, all of which took a while. Ruth was still in the cell block, and Rhodes hadn't had a chance to ask her about the lab work she'd wanted to tell him about.

"So she confessed to ever'thing," Hack said to Rhodes after Ruth had led Lily away. "No wonder those two women wrote a book about you. You really are one crime-bustin' lawman."

"You forgot *handsome*," Rhodes said.

"Well, I didn't forget, exactly."

"I forgive you. Anyway, I didn't get her to confess to everything."

"Same thing as. Aidin' and abettin', assault on an officer, and all the rest."

"Not all," Lawton said. "She didn't admit that she killed anybody."

"She did it, though," Hack said. "I've seen plenty of guilty folks walk through that door, and she's got the look if anybody ever did."

Rhodes wished he could be as sure about that as Hack. Although he'd talked to Lily for another half hour in the office at Truck's Trucks, she'd continued to insist that she had nothing to do with Helen Harris's death.

On the other hand, she had no alibi for the morning of the murder. Truck had gone to work early, as he always did, not long after seven o'clock, and Lily had been home alone. She told Rhodes that she'd eaten breakfast, watched television, and cleaned house, but no one had seen her, no one had called her, no one could vouch for her.

Rhodes's theory was that Mrs. Harris had found out about Lily and Thorpe. She'd confronted Lily, who'd picked up the stool and hit her. Rhodes could speak from personal experience about Lily's ability with a handy object used as a club. She had plenty of power to kill somebody with the right weapon, and the stool was certainly right for the job. Now all he had to come up with was a reason for Lily to be at the Harris house at the time of the murder.

Then something else occurred to him. It was possible that Thorpe hadn't been lying about paying Lily back. He'd planned to do it as soon as he got his inheritance from Mrs. Harris. She wasn't likely to die anytime soon, so Thorpe could well have decided to hurry her along. Lily might even have helped him.

"Maybe Ruth has somethin' for you," Hack said, breaking into Rhodes's thoughts. "She said she found some fingerprints at the Harris place. You need to talk to her."

Rhodes said he planned to do exactly that as soon as he had an opportunity. While he was waiting for her, he worked on his reports. He'd gotten most of them done before Ruth came back.

"Here she is," Hack said, just in case Rhodes hadn't noticed. "Maybe she's got the answers you're lookin' for."

It would be nice to think so, but Rhodes had never had a case that was solved by fingerprints or, for that matter, by any exotic method. Things like that were possible, he knew, but not very likely in real police work in a small Texas county.

People who liked to think that crime labs in reality were like the ones shown on popular TV shows should take a tour of any real lab, even the ones in big cities. Most of them were underfunded, and Rhodes didn't know of a one that had attained the almost supernatural status of those presented weekly on the cop shows. He'd read a lot of newspaper accounts of the woes of the Houston police department's crime lab, and the situation there, which had been years in the making, was almost like a comedy of errors, except that it wasn't at all funny. Overturned convictions abounded thanks to the many faulty results that had been used in evidence. After years of work, during which time testing had been farmed out to private firms, the lab still wasn't up and running again.

So Rhodes wasn't depending on anything that Ruth had learned to sew up the case for him. He just wished she could give him enough help to convince Lily to confess.

"I hope you're going to tell me that you found a hidden security camera in the Harris house," he told Ruth. "It would be great to have some clear pictures of the killer. Color or black-and-white. I don't care which."

"I wish I had something like that for you," Ruth said, "but I don't have anything nearly that good."

Rhodes would have been amazed if she had. He asked what she did have.

"Fingerprints."

"Not many, I'll bet."

"You'd win. How did you know?" Before Rhodes could answer, she said, "Oh."

"Oh?" Hack said, listening in as always. "What's that supposed to mean?"

"You ever visit Helen Harris?" Rhodes said.

"Nope. Never had the pleasure."

"If you'd seen her house, you'd know why there aren't any fingerprints. It's clean. Really clean."

"I didn't say there were *no* fingerprints," Ruth said. "There were some, where you'd expect."

"On the stool?"

"Yes, on the legs, and on the handle of the gate in the fence, too. There's a problem, though."

Rhodes knew what the problem was. Fingerprints are fine if you have a set to match them with. If not, they're worthless. To get a match, the fingerprints have to exist in the databases or be available some other way. Lily Gadney had just been printed, so Ruth could do a comparison. If the prints didn't belong to Lily, they'd have to do a search by computer. Brant had been in the service, so his prints would be on record. They might be the only ones of all those concerned.

That wasn't the only problem, however, as Ruth let him know quickly enough. There were no complete prints, only partials, and partials were harder to match.

"The surface of the stool is rough wood," Ruth said. "Powdering doesn't work so well on it. Even the spray isn't that good, so what I have isn't going to be easy to match with anything."

"What about the gate handle?"

"It's rough and rusty. Same problem. A tough job getting a match."

Rhodes hadn't expected much more. "What about the light-bulb? The broken one, too."

"They have Mrs. Harris's prints on them. It was an easy match."

Rhodes had known that the rest wouldn't be easy.

"Now what?" Hack said.

"That's simple enough," Rhodes told him.

Hack shook his head. "I don't see how."

"Me neither," Ruth said.

"We'll just have to get somebody to confess."

"Who?"

"I'd settle for anybody. I'd like to work on Thorpe, but he's not going to be able to confess to anything for a long time, if ever."

"Sure was inconsiderate of that fella to shoot him," Hack said. "Who does that leave you with besides Lily?"

"A couple of people at least, but Lily's a better bet. I need to get her to admit her part in it."

"How you gonna do that?" Hack said.

Ruth looked at Rhodes expectantly. "Do you have an answer for him?"

"Sure."

"What's the answer then?" Hack said.

Rhodes shrugged. "The answer is, I don't know."

"Bull corn," Hack said.

Ruth smiled. "There's one more thing."

Rhodes asked what it was.

"Mrs. Gadney wants a lawyer."

"Perfect," Rhodes said.

"And she wants Randy Lawless."

"Thanks," Rhodes said. "You just made my day."

"I'm glad to hear it. What do I do next?"

"You check out Lily's Explorer. It's at Truck's Trucks. See if you can find some soil samples that match the mud at the Tumlinson place."

"Where's the Tumlinson place? I'll have to go there, too."

Rhodes told her how to get there.

"What if the soil's just like the soil all over the county?"

"Let's hope it's not," Rhodes said.

"It's prob'ly not," Hack said. "Mostly white clay down there, and sticky old black gumbo around here."

"That would make it easy," Ruth said. "If we can get a match, it would help the case."

Rhodes agreed and added, "We need all the help we can get."

"Amen," Hack said.

Chapter 26

▼

Randy Lawless was the most successful lawyer in Black-lin County by just about any measurement Rhodes could think of. His clients were likely to escape conviction, he was rich, and he'd even served a couple of terms in the state legislature.

He was good-looking, he was tall, he had thick, black hair, and he drove an Infinti. His wife, Barbara, was an officer in just about every club in town and the star of an amateur theatrical production every year.

Lawless could even joke about his name, and often did, especially in court and especially before opposing counsel could work in some kind of snide remark.

If pressed, Rhodes might have admitted that Lawless was a pretty good lawyer, but he would have hated to do it, and he would never have said it to Lawless except as a joke.

"My client says you threatened her and then beat her," Lawless told Rhodes. "You could be in real trouble. Police brutality is a grievous offense."

"I like the way you can keep a straight face when you say things like that," said Rhodes, who also liked the use of *grievous*. "It's no wonder you do so well with juries."

"Don't try to change the subject, Sheriff. This is serious business."

They were in Rhodes's courthouse office, which is where Rhodes had told Lawless he'd be when the lawyer had asked for a meeting. Lily was already free on bond, and not a high bond at that. She hadn't been charged with murder, only with embezzlement.

Lawless looked at ease in his thousand-dollar suit. His custom-made cowboy boots had probably cost even more. Rhodes felt downright ratty by comparison.

"I know how serious it is," Rhodes said. "I don't suppose Lily mentioned that she hit me with her purse."

He was sorry he said it as soon as he saw Lawless smile.

"That's going to sound great in a courtroom," Lawless said. "I'll have to get you on the stand as soon as I can."

"I thought you told me the case would never come to trial."

"That was before I heard what your testimony was going to be. I wouldn't want the county to miss out on hearing how the sheriff let a woman with a purse get the drop on him."

Rhodes fingered the place on his jaw where decorations on Lily's purse had made an indentation. He decided that he didn't like Lawless now any more than he ever had. Less, in fact.

"As you know, my client claims she's not guilty of the charge you've filed against her, much less of the murder you've accused her of committing. If you'll have a talk with her husband, you'll find out that he's going to withdraw any charges of embezzlement. It was all a misunderstanding."

Lawless had talked with Truck, and Lawless was one smooth operator. He wasn't going to get Lily off that easily, however, not if Rhodes could help it.

"We'll see how it goes," Rhodes said. "This has just started."

Lawless stood up. Rhodes wondered how much his tie had cost. More than Rhodes had spent on ties in his lifetime, most likely.

"You're right about that, Sheriff. I hope you know what you're getting into."

Rhodes knew all right. He'd dealt with Lawless a few times, and Lawless hadn't always come out the winner. Rhodes had the edge, in fact, which he was sure didn't sit well with Lawless.

"I'll see you later, Sheriff. After I've had time to gather the facts and show you how wrong you are."

"I'm looking forward to that," Rhodes said, smiling.

Lawless smiled back. His teeth were depressingly perfect, a fact made all the more depressing because they were so obviously his own teeth.

"I just bet you are." Lawless turned to leave.

"I have one question for you before you go."

Lawless turned back. "I'm not promising an answer."

"This isn't a legal question. I just wondered if you had a cat."

"No. I don't have a pet."

"Then you need one. I have Helen Harris's black cat at my house, and I'm trying to find him a good home."

"Then you're asking the wrong man. I don't much like cats, and my wife likes them even less than I do. She says she's allergic to them."

"I've heard that's purely psychological," Rhodes said.

"I'm not saying it's not, but I'm not going to be the one to tell my wife that. If you want to do it, be my guest. Is that all you wanted to know?"

Rhodes said that it was, and Lawless left without offering to shake hands, which was fine with Rhodes, who didn't care to shake hands with him anyway.

Rhodes slumped back in his chair and wished he had something to prove that Lily was guilty, but he didn't. Ruth was working on the prints, but from what she'd told Rhodes so far, the only identifiable ones on the stool legs belonged to Mrs. Harris. Things weren't shaping up the way Rhodes had hoped.

There was a knock on the door. Before Rhodes could say "Come in," Jennifer Loam opened the door and stepped inside.

"Just the man I've been looking for," she said.

Rhodes fought the urge to slip even lower in his chair. He stood up. "What can I do for you?"

Jennifer sat down and got out her little recorder. "You can tell me all about the big fight you had with Leonard Thorpe and about how you captured Lily Gadney."

Rhodes sat back in his chair. "You don't really want to hear it."

"Oh, but I do."

Rhodes told her, being careful to say nothing to indicate that Lily Gadney was guilty of any particular crime. She was just "a person of interest" as the current phrase had it.

"You disappoint me, Sheriff. I never thought I'd hear you use that kind of government-speak."

Rhodes was a little disappointed in himself, too. "I got carried away. I wanted to make sure you knew she wasn't accused of murder. She has a good lawyer."

"Not Randy Lawless."

"He's the one."

"That should be a lot of fun. The editor will love it. We'll sell a few extra papers."

Rhodes said he was always glad to do what he could to assure the financial stability of the free press.

"Off the record," Jennifer said, ignoring his comment, "do you think she killed Mrs. Harris."

"*Off the record* would mean that you'd turned off the recorder." Jennifer clicked it off. "Well?"

"I think it's a good possibility, but only because I don't have any other suspects. She claims she's innocent."

"Maybe she is."

"Maybe. I'm not going to close the investigation, if that's what you're asking."

"Can I print that?"

"I'd rather you didn't. If there's someone out there who's guilty, he might be thinking he's off the hook. Thinking like that is what gets people caught."

"So you don't think Mrs. Gadney did it?"

"I didn't say that."

"I'm never sure what you're up to, Sheriff."

Rhodes said that he wasn't ever sure, either.

"And I never know when you're being serious."

"Most of the time," Rhodes said, "but not always."

"See? That's what I'm talking about."

"Sorry," Rhodes said, though he wasn't. "I'll try to do better when we're on the record."

Jennifer smiled. "I have enough of that now to write a good story. The handsome, crime-busting sheriff mud-wrestling the hardened criminal and then saving his life. That will sell some papers all by itself."

"It didn't happen exactly like that."

"That's what it will sound like, even in a straight account. You might as well get used to your new role."

Rhodes didn't like the idea of having a new role or of having a role at all. He just wanted to do his job.

"Will you be at Helen Harris's funeral tomorrow?" Jennifer asked.

Rhodes said that he would. He didn't like funerals, but he nearly always went.

"Do you think Mrs. Gadney will be there?"

"No," Rhodes said, "I don't. What are you going to do about Alton Brant? Write a story about his masquerade or forget about it?"

"I'm not going to forget about it, but I'm not going to write a story. Not for the time being, anyway. The editor didn't think it would serve any useful purpose to run one."

Rhodes supposed Brant's assumption of rank had been innocent enough.

"We won't be doing any more interviews with him on Veterans Day, though," Jennifer said.

"That's probably a good idea."

"Yes. It probably is."

The rest of Rhodes's afternoon, what was left of it, was taken up with routine things, the most interesting of which was a stolen-car caper that Buddy worked, although the car hadn't actually been stolen.

"It was just a sale gone bad," he explained to Rhodes.

"That ain't what Dora Aman told me when she called it in," Hack said. "She said it was stolen right out from under her."

"You told me that, too," Buddy said. "Which is why I wound up chasing Ron Alvarez about five miles down County Road 178. You know Alvarez?"

Rhodes said he didn't, and Hack shook his head.

"Has a little place out close to Obert. Cuts hay and does some shredding. He was trying the car out, so he says, when I got after him. Nice little Chevy. Clean. Low miles. Runs like the dickens, even on that dirt road. Good suspension, too. Didn't bounce all over the place."

"You sound like you're sellin' it yourself," Hack said.

"Just trying to give you an idea of what happened and why. Anyway, I came up behind him and put on the siren. He took off. Maybe he wanted to see if he could get away just for the fun of it. He couldn't, so he finally pulled over. I talked to him about the car, and he said that it was his. Claimed he'd bought it from Dora Aman this afternoon and paid her cash money for it."

"Did he have any proof of that?" Rhodes asked.

"He sure did. He had the title with Dora's signature on the back. He was telling the truth. He'd bought that car fair and square."

"So how come she said he'd stole it?" Hack said.

"I went back to her place and asked her about that. She hemmed and hawed and finally said she'd changed her mind and didn't want to get rid of the car. It was in such good shape that it was probably better than a new one."

"She admitted that she'd sold it to him, though?" Rhodes said.

"Yeah, but she claimed she called him and said she'd changed her mind and wanted it back. He said no way, so she reported it as stolen. She says that if he wouldn't let her change her mind, it was the same thing as stealing. She wanted me to arrest him and lock him up, and she wanted her car back."

"What did you tell her?" Hack said.

"That I gave him a speeding ticket."

"I bet that didn't satisfy her."

"It sure didn't. Just made her madder. She says she's gonna sue Alvarez, and me, too."

"What did you say to that?"

"I told her to get a good lawyer."

"Who'd you recommend?" Hack said.

"You know we don't do that kind of thing."

"Yeah, I know. I'll tell you who I'd get if it was me."

Rhodes had a feeling he knew what was coming next.

"Who?" Buddy said.

"Randy Lawless," Hack said. "Who else?"

Chapter 27

▼

WHEN RHODES GOT HOME THAT EVENING, THE CAT WAS STILL there in the same place in the kitchen near the refrigerator. As far as Rhodes could tell, it hadn't moved more than a couple of inches since the last time he'd seen it that morning.

"He gets up and walks around," Ivy said, a little defensively, Rhodes thought, when he commented on it. "He doesn't just lie in one spot all day."

What disappointed Rhodes was that Yancey, who had come bouncing to the door to meet him, seemed to have come to accept the cat as a permanent resident. Yancey's behavior had reverted to exactly the way it had been before the cat had arrived, with all the same nervous energy and barking.

That wasn't the only thing that disappointed Rhodes. The other was that the cat seemed perfectly at ease with Yancey's antics. When Yancey bounced over to him and barked right in his face, the cat didn't turn a hair.

"They're good friends now," Ivy said.

Rhodes said he was glad to hear it.

"I can tell." Ivy gave him a look that was heavy with suspicion. "Have you been trying to give Sam away again?"

Rhodes denied it, but Ivy didn't believe him.

"Well, maybe I mentioned to a couple of people that he was available, but nobody took me up on the offer."

"It's just as well. Sam has a home here now."

Ivy looked over and smiled at the cat, who was lying there purring while Yancey barked around her ankles.

Maybe having a cat wouldn't be so bad, Rhodes thought, and then he sneezed.

"Don't start that again. You're not allergic to Sam. You can't fool me."

"I'm not trying to fool anybody," Rhodes said, stifling another sneeze. He'd skimped on lunch, and he was feeling a little peckish. "What's for supper?"

"I thought it might be nice of you to take me out."

"Mexican food?" Rhodes tried not to sound too hopeful.

"That sounds good."

It sounded good to Rhodes, too.

Later that night, trying to sleep, Rhodes thought about the case against Lily Gadney. It wasn't a good one, and it left too many things unexplained. Thorpe was looking like a better suspect all the time.

Ruth Grady had gotten some soil samples from beneath Lily's Explorer, and she'd gone out to the Tumlinson place for samples near the house. She'd run some tests tomorrow, although the samples didn't look at all similar to Rhodes. Everything from under the Explorer looked like black gumbo, while the clay from the Tumlinson place was almost white.

Even the lack of a match wouldn't have bothered Rhodes so much if he could figure out what had happened to the will. He couldn't, however. It hadn't turned up anywhere, and it didn't seem likely to.

With all that running through his head, Rhodes couldn't get to sleep for a long time, and when he started to drift off, he thought about the cat, which he was sure would jump up on the bed at any minute and glue itself to his back.

It didn't happen, however, so to keep himself from worrying about it, Rhodes got up and went to the kitchen for a drink of water.

The cat wasn't in its usual spot. Rhodes looked around the room and didn't see it anywhere, so he stepped out onto the small enclosed porch. He could see Yancey's basket, where the little dog was sound asleep.

In the basket with him was the cat, also asleep. As Rhodes stood there watching, it raised its head and opened its eyes, looking directly at Rhodes. It wasn't smiling, but Rhodes thought it would have been if it could have.

After a second Rhodes said, "You think you've won, don't you?"

The cat gave him another smug look, then lowered its head and closed its eyes. Yancey never moved.

Rhodes went back to bed and eventually fell into a fitful, unsatisfactory sleep.

The funeral was held at the "new" First Methodist Church, which had been around for something like forty-five years, as opposed to

244

the "old" First Methodist Church, which had been around for forty years or so longer.

The old church was in fact no longer a church. It had been sold to a nondenominational group when the new church was built, but that hadn't lasted long, and the building had been used since then for a number of purposes, none of them related to religion. It had even been a coffeehouse at some point in the early 1970s.

The new church was, of course, no longer new, except in comparison to the old one, but it had been well cared for and showed few signs of age.

Rhodes and Ivy arrived a little late and sat in a pew near the back after signing the register. Rhodes wasn't sure why they'd bothered to sign. As far as he knew, Mrs. Harris's only relatives were her brother in Montana and Thorpe, who couldn't have cared less who attended the funeral, even if he'd been conscious, which he wasn't. Rhodes had called the hospital to check before he'd gone by to pick up Ivy at the insurance office.

The church was full, as Rhodes had expected it would be. He saw most of the OWLS sitting together on what some people called "widows' row," even though not all the OWLS were widows. Quite a few of Mrs. Harris's former students were scattered around the church. Rhodes recognized them because they were younger than most of the others.

Because Mrs. Harris had no family members, Alton Brant was the only person sitting on the pew reserved for relatives. He was wearing a suit, not a military uniform.

Rhodes thought the funeral was acceptable, which meant a closed coffin, a short eulogy, a few scriptures, and no sermon at all. He knew there'd be a few complaints about the closed coffin afterward. Some people always wanted to know if the dead person "looked natural," but Clyde Ballinger always put the top down if there were no instructions to the contrary.

Rhodes was pleased that the songs played before the funeral were old gospel tunes that he recognized, and they were played at the proper upbeat tempo, not some lugubrious pace that made them sound depressingly mournful.

After the service, the casket was wheeled out and placed in the back of the black ambulance for transportation to the cemetery, and Clyde Ballinger ushered Alton Brant into the front seat of a black limo for the trip. Rhodes saw the OWLS standing together nearby, having gone over to offer some comfort to Brant.

These days not everyone wore black to funerals, but Thelma Rice did. Even fewer people wore hats, but Thelma had one on. It was black and small, nothing at all like the red one she'd had on the time Rhodes had seen her at the club meeting.

"It's nice to see you, Sheriff," Thelma said when Rhodes walked over to the group. "You, too, Ivy, even if your husband has been arresting our club members."

Ivy smiled, and Rhodes said he was sorry about the arrest but that was his job. Some of the other OWLS edged away from him, as if they thought he might arrest them, too. Francine Oates was among them, but Rhodes made it a point to speak to her.

Francine Oates wore a gray pantsuit. Rhodes could remember a time, not so long ago by his reckoning, when women wouldn't have considered wearing pants to a funeral, but times had changed. He could even remember when women would never have considered leaving the house for even a shopping trip without panty hose, but now bare legs were the thing. Rhodes wouldn't have been surprised to see someone at the funeral wearing flip-flops, though certainly not among the OWLS.

Rhodes didn't know the rules about jewelry at funerals, if there were any rules. Francine wore gold earrings, plain circles that matched her wedding band. She didn't have much to say to Rhodes, and he didn't want to press her, not at the moment. Still, he wanted to talk to her again to see if she'd remembered anything more about the morning Mrs. Harris had died.

"I have a question for you, too," she said when he mentioned having something more to say to her. "But this isn't the time for it."

Rhodes said he'd drop by her house later in the afternoon, and she said that would be fine.

"Are we going to the cemetery?" Ivy said.

"All right," Rhodes said.

The graveside service was short, if not sweet. The sky was blue, the sun was warm, and a light breeze ruffled the edges of the tent set up near the open grave. Rhodes could smell the damp earth that was piled by the side of the hole, covered with fake green turf that did nothing at all to disguise what was beneath it.

The minister read the twenty-third psalm and said a prayer. Alton Brant choked back tears as the coffin was lowered into the ground, and Rhodes heard some sobs from the others gathered under the tent. Not many, however. Helen Harris had been well enough liked, but she'd had few close friends other than Brant.

After the coffin was lowered and people had begun to leave, Rhodes said a few words to Alton Brant.

"Thorpe should be in that coffin, not Helen," Brant said. "It's not right that you haven't done anything about him."

"He's not what you'd call a free man," Rhodes said. "He's still in a coma."

"How much of a chance do the doctors give him?"

"They haven't been specific. It could go either way."

"I want him to recover and stand trial."

Rhodes decided not to mention his suspicions about Lily Gadney. Besides, he was beginning to think Brant might be right about Thorpe.

"He hasn't even been accused yet," Rhodes said.

"Well, he should be. You need to do your job and find the evidence against him."

Rhodes didn't have a snappy answer for that one, so he just went to join Ivy, who was talking to Thelma Rice.

"That Alton Brant was acting snippy, wasn't he," Thelma said. "You can't blame him. He and Helen were very close. He visited her just about every day."

"What time of day?" Rhodes said.

"You're always working, aren't you. I don't know the time. I just know he visited her."

Ivy took Rhodes's arm. "Sometimes I think you work too hard."

"It's his job," Thelma said. "That's what he told me."

"You should have to live with him," Ivy said, tugging Rhodes's arm and steering him toward the car. "Time for us to go."

As they drove away, Rhodes looked back to see Alton Brant standing alone at the edge of the open grave. They'd wait until he left to start filling it in. The backhoe was parked at a discreet distance, but it was impossible not to see it. The operator was standing in the shade beside it, smoking a cigarette.

He was a young man. Sooner or later, he'd be waiting to cover Rhodes's grave, he or someone like him. Rhodes hoped it would be a lot later, and he thought of Helen Harris, who'd been rushed into the grave by a person or persons unknown. It might have been Lily Gadney, but Rhodes was growing less sure of that all the time. He wished again that Thorpe was conscious and talking.

"Don't worry," Ivy said. "You'll find out who did it."

"How did you know what I was thinking?"

"I always know."

"If that's true, I'd better be a lot more careful with my thoughts."

"That," Ivy said, "would be a really good idea."

Chapter 28

▼

SOMETHING ABOUT THE FUNERAL WAS BOTHERING RHODES, BUT he couldn't figure out what it was. When he parked at the insurance office to let Ivy out of the car, he asked if she'd noticed anything odd about the service.

"No, I thought it was fine. Your friend Ballinger is going to get complaints about that closed casket, though. Maybe that's what you're thinking of."

"No, that's not it. Anyway I'm sure there was a viewing at the funeral home. It was something else. Something was out of place."

"Well, I didn't see it, and I have to go to work."

She got out of the car, and Rhodes watched her walk into the office. He still couldn't figure out what was nagging at him, but maybe it would come to him later.

It was a little soon to go by and talk to Francine Oates, so he stopped at the jail. Nothing was going on, but Ruth had left the results of the soil comparison test on his desk.

"Not a match," Hack said, saving Rhodes the trouble of reading it. "You'll have to find yourself another suspect."

"Maybe not," Lawton said. "How many cars you think Truck has on that lot of his? I'd guess about half of 'em run. She could've taken any of 'em. If this was the *CSI,* you can bet they'd check out ever' car there, and they'd find the one that matched, too."

Rhodes didn't see the point of checking all the cars. Hack was right. He'd have to find another suspect, not that he didn't have a couple of them already. For all he knew, Thorpe had killed Mrs. Harris for the inheritance. Brant thought so. Brant himself might have done it, and it might be time to talk to Billy Joe Byron again.

"How was the funeral?" Hack asked.

"It was all right, as funerals go."

"I don't like 'em, myself. Too sad, specially when you get to be my age and start thinkin' it might be you next week lyin' up there in the front of the church."

"Church might not let you in," Lawton said. "They don't take heatherns. You'd have to be buried out of the funeral home. That'd be all right. It'd be plenty big since nobody'd come anyway. Me and the sheriff'd be there, though. You could count on us. Unless we happened to be needed here at the jail or out on the street to do some crime bustin'. Otherwise, though, we'd be there. Right, Sheriff?"

"Right," Rhodes said. "You don't have to worry about that, Hack. I'm pretty sure Ruth would come, too, and maybe Buddy, if I didn't have to send them off on an investigation."

"You two are reg'lar Jerry Lewises," Hack said.

"Who's that?" Lawton said. "Must've been before my time."

"Or after," Hack said. "Maybe I should've said you were a reg'lar Eddie Cantor."

"Never heard of him."

"How 'bout Lillie Langtry? She'd be more from your era, I guess."

Rhodes had had enough of the witty repartee, so he told them he was going to see Francine Oates.

"She gonna tell you who the killer is?" Hack said.

"Somebody better," Lawton said. "I can tell he's gettin' frustrated over this."

"How?" Hack said. "He's not gettin' touchy yet."

"Just by the way he looks. He'll be gettin' touchy by tomorrow."

Rhodes grinned. "You two know me too well."

"We spend too much time together," Lawton said. "Me and Hack need to get out more."

"Speak for yourself," Hack said. "I get out plenty."

"I'm going out right now," Rhodes said before they could get started again. "I'll be at Mrs. Oates's house if anybody needs me."

"We'll be sure and get in touch," Hack said.

Rhodes drove by his own house first to check on Speedo, Yancey, and the cat. They were all fine, especially the cat, which was still in the kitchen. It was grooming itself when Rhodes came in, and it didn't bother to acknowledge his presence or that of Yancey, who acted as happy to see Rhodes as if he'd been gone for years instead of just a few hours.

"You should play with the cat," Rhodes told Yancey. "Maybe he'd enjoy getting a little exercise. Chase him a little. Bark at him."

The cat kept right on grooming, and Yancey didn't seem interested in getting involved with him, so Rhodes left them there and went outside to play ball with Speedo for a few minutes. The collie enjoyed running after the ball and bringing it back for Rhodes to throw again. Sometimes the dog liked to hold on to the ball and make Rhodes take it away from him, but today wasn't one of those days.

Rhodes didn't have to concentrate on the ball, so he tried to clarify his thoughts about Helen Harris's death. After ten minutes he hadn't come to any conclusions, but Speedo had gotten tired of playing and gone to lie in the shade of a pecan tree with his ball between his paws.

"We'll play again," Rhodes said, and Speedo thumped the ground with his tail to show his pleasure. Rhodes wished that humans were so easy to read.

Francine Oates answered the door still dressed as she'd been at the funeral, and with his first look at her Rhodes knew what had been bothering him after the service. Everything that had been twisting around in his mind sorted itself out and rearranged itself into an understandable pattern. He didn't have all the answers yet, but he hoped that Francine would provide them for him.

"Would you like a Dr Pepper, Sheriff?"

Rhodes declined, and Francine suggested that they sit in the living room. It was a little formal for Rhodes's taste, and he doubted that it was used more than once or twice a year. It was almost as neat as if Helen Harris had straightened it. The chair that Rhodes sat in had a rounded back and a slick seat cover. He hoped he wouldn't slide off.

"You said you had a question for me," Rhodes said when he was sure he was stable. "Why don't you go ahead and ask it."

"I hope you won't consider it unseemly. In view of the circumstances."

Rhodes said he wouldn't pass judgment. By now he even thought he knew what the question would be.

"You see, I've been wondering about Helen's will," Francine said.

"So have I. It's missing."

"I know. We know there was one, however. Alton Brant and I witnessed it. We even know what it said."

Rhodes knew where she was going, so he just waited.

"I was wondering, if two witnesses testified to the will's contents, would it be valid?"

Rhodes told her that he had no idea. "It's not something that's ever come up. You'd have to ask a lawyer about that. Otherwise Mrs. Harris's brother up in Montana will inherit."

"They didn't get along. It doesn't seem fair that he'd get her land and those wells. He hasn't visited her in years. Leo Thorpe lives right here in town, and he and Helen saw each other all the time."

"That wouldn't matter. The brother's next of kin, and if there's no will, he'd inherit."

"I just don't think that's right."

"You could check with a lawyer about the witnesses testifying to what was in the will. It would be a lot easier if the will happened to turn up. But it won't, will it."

"Why not?"

"Because you took it."

"I . . . what did you say?"

"You took the will. I don't know why, but I'm sure you did." Rhodes looked at her ring finger. "You took it when you got the wedding band."

Francine's hands fluttered. She clasped them together and stuck them between her legs, hiding the ring. "I . . . I don't know what you're talking about."

"I think you do. You weren't wearing a wedding band when I talked to you the other day, but now you are. Putting it on was a mistake, but maybe you thought no one would notice. You took it off the bookshelf in Mrs. Harris's house. You made another mistake, too."

"I . . . another mistake?"

"The first time I talked to you, you told me that you witnessed the will but didn't look at it. Now you say you remember it well enough to testify to what it said, and you implied that Leo Thorpe's the heir."

"I . . . just remembered."

"You've been wearing a lot of long-sleeved outfits lately, even though it's warm. I'd like to have a look at your arms."

Francine recoiled. "Well, I never!"

"The cat scratched you. You don't like cats, and he doesn't like you. You're the one who let him out. You tried to grab him to keep him inside, but he scratched you and got away. He must have done a pretty good job on you, since you're still covered up."

"You can't . . . I didn't."

"You're the woman Thorpe dumped Lily Gadney for all those years ago." It was all becoming clear to Rhodes now. "You worked at the elementary school, and Thorpe seems to have cut a swath there. It embarrassed Mrs. Harris then, and it must have embarrassed her even more now for Thorpe to be making a fool of you.

And her. My guess is that you and Thorpe met a time or two at the Tumlinson place recently, and you lost the wedding ring there. No wonder Mrs. Harris was so delighted to find it, and no wonder she wouldn't tell anybody what she'd found. She must have suspected that you and Thorpe were fooling around, and now she had the proof."

"I don't know what you're talking about."

"She put it out in plain sight to torment you," Rhodes said, "but you got it back when you killed her."

He expected Francine to deny the last statement, and she didn't disappoint him.

"You're completely wrong about that. Helen had an accident. You told me so."

"That's what I was supposed to believe. Did you set it up, or was she changing the bulb when you came in?"

"You don't know I was there."

Rhodes leaned back in the chair. It wasn't conducive to that, so he straightened and slid a little forward on the seat.

"Do you ever watch *CSI*?"

"I . . . what does that have to do with anything?"

"If you watch, you know all about modern police methods. You know that the cat will still have traces of your blood on his claws and in his fur. We'll get a sample and prove it."

Actually Rhodes had no idea if that was possible. What with the cat's habit of grooming itself, all traces of blood might well be gone by this time, but it sounded convincing. Besides, it was nice to think the cat might be good for something.

"We'll check your car for soil samples, too, and prove you went to the Tumlinson place. It *was* you who took Thorpe his clothes and pistol, wasn't it? Thorpe's neighbor saw you at the trailer, and he'll be able to identify your car." That wasn't true at all, but Rhodes didn't mind exaggerating a little more if it would persuade Francine to tell him the truth. "Your fingerprints are on the stool legs, too. You can't get out of it."

Francine looked at him. Her face was crumpling. It was sad to see, but Rhodes had to go on.

"You must have been pretty upset with Helen. She had your ring, and she was taunting you with it. I don't blame you for getting upset with her, but you shouldn't have hit her. And you shouldn't have hit her so hard. Assault is bad enough. Murder's a lot worse."

"She wasn't taunting me," Francine said. "Not with words. She just put the ring on that shelf and called my attention to it. 'Look what I found, Francine. I wonder who'd be silly enough to lose a wedding ring out in the country at some sleazy rendezvous.'" Francine removed her hands from between her legs. She looked at the ring and then at Rhodes. "What Leo and I had wasn't sleazy at all. You can see that I had to do something, can't you?"

"Sure. She went too far, and the stool was right there. You didn't know what you were doing." He paused. "I need to tell you a few things before you go on." He gave her the standard Miranda warning. "Now you can tell me how it happened."

"It was the will."

Rhodes had wondered when they'd get around to that. It was the one thing he hadn't figured out. He wanted to know about the will.

"You took it."

"Yes, I took it."

That's what he couldn't figure out, since Thorpe was the heir. He asked her why.

"Because she'd changed it."

That explained a lot, Rhodes thought, and he asked her what the change was.

"Helen made an entirely new will naming Alton Brant the heir. She called me to ask me to witness the change, just rubbing it in. That was so typical of her. She had no idea of manners."

"You went over and witnessed the will? What about a second witness?"

"She didn't have one. She didn't want Alton to know about the change."

She shouldn't have let Francine know, either. Rhodes thought the will might have been more a part of the motive than the ring.

"So instead of witnessing the will, you took it."

"That's right. Helen said she'd destroyed the old one, but I couldn't allow her to make Alton the heir. Leo deserved that money. He'd just started a new business that was going to be a big success, but he needed the money he'd inherit, just in case it didn't work out."

"Lily Gadney was his backer at the Royal Rack. She'd cut you out."

Francine gave a sad, tired smile. "How little you know. He was just using Lily, as he had before. I was always the one he cared about."

Rhodes didn't believe that Thorpe had ever cared about anybody except himself. He'd used women all his life, Lily, Francine, Helen. Probably others that Rhodes didn't know about.

"Was it Leo's idea for you to get the new will?"

"He didn't know about it. She called me there to witness it that morning."

"When you hit her."

"Yes, all right, I hit her. The ring, the will, she shouldn't have treated me that way. It wasn't ladylike at all."

Rhodes wanted to ask her if sneaking around with someone like Thorpe was ladylike, but he didn't think she'd get the point. Something else occurred to him.

"You're the one who sent Brant after Truck Gadney, aren't you. I should have thought of that. Somebody had to tell him, and you were there in the library when I was asking Lily about her and Truck's quarrel with Mrs. Harris. You thought that you could sic Brant on Truck and distract me from you and Leo. Is that right?"

"I called him. I was afraid he'd tell you, but I suppose he didn't."

"I didn't think to ask him. My mistake."

"Will I have to go to jail?"

"Yes. You will."

"For a long time?"

"That'll be up to the judge and jury."

"She taunted me. Helen. She made me do it. It wasn't my fault."

It was always good to start working on the case for the defense, Rhodes thought.

"Are you ready to go?"

Francine stood up. "She made me do it. I would never have hit her otherwise. You see?"

"What I see doesn't matter. I just make the arrests."

"I'll be out soon. I know a very good lawyer."

Rhodes had a sinking feeling in his stomach. "Randy Lawless?"

"Yes. How did you know?"

"Just a lucky guess."

Chapter 29

▼

"I FEEL SORRY FOR FRANCINE," IVY SAID THAT EVENING WHEN she and Rhodes were eating their meal of three-bean vegetarian chili, which Rhodes was glad wasn't as bad as it sounded. "I feel sorry for all of them."

By *all of them* she must have meant the women involved with Thorpe in one way or another, Rhodes thought.

"Look on the bright side," Rhodes said. "Francine will have plenty of time to finish writing that romance novel of hers while she's serving her sentence."

"It was really Leo's fault," Ivy said, ignoring Rhodes's comment. "And he's not even going to jail."

Thorpe was still in the hospital, still in a coma.

"He's not exactly living large." Rhodes took a mouthful of the chili. "Not like us."

Ivy didn't smile.

"I love the chili." Rhodes took another bite to prove it. "You know that."

"What about Sam? Do you love him?"

Rhodes looked over at the cat. It had one leg stretched out and was licking it.

"Do I have to love him? Can't I just tolerate him?"

"Well, all right. That will do if you promise to stop trying to give him away."

Rhodes didn't want to make any promises he couldn't keep. He said, "I haven't sneezed in a while."

"I told you that was psychological."

Rhodes was reserving judgment on that.

"After all," Ivy said, "he helped you solve the case. All that DNA evidence on his claws and fur."

"I don't know if it's there. It's probably not. We're not going to look for it now. We don't need it. That was just a way to convince Francine to tell me the truth."

"You'd never even have found Helen's body if it hadn't been for Sam. Someone else would have come along and spoiled the crime scene. You might never have known about the murder."

"It's a possibility. A small one."

"Come on. Sam's a hero. You just don't want to admit it."

The cat had stopped licking and was looking at Rhodes as if waiting for him to comment.

"Say it," Ivy said. "Say his name."

Rhodes opened his mouth, but nothing came out.

"You can do it. It's an easy name. Sam. Give it a try."

"Sam."

Ivy smiled at Rhodes. "See? I knew you could do it. Aren't you glad he's here? We needed a cat."

"We didn't need a cat. We have dogs."

Both dogs had come to Rhodes by way of cases he'd worked on. He was beginning to feel as if he might be running an animal shelter. He might have to arrest himself for not having a license.

"And now we have a cat," Ivy said. "Sam."

Rhodes was saved from further discussion of the cat when the phone rang. Ivy answered it, listened, laughed, then called to Rhodes.

"It's Jan. She wants to talk to you about the book."

Rhodes didn't want to talk about the book any more than he wanted to talk about the cat.

"She and Claudia had a call from their editor. The editor feels the book is lacking something."

"Is that bad?"

"Maybe not. It can easily be fixed. That's what Jan wants to talk to you about."

Rhodes stood up. "What's it lacking?"

Ivy laughed again. "A cat. It lacks a cat."

Rhodes looked over at Sam, who dragged a paw along the side of his nose, brushing his whiskers.

Rhodes sneezed.